OFF
YOUR
GAME

OFF YOUR GAME

SUSAN RENEE

PAGE
— & —
VINE

To Chels at TikTok's @babesreadingromance,
Thank you for giving me the inspiration
for the very first line of this book.
Okay, maybe the second line of the book!
I am forever grateful for my TikTok friends
and their creative minds!

CHAPTER 1

Colby

"Fuck me. They could've at least called us good girls before spanking us like that." Dex tosses his stick against the wall, missing the rack completely as we storm off the ice and into the locker room. Having nothing good to say, because I'm pissed as hell about our horrible defeat, I bite my tongue and remain silent. I just want to get the fuck out of here as soon as I can. I'm not in the mood for the ass-reaming I'm sure we'll get from Coach, and I'm not interested in hearing the excuses and the blame shooting from one player to the next.

The fact is, we lost.

Again.

And it's really pissing me off.

Coach follows us in and heads straight to his office, slamming the door. It's rare that he doesn't say at least something after a game. That's how we all know how pissed and disappointed he is with our performance tonight. Can't say I blame him. Anyone watching would've thought we were a bunch of rookies out there on the ice for the very first time.

Embarrassing is what it was.

A clusterfuck of chaos.

The Seattle Sea-Brawlers are a tough team, but we've dominated in past games, so whatever the hell happened tonight is a shock to my core. It's also my fault, and nobody will be able to convince me otherwise.

I didn't eat my Lucky Charms before the game.

No, really.

I fucking ran out this morning and didn't have time to grab another box. Assuming I had one stored in my locker like I always do, I came in early to grab a bowl before my pregame workout, but there was not a fucking Lucky Charm to be seen in or around my locker. The guys know it's my routine—a bowl of Lucky Charms every game day before I start my preparations and warmups.

Of course, I know it's not good for me. Of course, I know it's nothing but a mound of sugar floating in milk, but after consuming a bowl of the marshmallow goodness every damn day for more years than I can count, it's kind of a habit now. And no way in hell was I going to tell the team I didn't get my Lucky Charms today and ruin any sense of confidence they had going into tonight's game.

Instead, I ruined my own confidence for the night. I told myself I didn't feel right because I didn't down a bowl of sugar cereal before hitting the ice. Like that really matters.

But to me, it does.

Did we all make some ridiculous mistakes out there tonight? Yeah, we did. In my brain, I know tonight's loss isn't all on me, but in my heart...the loss is mine.

"What the fuck was with McClacken tonight?" Milo asks, ripping through the laces of his skate and pushing it to the floor.

"I don't know." Quinton shakes his head. "I wanted to shove his goddamn stick so far up his ass he'd feel the splinters on his fucking tongue! That guy's a piece of work."

Hawken throws his jersey into the laundry bin in the middle of the room and continues to strip down. "He's all over the tabloids lately, have you seen? Threatening his girlfriend or cheating on her or some shit like that. He's a high-quality, grade-A douche, that's for sure. Doesn't even seem to care that his dirty laundry is being aired to the world."

Zeke, our star goalie, nods. "He's a PR nightmare, I'm sure. Sucks to be whoever handles that guy."

Still brooding over our performance, I hit the exercise bike to rid myself of the rest of my adrenaline and then head for the shower, hoping my body and my attitude will cool off before going home. Reviewing play after play in my mind — the number of times I sat in the damn sin bin, coupled with only one assist under my belt for the night — none of it is sitting well with me.

I'm better than this.

I work too hard to fuck up the way I did today.

"Fix your face, man," Zeke murmurs, stepping up to the shower next to me and turning on the water. "You haven't said a word since we left the ice, and I know what you're thinking. You know this loss isn't your fault, right?"

With a huff, I squeeze my eyes closed and wipe the water from my face. "It's always my fault, Zeke."

"How do you figure?"

"Because I'm the oldest one on the team. I'm the fuckin' captain, and if I'm doing a piss-poor job of performing, how can I expect the guys to step up?"

"Uh, it's called teamwork, Colby. It's what we get paid to do. We cover each other's weaknesses. We're all allowed to have a bad day."

"Yeah, well, I'm having a bad two weeks. I've fucked up my part in the last four games."

"So, what's eating you? You don't usually have bad games. You want to talk about it?"

"Not particularly."

"Good. Let's begin."

Zeke is great at never taking no for an answer. Plus, he's one of my best friends, so he doesn't put up with my shit.

With a heavy sigh, I reluctantly answer, "I didn't get my fucking Lucky Charms today."

He chuckles softly. He and Milo are the only ones, except my brother, Elias, who know the meaning behind my Lucky Charms habit.

Habit?

No.

Ritual.

I don't eat them for no reason.

It's a ritual.

An homage.

The only way I know I can keep the memory alive.

"You seriously don't think that's why—"

The look on my face stops him before he finishes his sentence. He raises his hands in defense. "All right. Lucky Charms in bulk. Noted." His voice softens when he asks his next question. "But, Colbs, I don't think a box of cereal is what's really causing whatever it is going on in your mind lately. You know it and I know it. And really, the guys know it by now too. So, tell me, what makes this season different from any other season?"

My shoulders slump as I lean against the shower wall. "I don't know. For some reason, I'm stuck in my head about it more this year, and I can't shake it. It's been twenty years. I should be goddamn over it by now. Instead, the nightmares are coming back, and I'm not sleeping much."

"Twenty years. You're right. I'm sorry, I guess I kind of allowed myself to lose track of time. Also, I don't think it's something you can ever truly get over. Grief comes at unexpected times. I know you know that. You just need to not be so hard on yourself. Let the team carry the burden a little. You don't have to feel so overwhelmed. Get back to enjoying the game instead of feeling like it's your job to be out there."

"But it is my job to be out there. It's my job to be in my best form, and it fucking sucks when I'm anything but."

Milo steps into the shower next to us, picking up on our conversation.

Zeke gestures to me with a nod of his head. "Milo, will you please tell Colby our loss isn't his fault?"

"Not your fault, Colb," he says. "Technically, we could blame Zeke. He's the one who failed to block their pucks."

Zeke's shoulders fall, and he shakes his head. "Ouch. Touché, man."

"See, Colby? We all have parts to play. We're a team. It sucks for all of us when any of us have bad nights. I'm just trying to say our loss isn't on you and you alone."

All three of us are quiet for a few minutes while we scrub the stress of the loss from our bodies, but then Zeke finally speaks again.

"Have you tried talking to someone about it?"

"You mean like a head doctor?"

Milo rolls his eyes. "I think they call them therapists, Colby."

"No. Quite frankly, I don't want to rehash the past. Keeping busy helps keep my mind...healthy."

"So do therapists," Zeke adds

"I guess I'll have to take your word for it."

"So, you need to let off some steam instead of going home and brooding about tonight's game."

"Yeah?" I roll my eyes, knowing what Milo's going to say before I even ask the question. "And what did you have in mind for letting off steam?"

"The guys are heading to Pringle's Pub. Come with us." He shrugs. "Maybe find someone to help you release some energy. When was the last time that happened?"

"Sex?" I shake my head and blow out a breath, turning the water off and grabbing my towel. "Hell if I know. Last time we were on that long away stretch—Virginia...New York maybe? Makayla? Mackenzie? Michelle? I can't remember her name."

Puck bunnies are always hopping around the local bars after our games in hopes they'll catch a player or two and sink their horny teeth into one of us. Several of them are successful, since only one of us on the team is committed. I'd be lying if I said they were annoying, because, quite frankly, a quick fuck beats having to dip into my spank bank to get myself off when a pair of warm lips and a tight pussy are willing and waiting. The sex is average at best, but the view is usually better than my fist, so I don't complain.

"All right, it's been a few weeks at least," Milo reminds me. "Let's go find you a hot body to bend over or a sexy pair of legs to stick in the air. You spend too much time alone."

I glance at Zeke and raise a brow. "You're heading to Pringle's to grab some ass?"

He chuckles. "Fuck no, are you kidding? No, thank you. I like my relationship with Lori too much to mess it up. Plus, I happen to know she went to Victoria's Secret yesterday so I'm pretty sure I've got something nice waiting for me at home."

I know they're trying.

I know my best friends want what's best for me.

They want to see me happy. On and off the ice.

"Thanks, Milo, but I'm just not feeling it tonight. I don't want to bring the guys down any more than I already have." I pull on my boxer briefs and jeans, and slide my long-sleeve Henley over my head. "I'm heading home, well, after I find myself some cereal."

Milo gives me an understanding nod, and I want to tell him how appreciative I am he's not pushing me on the issue as he usually does. I get that's what best friends are for, and I love him like crazy for sticking with me all these years, but sometimes I just want to be alone.

To wallow.

To reflect.

To be pissed off.

To jack off.

Whatever the hell I want to do to feel better without the judgment of someone else.

I pull my car into the nearly empty Meijer parking lot, realizing it's almost time for them to close for the night. Adjusting the gray beanie on my head in hopes I won't be recognized and forced to make small talk with fans, I quickly jog inside. This won't take more than a minute to grab a box of Lucky Charms and be out of their hair.

I find aisle ten, where all the cereals are, and run into what seems like the only other shopper in the entire store...and she's holding a box of my favorite cereal.

Thank God! They have some in stock.

"Excuse me," I murmur, only making eye contact for a moment. Smiling at the woman politely, I step past her to get to the product I'm looking for.

"No problem," she says, tossing the box of cereal into her cart and walking down the aisle.

I lean down to grab some Lucky Charms for myself but realize the bottom shelf is now empty.

"Shit. Are you..." My words are a whisper as my head snaps up toward the woman walking away from me.

"Wait! Ma'am?"

The stranger turns. She's...fuck, she's beautiful, which catches me off guard. A petite woman, she can't be more than five-two or five-three, max. Her toffee-brown hair frames her face in soft shoulder-length waves, and her dark chestnut eyes catch mine as she turns around. Her face is slightly oval in shape, the pinkness in her cheeks from being outside accentuating the freckles bridging her nose. I can't see all the goods with her winter coat covering her body, but she has a tight little ass. That, coupled with the rest of her, would seriously put her on my radar on a normal day — and I haven't had those thoughts for a long time. Thank God she appears pleasant enough to hopefully give me what I'm about to ask for.

"Yes?"

I gesture to the shelf beside me. "Was that the last box of Lucky Charms?"

She gives me a sympathetic nod. "Yeah, I think so. Sorry." She shrugs and turns back to head down the aisle.

Without thinking, because all I came for was that damn cereal, I blurt out, "Can I have it?"

"I'm sorry?" She turns again, her brows narrowing.

"Your Lucky Charms. Can I, uh... Can I have them?"

"Uh..." She smiles awkwardly, and my body tenses because

I can already tell what she's about to say. "I'm sorry. This is one of the only things I came in here for. Tony's was out, so I had to travel to this end of town to find some. Maybe try the Meijer across town?"

My shoulders sag, and I tilt my head, frustrated. "At this time of night? Doesn't matter how fast I drive, they'll be closed by the time I get there."

She winces. "Hmm. You're probably right."

"Look, can I just pay you for that box?" I pull my wallet from my back pocket. "I'll pay you...double...no, triple what you would pay. How's fifty bucks sound?" I pull out a few bills and hold them out to her.

The woman juts her hip out and looks at me like I'm crazy. She might be right, but I hold firm, waving money in her face.

"You want to pay me fifty dollars for a box of kid's cereal?"

"Yes." I nod fervently. "It's for my, uh...my kid. Yeah. He's very sick, you see. And he's been crying for Lucky Charms, and I just got off work, and I'm trying to find some for him before I go home."

A brow raises above her left eye, and her smile fades. "Does that story usually work when you really want something? Because I believe they're having a sale on tiny violins in aisle six, if that's the case."

Yeah. I should've known it wouldn't work.

"All right, you drive a hard bargain." I pull out all the money in my wallet. It's a couple hundred bucks. "How about all my money? You could buy several boxes with this."

"You're right." She nods. "So, you go ahead and do that. My Lucky Charms are not for sale."

"But they are for sale." I roll my eyes, annoyed we're even having this conversation when she could just be nice and give me the box. "You just haven't paid for them yet."

"Are you really serious right now?" she asks, looking around as if I might be pranking her and, any minute now, the camera crew is going to step out and have a good laugh.

"Look, I'm really sorry you were about thirty seconds too late getting here, and I beat you to the last box of cereal fair and square. I took the time to travel across town to get it, so I'm going to pay for it now and take it home so tomorrow morning before I start my new job, I can enjoy a bowl of my favorite cereal. I'm sorry about your luck." She gestures to the shelf next to me. "Try the Magic Oats. I hear they taste the same."

"Like hell they taste the same." I gawk. "Everyone knows the generic version is shit." My nostrils flare as I glare at the evil woman, whose only purpose now, I'm quite certain, is to make my night a living hell —even more so than the evening I just endured. I grit my teeth and try to keep the vein that pops out of my forehead when I'm angry at bay.

"Okay, what is it you really want? A date? Is that what you want? A nice meal and maybe a little tongue action in exchange for the cereal?" I size her up from head to toe, bobbing my head. She definitely checks all the marks in the attractive department, but hell if I'm going to admit that to her. "You've got enough for me to play with. To hold on to. I could make it happen, if it's what you want."

Her confidence and sass are sexy enough that I wouldn't even have to pretend.

Her mouth falls open, and she slaps me across the face. "Who the hell do you think you are?"

I laugh aloud. "Like you don't know." Our eyes meet and her expression is still the disgusted, questioning look it was a moment ago. When she doesn't say anything, my brows pinch. "Wait...you really don't know who I am?"

She scoffs. "Uh...unless you're Ryan Reynolds specifically dressed in his Deadpool costume and whispering ridiculously vulgar words in my ear before fucking my brains out, then I don't give two shits who you are."

"Ryan Reynolds kink, huh? Lady, you're a piece of work. You know that?"

"Seriously? Because I won't bend over and give you a fucking box of cereal? And you're calling me the piece of work?"

Forget annoyed. Now I'm irritated. "Yes! I don't know why you're being so damn difficult. It's not like I didn't ask nicely the first time, and I'm offering you a shit ton of cash."

"Right." She flails her arm. "You only offered dinner and, quote-unquote, tongue action for the box. My bad for not giving in to the ridiculous temptation standing in front of me."

"Your loss, princess." I roll my eyes. "Women throw themselves at me like candy in a parade just about anywhere I go."

Her cheeks bulge, and she pretends to gag. "Oh, sorry. I just threw up in my mouth a little."

"You know what? Fuck it," I murmur. "You're impossible."

"And you're just some sexy guy with a full wallet, a sick kid, and..." She tsks. "Aww, no Lucky Charms to take home to him." She smirks as she shakes her head. "Hope you have more luck somewhere else."

The evil cereal witch has the audacity to wink at me before she turns for the final time and heads to the checkout counter. Standing here watching her, I'm wondering what would happen if I literally threw myself over her cart, grabbed the cereal, and high-tailed it out of here.

That would be a PR nightmare tomorrow.

Coach would bench me for sure.

Fuck.

"Excuse me, sir? Is there anything we can help you find? We'll be closing in about five minutes." A young man, who can't be much over twenty years old, stands next to me in his Meijer polo shirt.

"Uh...no. I, uh..." Came for some goddamn Lucky Charms. "Stopped for some beer. I'll just be a minute."

By the time I grab a six-pack and head to the checkout, the woman is gone from the store. Guess I won't be mugging anyone tonight.

Not that I mug people regularly.

Or ever.

But if I had given it some serious consideration, I think I

could've actually done it tonight.

As I climb into my car and turn the key, I stare out the window, thinking back on the woman in the cereal aisle.

"And you're just some sexy guy with a full wallet, a sick kid, and..." She tsks. "Aww, no Lucky Charms to take home to him."

Well, I suppose if there's one positive thing about the night, for as evil as she was, it's that she called me sexy.

Damn right I am.

"Alex!"

"Eli, help him!"

"I know, Colby! I fucking know! Stay there!"

Fear washes over me as I sit in the mound of snow, unable to see much in the darkness, the lake only illuminated by the luminous glow of the moon. It wasn't like this, though.

In reality.

My mind knows this, but it's not changing the picture in my head.

I hear the breaking of the ice and the furious splashing of water.

The coughing.

The gasping.

"Colby, go get Dad!"

Running.

Running so hard through the drifted snow, my legs can barely keep up. I'm tiring quickly, yet I still have so far to go.

I'll never make it.

I try anyway.

"Dad! Where are the Lucky Charms?"

I spring up in my bed, darkness invading my senses, my chest tight, a sheen of sweat on the back of my neck. My breathing is jagged. I try to catch my breath, reminding myself it's over.

Just a dream.

In my past.

Not real.

Not entirely.

My mouth is dry when I try to swallow, so I reach for the water bottle on my nightstand and gulp its contents. The clock on my phone reads four thirty in the morning.

Fuck.

There's no way I can go back to sleep now. I need to be at the gym early anyway. This is obviously the universe's way of telling me I need an extra workout today. A punishment for not getting a good night's sleep? A punishment for losing him.

For not being fast enough.

For not having strong enough legs.

All of it, my punishment for playing hockey.

CHAPTER 2

Carissa

> **Chelsea: I'm eating a bowl of Lucky Charms just for you, girl! Good luck on your first day! You're going to be great!**

Snapping a picture of my nearly empty cereal bowl, I text it to my best friend with a smiley emoji, thanking her for the encouraging message.

> **Me: Me too! I'm going to need all the luck I can get.**

> **Chelsea: Nah. You'll be fine. It's no different from your campus job. You're just getting paid more. *high five emoji***

> **Me: Yeah and working with millionaire jocks who probably think their shit doesn't stink.**

Chelsea: Oooor...they're a bunch of down-to-earth, super-hot sexy athletes who are actually fun to be around. Let's shoot for the positive!

Me: You're right. No negativity here! It's going to be a great day! Also, good luck handling Gretchen today. Sorry I won't be there to help you.

Chelsea: You are absolutely not sorry. And it's ok. I forgive you. Now go slay bestie! Love you girl!

Me: Love you! Drinks tonight to celebrate?

Chelsea: Hell YES!

Gretchen Prong is one of the girls I am all too happy to finally be free of. She and I were the only two students hired on as PR staff for DePaul University when we graduated. We've worked together there for the past eight years, and although we've worked pretty well together most of the time, I've always felt this sense of competition with her. Like she always felt she needed to have one more social media post than I did on a particular day, or she would somehow weasel her way into assignments that were mine in years past. Sometimes it felt like she wanted to get under my skin on purpose, but other times I think she just wanted to feel like she was the best at something.

"Well, you're the best now, Gretchen. I concede. You can keep the job. I'm moving up in the world, starting today."

I place my now empty bowl in the sink, promising myself I'll wash the small pile of dishes tonight when I'm home, and then reach for the cereal box on the table. My eyes sweep over the Lucky Charms as I shake my head, laughing about the asshole from last night who looked like he couldn't decide whether to fuck me or murder me over a box of cereal that's basically Cheerios with marshmallows.

"And that's why you don't go shopping at night, Carissa," I murmur to myself. "The crazies only come out at night."

I slip the colorful cereal box back into my pantry and grab my coat from the hook by my door. They don't call Chicago the Windy City for nothing, and today is no joke. The rattle of my windows and the air leaking through the unsealed edges tells me it's an ice-cold day in Hell out there. We don't always get the luxury of delighting in a beautiful snowy day in the city. When the wind whips off the lake and bites you in the face, it's all you can do to not cry. And you definitely don't want to do that, lest you end up with frozen tears stuck to your face.

Wrapping my scarf around my neck and slipping on my gloves, I grab my purse and shoulder bag that, for now, carries a couple notebooks, a few pens, and my planner, and head outside. With any luck, I'll walk fast enough to make it to the L in plenty of time before it departs.

"Good morning, ma'am," an older white-haired gentleman says, nodding with a friendly smile when I enter the Alliance Arena, my cheeks pink with windburn. "How can I help you this morning?"

"Uh, good morning," I answer. "I'm starting a new job here today—with Valerie Wellman?"

"Oh yes, Mrs. Wellman. Very good. You'll simply go straight around on this floor and proceed down the hall to the right. Her office is the third door. Welcome to the Red Tails family."

"Thank you so much."

"You're welcome." He smiles as I step past him and head off to meet with my new boss.

My nerves creep up as I make my way down the hall as directed. This could be a great opportunity for me, or it could be a huge flop.

It won't flop.

Don't even think it!

I might not know much about hockey, but I'm a quick study, and I'm confident in my social game. It feels great to finally feel like I'm in a real job. Not that what I did on a college campus wasn't a real job. It was. But since I went straight from graduation into the social media public relations post, the only thing that really felt different was moving into a campus apartment paid for by the university in return for also being a Resident Director. I think the fact that I never truly left after graduation made me feel like I was still a student there, even if I wasn't.

The greeter's directions were flawless, as I'm able to find Mrs. Wellman's office without any trouble. Standing just outside, I knock three times on her open door. When she looks up, she greets me with a full smile.

"Good morning! It's Carissa, right?"

I nod. "Yes, ma'am."

She extends her hand, shaking mine and welcoming me into her office. "It's great to see you again. I am so excited to help get you started today. Congratulations again on the new appointment. I imagine this is quite the promotion for you."

"Yes, it is. Thank you very much. I'm eager to get started."

"Good. We like hard workers here, and Doctor Sweeny at the university had amazing things to say about your work for the school over the last several years."

A warm, appreciative smile spreads across my lips. "I enjoyed my time at DePaul very much and loved working for them after graduation."

It's been eight years since I graduated from DePaul with my degree in public relations. Before graduation, I was offered a summer internship that would turn into a full-time job if I showed I was a strong enough candidate, which I did easily. The following fall, the university offered me a contract to be their social media manager. It was a fantastic opportunity to pad my résumé while feeling like I was still at home on a campus I loved and respected so much. But when the opportunity to work with the Red Tails came up, I knew it was time to move on, stretch my wings, and become an honest-to-goodness adult.

It was time to get my own apartment.

Pay my own rent.

Do all the things adults do.

Even though my parents were making it exponentially harder for me to do so.

Valerie gestures to one of two chairs in front of her desk. "Why don't you have a seat, and we'll go over a few particulars before I show you around."

Unbuttoning my coat, I slide it off and lay it across the chair next to me, along with my purse and bag. Valerie, my boss, goes over the details of my day-to-day responsibilities and explains the hierarchy around the office. There are a few other public relations specialists, but I'm the one assigned to digital content and engagement.

"On their off time or particularly when they're not in a focused practice with their coaches, you'll have free rein of the players on the team," she explains. "Obviously, our fans want to see their favorite players, and we want our fans to see that not only are our players relatable, fun guys, but they're also consistent philanthropists. So, anything you can dream up to help the guys portray a solid image to the hockey community is a win in our book."

"I see. And are there some, more than others, who need a shinier social media reputation?"

Valerie nods, rolling her eyes with a smirk. "There are always one or two who need the positive limelight more than others. And it changes throughout the season. We're all human. Some guys get more upset at losses than others, and although we try to keep drunken mistakes to a minimum around here, some of them will go out and make questionable choices, win or lose. Some will say the wrong thing in a post-game interview, and we have to make sure they're seen in a better light than the slight in their character that happens every once in a while. Yes, the world likes to feed off drama, but more than anything, they like to believe the athletes they root for are more like heroes. So, we do our best to help them appear that way."

Really, she's saying angelic, well-mannered winners equal dollar signs for their franchise.

"Gotcha. I think I can handle that."

"I'm confident you can." She leans forward on her desk. "Now, I know probably don't need to say what I'm going to say next, but I feel like if I don't at least say the words, I'm not doing my job correctly."

Chuckling, I nod. "Okay."

Her eyes narrow, and her head tilts. "First of all, Carissa, how much do you know about hockey?"

My cheeks may have been pink from the chill outside, but now they're full of heat from uncomfortable embarrassment. "Uh...not that much, actually. I mean, I know how the game is played—in that a puck in the net equals a goal—if that's what you're asking."

She throws her head back, laughing. "Oh, you poor thing."

"I'm sorry," I tell her, cringing. "I was told a strong hockey knowledge was not a requirement for the job."

Oh God. Am I fired before I even get started?

"No, no. You're right. It's not." Valerie waves her hand dismissively. "Not at all. Your social media knowledge and experience are what got you this job, and that's what we need. Anyone can learn about hockey, but your lack of hockey knowledge and probably, therefore, knowledge of the players themselves..." She stops. "Correct?"

I nod.

Good Lord, I couldn't name one player to save my life.

"Yeah, that's what I thought. Okay. So, first and foremost, don't let yourself get pulled into the players' bullshit." She chuckles. "They're a great group of guys, but they will definitely tell you how great they think they are, and don't be the least bit surprised if they tease you a little or give you a hard time about how little you may know about hockey. These guys are well-paid and pretty damn popular, if I do say so myself. It's your job to keep them from doing anything stupid that might go viral online and damage their reputations."

"Squeaky-clean hockey players." I nod. "Got it. No problem."

"Be careful around the guys after a game. Specifically, a game they've won. Adrenaline is high. They need the release, and some of them will take it any way they can get it."

My eyes widen. "Oh my God! Do you mean... Do I need to carry mace or something?"

She chuckles again. "No, though mace isn't a bad idea. We do live in Chicago, you know."

"True."

"I am talking about sex, though, yes. Spend enough time with the guys, and they will undoubtedly start to flirt with you, whether you're single or not. I'm not saying it's not harmless behavior between working adults, but when the adrenaline is high and the alcohol flows, some of them would gladly take what you might offer. And please, for the love of God, do not offer." She laughs awkwardly. "That's more drama than I get paid to handle, so do me a solid and don't cross the line. Leave that to the puck bunnies of the world."

"Puck bunnies?" My brows pinch.

"Oh. Right." She shakes her head, remembering I have little to no knowledge of hockey.

"Puck bunnies are the tramps who hang out at bars or hotels after games looking to hook up with a player. Some are in it for a quick lay with a hot, rich athlete, and some think sleeping with one will make them equally as famous."

My jaw drops. "That really happens?"

She laughs. "More than you could ever know. You're bound to see some of the guys give in to a puck bunny or two during our travels throughout the season. So, now you know and won't be shocked when it happens. You ever hear how much sex happens at the Olympics because the athletes just need a way to release their energy and tension and adrenaline?"

"Yeah."

She nods. "It's the same thing here with our athletes—meaningless sex as an adrenaline release." She watches me take in her explanation and then continues. "In fact, if you're ever hanging out with the guys after a game, filming for posts or whatever, it wouldn't be a terrible thing to remind them to be protected. The last thing we want is to have to cover up an accidental pregnancy scandal."

I cringe. "Ew. No, you're right. No fraternization. Try to keep them out of trouble," I note. "No problem."

I don't know how she thinks I'm supposed to control a group of horny, hunky athletes drunk in a bar after a game, but I'll nod and agree to anything at this point. Hopefully, she's exaggerating just a bit.

"Good." She smiles. "Other than that, it's just the basics. Think before you post, and don't post anything that puts any of the guys in a bad light. We're busy enough trying to put out fires that outsiders try to start. You know how crazy people can get."

My thoughts float back to the weird guy needing a Lucky Charms fix last night. "I totally get it, and I can assure you, you've put your faith in the right person. I won't let you down."

"I'm sure you won't. I'm excited to see what you can do for the team. We're glad to have you as part of the Red Tails family, Carissa. Welcome aboard. I'll show you to your office, and then I think we should meet the team, don't you?"

She stands from her desk, and I do the same, picking up my coat and bags. "I think that sounds great."

Valerie leads me down a few sets of stairs and through a couple of long hallways, each one decorated with Red Tails banners, logos, historical moments, and other memories of the team. It's red and black everywhere I look. The sounds of gym weights clanking and whistles blowing can be heard up ahead, and I suddenly get goosebumps along my skin.

Excitement blooms in my stomach.

This is where the action happens.

We stop just outside a set of doors, and Valerie pulls one open to reveal a group of office suites, each one with a long back window that overlooks the ice below.

"Wow!" I gesture toward the rink. "This is my view every day?"

Valerie shrugs. "Unless you don't want it to be, in which case you can simply pull the blinds. Someone in charge of social media marketing needs access to everything and everyone if she's going to pull off an engaging team account. It's not huge, but—"

"It's amazing!" I blurt out, stepping into my new office with a giddy smile. "Thank you so much for this."

"It's my pleasure, Carissa. Do whatever you want with the space. Make it your own so you're comfortable. Why don't you put your things down here, and I'll introduce you to the team."

"All right."

Following Valerie once again, we walk back down the hall to a meeting room where it looks as if the team is studying their plays from recent games. She darts her eyes around the room and then asks, "Where's Nelson?"

"Finishing up a second workout with Landric," one of the guys tells her, eyeing me. For a moment, I feel ridiculously small standing in a room with a group of large burly guys sprawled out on the furniture, but then I remind myself why I'm here and stand up a little taller.

"Carissa, this is Coach Denovah." Valerie gestures to a man who looks to be in his mid to late fifties, slightly shorter in stature from the other guys in the room, with a receding hairline and five o'clock shadow. His physique suggests that he was once an athlete himself in the way he's built. He offers me his hand, and I shake it.

"Pleasure to meet you, Mr. Denovah."

"Likewise, Carissa. Everyone around here calls me Coach.

You may as well do the same."

I give him a friendly smile. "All right. Thank you."

"Carissa is our new PR social media specialist," Valerie explains. "So, she'll be spending a good bit of time with the team. I thought I would introduce her to the guys."

Coach nods. "No problem. We need to wait for Nelson and Landric anyway. You got a last name, Carissa? It's not uncommon to go by last names around here."

"Oh, right. My last name is Smallson."

"Carissa Smallson." He nods and then raises his arm out to the side, gesturing to the guys in the room. "Welcome to the team. Shall I do the honors?"

"Of course! Please."

Coach Denovah goes through the guys one by one, telling me their names and what positions they play as if I know everything there is to know about hockey. Rather than make my lack of knowledge known, I simply take it all in stride, smiling and trying like hell to remember at least a few of the names being thrown at me.

"This here is goalie, Zeke Miller, right wing, Hawken Malone and Dex Foster, he's a defenseman." Each of the three guys raises his hand in a slight wave and friendly nod, my nerves relaxing with each smile.

"That guy over there is left wing, Quinton Shay," Coach says, pointing to the man in the corner of the room. "And the last two should be here any minute."

Well, they don't seem so bad.

I wave at the group of guys and feel their eyes taking me in like it's been years since any of them have seen a woman. That Dex guy even licks his lips, but I pretend not to notice.

Good Lord, I'm like a piece of meat sitting in front of a den of hungry lions.

"Hey, everyone. I'm Carissa. It's great to meet you all. I'm sure we'll be getting to know each other very well in the coming weeks, and I'm excited to get started."

"Get started with what?" a voice says from behind me, to my right. All heads turn, including my own as two guys step into the room, sweat towels hanging from their necks. I have to assume they're the last two players everyone has mentioned, but when one of them makes eye contact with me, he stops dead in his tracks.

He looks familiar.

Where do I know him from?

His eyes narrow as he looks me up and down with a frightfully serious expression before his frown morphs into a dickish smirk. "So, you do know who I am, huh? What? Did you feel guilty and stop by to bring me my cereal? How did you even get in here?"

Oh God.

It's him.

The asshole from last night.

Shit.

Why does he have to make it super awkward?

What do I do?

What do I say?

Play dumb or acknowledge?

Play dumb or acknowledge?

Play dumb, Carissa.

For the love of God, play dumb!

Shaking my head slowly, I furrow my brow and give the biggest Oscar-worthy performance of my life. Okay, Emmy-worthy at least.

"I'm sorry, do I know you?"

"Uh, yeah. You do. You took my cereal," the sweaty guy tells me, his brandy-colored eyes piercing my own.

He's wearing a pair of black athletic shorts and a gray muscle shirt with the Red Tails logo on the front, his well-defined biceps on display for my suddenly parched eyes.

I didn't notice his hair last night as he was wearing a hat, but today it's a mess of dark brown strands that flop every which way when he runs his hand through it. He has a prominent square jaw covered in the shortest of beards, and a slightly crooked nose that

I can only imagine has been broken a time or two in game play. My eyes slide down to his taut shoulders and solid body. What I wouldn't give to peek under that shirt.

There's no way he doesn't have a solid twenty-four pack under there if that's even a thing.

Speaking of pack...age...package...

I bet he has a worthy package.

I could sneak a peek.

No, don't look!

I kinda want to look, though.

Do NOT look, Carissa!

Dammit!

Why does he have to be so attractive?

Good Lord, he could easily give me the ride of my life, so someone please tell me again why the sexy ones are always pricks?

Ugh.

He clears his throat and crosses his arms over his chest, and I shake my head again, willing myself not to make eye contact with the area I so badly want to check out.

"Your cereal?" I laugh nervously.

Is it hot in here?

"I don't...I'm sorry. I don't know what you're talking about." I turn to Valerie. "Was I supposed to bring cereal?"

She nearly snorts and grasps my forearm. "Goodness, no. These guys have all the food they could want prepared for them in the café." She turns to the cereal addict, who is giving me the stink eye. "And there's plenty of cereal down there if you..." Her brow pinches in a look of both confusion and disgust. "Need it."

Coach Denovah steps in. "Carissa, this is Milo Landric and Colby Nelson, the last of the team members. Milo's our center, and Colby here is a defenseman. He's also the team captain. Gentlemen, this is Carissa Smallson, your new PR manager."

Milo looks to his broody teammate, who is still staring at me, and offers his hand along with a beaming smile. "Carissa. It's a pleasure to meet you."

"Likewise, Milo. Thank you."

Milo elbows Colby, who is standing next to him, and whispers, "Shake the woman's hand, dumbass. Don't be a douche."

His eyes still narrowed, watching me, Colby finally releases his arms and shakes my hand. "Colby Nelson."

His large hand is surprisingly warm and soft as it covers mine. I make sure to squeeze firmly because hell if I'm going to let him try to intimidate me. "Nice to meet you, Colby."

"Uh-huh." He rubs his cheek right where I slapped him last night, my eyes following his movement. "Do you know anything about hockey?"

My jaw falls open. I want to slap the prick all over again for purposely trying to humiliate me on my first day. Thankfully, Valerie saves me.

"What she doesn't know, she'll learn. You'll just have to show her the ropes around here, Nelson."

Coach chuckles. "Carissa, I think you have your work cut out for you. Colby here has had a rough couple of weeks and could use a little positive PR these days."

Before I can respond, Colby rolls his eyes and steps over to an empty chair. "Thanks, but no thanks. I think I can handle myself just fine."

As he sits down, I hear Milo scoff quietly beside me. "Tell that to our losing streak."

Milo shakes his head as he takes the last seat on the other side of the room.

"Well, we'll let you get back to your work, Coach. Carissa will be around to meet with the guys later."

All of the players in the room wave goodbye or smile and nod, but one does not. Colby stares at me from his chair, his expression hardened, and doesn't say a word until I'm out the door. From the hallway I hear someone say, "Dude, what the fuck's your problem?"

CHAPTER 3

Colby

"How many times are you going to work out today, man?" Milo stops short as he passes by the gym and spies me on the bike for the second time today. Quinton, Zeke, and Hawken are right behind him, coming in for the workout before today's practice.

"What difference does it make?"

"Dude, it's your third workout of the day," Quinton reports. "Keep it up and you won't have anything left for practice."

I shake my head. "Don't worry about me. Just clearing my head."

Zeke struts forward and grabs the same handlebars I'm holding onto, leaning in close. "You want to tell us what it is you need to clear your head of?"

"Nope." I shake my head. "Not particularly."

"Is it about the new girl?" Dex asks.

Hawken frowns. "What new girl?"

That earns him a teasing slap to his bicep. "The new girl, dipshit. Cassie? Carsie?"

"Carissa." Her name drips off my tongue like poison, though her face flits through my mind on repeat. Her freckles. Her pink cheeks.

"Yeah! Carissa." Dex's eyes light up. "She was a pretty little thing, wasn't she? Bet she'd look hot in a jersey."

Something turns over in my gut, and it doesn't feel pleasant.

"Oh yeah! What was that all about, Nelson?" Hawken asks as he adjusts the weights on his machine. "Do you know her?"

Milo gasps. "You said the words 'last night' when you were talking to her earlier. Did you sleep with her? That was fast, dude. How did you even—"

"No. It's not like that." Realizing they're not going to let it go, I release a sigh but continue digging into the pedals on my stationary bike.

"She stole my Lucky Charms last night."

Milo's eyes narrow and he tilts his head. "Come again?"

Dex scoffs out a laugh. "He'd have to come a first time, and well, we all know that ain't happening."

"Shut up, Dex." Zeke waits patiently for an explanation, his arms crossed over his chest as he watches me. "Do you really know her, Colb?"

I shake my head. "No, I don't know her. I stopped at Meijer last night on the way home right before they closed, and she was there. You know what she bought?"

"Let me guess..."

"The very last fucking box of Lucky Charms."

Dex cringes. "Ooh, that blows."

Zeke lowers his shaking head, and then slowly looks back up at me. "Are you sure it was her?"

"Of course, it was her. She was..." I let out a heavy breath. "She was attractive, all right? And I noticed. Same face. Same hair. The freckles across her nose. The tight little ass. Everything. Yes, any other time I might have been interested, but last night, she was like this demon witch who refused to even consider giving me the box. I even offered her all the cash in my wallet."

Dex laughs. "And she still wouldn't budge? Did she know who you were?"

"I assumed she would, but if she did, she pretended not to. Just like she did this morning when I brought up the cereal."

"Well, in her defense," Quinton starts. "I wouldn't want to admit to an altercation with one of the Chicago Red Tails players on my first day of work...especially in front of the whole team."

"And her boss..." Hawken adds.

Dex nods. "Right. And the coach."

Frustration rolling off me in waves, I glare at them both. "Yeah, yeah. I get the point."

Hawken positions his legs on the leg press machine. "Or...she isn't your girl. Maybe a doppelganger?"

"Oh, she's the girl. Trust me." I can feel it in my chest.

"All right, so she didn't want to give up her box of cereal. She got to it first. What's the big deal? You know you're starting to sound like a crazy drug addict with your obsession."

"It's fine. I know," I spit out. "She didn't really do anything wrong. She just...got under my skin. I was pissed enough after last night's game, and she didn't help matters any. I assumed she might know who I am, and when she didn't fangirl all over me like all the rest of the female population, I assumed she would..."

Milo's brows shoot up. "The rest of the female population. That's impressive."

I know he knows what I mean. Women try to get with us anywhere we go. Sometimes it's heaven. Other times it's straight up annoying.

"Wow. Someone is quite full of himself this morning, eh?" Zeke laughs. "Lori would beg to differ. Do you know what I think? I think the girl's got balls. Took no shit from you, and you're struggling with that." He chuckles again. "Fuck, she'll fit in here just fine."

"Fuck you, Zeke." I don't really mean that, and he knows it. That's why he throws his head back laughing even harder.

"She's good for you, Colby. I'd bet anything on it. I'll see ya for lunch, asshole."

My phone rings from my locker as I slip my shirt on after practice. For the first time in a while, I've felt good about what I was able to accomplish on the ice this afternoon. After studying my plays from the last three games earlier today, I discovered I was leaning too much toward the weak side of the ice instead of getting in front of the net and protecting my goalie. I honestly don't know what I was thinking, because assisting the puck carrier is my job, and the decisions I made out there were straight up bad decisions.

At least it's something I can focus on now.

Something I can fix.

I grab my phone and see my agent's number on the screen. "Yeah?"

"Colby. How was practice? You feeling good for tomorrow?"

"Feeling solid. Yeah. I think things are going to turn around."

"Good. We need you fresh and ready, man. We want your fans loving on you, not looking for your ass to be benched."

Startled by his words, I shift my eyes around the locker room to see if anyone is watching or listening to my conversation. "What's that supposed to mean, Aaron?"

Aaron Strongfield has been my agent since I was brought into the NHL at the young age of twenty-one. I was a baby then. Nine years later, and I'm more of a seasoned pro than many on my team. Aaron has always had my best interest at heart and has never steered me wrong so when he speaks, I usually take him pretty seriously. This time though? The idea of my being benched...or worse...traded. What's that all about?

"Look, Colby, it's no secret you've been struggling these last few games."

Not wanting to have this conversation in the room with my teammates, I step out into the empty hallway. "Yeah, So? Can't someone have a goddamn dark moment once in a while?"

"Of course, they can. And they do. You know that. Don't get your panties in a twist, all right? We're going to fix this."

"Fix what?" I spit out, a feeling of unease shooting through me. "I've got a great reputation and a squeaky-clean record. I've never done anything illegal. I don't cause drama and I—"

"You're a crabby asshole lately, Nelson. Your head hasn't been in the game. Or maybe it's been too much in the game. I don't know, but we don't want people to take notice and start giving you a hard time, so there may come a time when we need to remind them who you really are."

Who I really am.

I know who I am.

I'm Colby Fucking Nelson.

I let out a dramatic sigh. "What are we talking here? A few meet-and-greets? Photo opportunity with kids?"

"I hear you guys just hired a new PR girl, right?"

Ugh. I already don't like where this is going.

"Yeah. We've met."

"Fresh eyes like hers could be good for you, for the team, so listen to her. And just go with it, all right? Give the fans what they want."

"What they want is a strong captain who can lead the team to victory."

"Yeah," Aaron says. "And they also want someone they feel they can relate to and look up to. They want a hero, Colby."

"I'm no fuckin' hero, Aaron."

"Sure, you are. Everybody is somebody's hero. Think about it. Go with it. Relax and enjoy the game. Pull that stick outta your ass a little, all right?"

"Yeah, yeah."

"I'll catch you later, Colbs. Hang tight."

He doesn't say anything else before he disconnects our call. Pocketing my phone, I turn back to the locker room to grab my socks, shoes, and coat, but the clickity clack of heels about to turn the corner down this hallway distracts me. The moment I turn my head I see who it is, clipboard under her arm, phone in hand. She's not watching where she's going, so I stand in the middle of the hall with my hands in my pockets and watch her.

She's wearing a pair of tight black pants that hug her hips and ass. A lilac blouse, with two big ruffles flowing down each arm, is tucked in at her waist. Her brown waves coast across her shoulders. It's not the stuffy, rich-girl professional look I'm used to seeing around here with some of the other staff —no pencil skirt and suit jacket. She's a little more casual. It's not a bad change at all. She looks...feminine. Pretty.

Normal.

Which, ironically, is disappointing when I think about it. She's pretty to look at and has a body I don't mind checking out, but that attitude she carries can suck it.

She's deep in thought as she texts someone on her phone, walking with a hurried pace right smack dab into—

"Oof! God, I..." When she collides with my body, I don't move an inch, but I feel everything. The moment her chest brushes up against mine. The grasp of her fingers when she grabs onto my arms to steady herself. She looks up, her eyes finally meeting mine. Her mouth falls open, but she quickly regains her composure. Her hands go to her hair, then swipe down her shirt as if she's checking to make sure she's still put together. I guess I'll bite my tongue and not tell her how much her nipples have hardened under that blouse.

What she doesn't know won't kill her.

Though it might kill me.

Her pupils dilate, and she gulps. "I'm sorry."

"Yeah, well, maybe you should watch where you're going." I know I could be nicer, but seeing her get all pissy is kind of fun.

She raises her chin. "And maybe you shouldn't take up the whole darn hallway."

"I won't apologize for my size, Smalls."

"Smalls?" She cringes, her hands on her hips. "I have a name you know."

"Carissa Smallson. I remember... Smalls," I repeat deadpanned. "I think it's a fitting nickname."

"Well, I hate it."

"I didn't ask you."

She huffs. "Can I ask you something?"

"No," I tell her, turning to go back into the locker room.

She asks anyway. "Are you always this much of a dick?"

What the fuck?

"Excuse me?" I turn on her.

"You heard me, Nelly...er...Nelson." She shakes her head, embarrassed at her lame nickname attempt, and mumbles, "Sorry, that didn't sound right in my head either."

I step up to her, flaring my nostrils as I stare down into her face. "Let me give you a piece of advice, princess."

She scowls at her second nickname, but she breathes heavily against me, keeping her chin up as if to not be intimidated by me.

Good girl.

She's strong-willed.

I'm mildly impressed.

But hell if I'll tell her that.

"If you're going to want the respect and cooperation of those of us on the team, it might be helpful to actually get to know us and that starts with our names."

"This has nothing to do with your names, and you know it." She scoffs. "Are you seriously that butt-hurt over some Lucky Charms?"

Yes. Yes, I am.

"You don't know a damn thing about me, Smalls, so I'm not going to justify my words or actions to you in any way. I owe you nothing."

She shrugs. "I mean, except an apology for the sexual harassment in the middle of the cereal aisle last night, but we can save that for later."

"So, you did know who I was! I knew you were lying this morning."

"Oh, my God. No, I really didn't know who you were, but regardless, how could I not lie?" She juts her hip out, clearly irritated. "You almost ruined my first day on the job, and I had only been here an hour!"

"Not my problem."

I watch her take a steadying breath and raise my brows in curiosity of what she could possibly say next.

"Look, we got off on the wrong foot. Last night wasn't my

best moment, and I'm sure after your big loss last night, it wasn't yours either."

Big loss?

Fuck that. We only lost by two.

"So, we could call a truce? Or start over? I'm really quite pleasant to work with, and I see no reason why we can't put this behind us and be friendly from here on ou—"

"Yeah, I'm going to stop you right there because this..." I gesture between us. "Us? We are not friends. We never were, and we never will be. You work for the Red Tails, just as I do, only your job requires you to follow me around and make me look good. Other than that, I owe you not a goddamn thing, so let's get one thing straight. I'm not here to be your friend. I'm here to do a job, and that job is to play hockey and win games. You don't have the faintest idea what kind of pressure I'm under or what I have to accomplish daily to keep myself and this team in good standing across the board."

"I get—"

"And if you think there will ever be anything friendly between us," I interrupt, "you will be sorely disappointed."

I stare into her deep brown eyes, daring her to say something else, but she doesn't. Her cheeks hollow, and I can tell she's biting the inside, probably to keep from saying something she knows she'll regret.

"One more thing..."

To put the cherry on top of this Carissa sundae, I lean into her ear and whisper something I know will piss her off.

"Might want to bring a sweater when you're at work, Smalls. You work near the ice, and your tight little nipples are screaming at me through that shirt."

Her mouth falls open in a gasp, making me bite my tongue, lest I make another lewd comment about what I could do to them with my tongue. Without another word, I turn and pull open the door to the locker room, leaving the pretty new girl speechless and perhaps mortified in the hallway.

A small piece of me, and I'm talking ever so tiny, feels bad that I was a complete dick to a woman when I didn't really need to be. But a greater part of me, and the part I easily give in to, thinks she didn't get anything she didn't deserve.

I have work to do.

The last thing I want to do is play nice with the help.

CHAPTER 4

Carissa

"Whoa! He said that?" Chelsea's jaw hangs open before she takes another swig of her beer.

I nod. "Swear to God, he all but thanked me for his invitation to the nipple show." I cover my face in embarrassment, but Chelsea laughs.

"Oh, this is too good! The hot, sexy hockey player talked about your nipples, Rissy!"

"Yeah well, he also said we are not, nor will we ever be, friends. Not that I was thinking we would be besties or anything but what the hell? The guy was a complete ass."

"I mean..." She shakes her head in wonderment. "What guy wouldn't be a complete ass when you fuck with his Lucky Charms the way you did?"

We both fall into a fit of giggles about a grown-ass man throwing a tantrum over a kid cereal.

"So, other than the newest douche in your life, did the rest of the day go all right?"

"Yeah, it really did. My boss seems nice. Eager for me to show her what I can do. And just from walking around and watching the team during today's practice, I already have several ideas for some new social media posts that I think the fans will love. You know, if the players cooperate with me."

"I'm sure they'll be fine. They can't all be douchey assholes, right?"

"You would think. Milo Landric seemed nice enough, and

Dex was pretty friendly."

"See? I told you. It'll be fine. And I'm sure cereal guy... What's his name again?"

"Colby Nelson. The team captain."

"Right, Colby. I'm sure Colby will come around. He just needs his losing streak to end." She winks at me as the side of her mouth curves up. "Maybe you can give him some pointers."

I burst out laughing. "Right. Me. The girl who knows next to nothing about hockey except that puck in the other net equals good. Puck in our net equals very bad. Plus, the guy hates me. God, if you could've seen his face before he walked away..."

His piercing stare was enough to make me feel like half a person. He made me want to cry in that moment, but no way was I going to let him know he had beaten me.

"Hey!" She waves her hands in front of me. "Earth to Carissa. Since when are you a Negative Nancy? I'll answer that for you. Since never. You're a badass, confident, strong-willed woman, and you're damn good at your job. Don't let one bad apple spoil your whole bushel. You can do this."

Her words seep into my brain, fueling me. She has always been my personal cheerleader. Since the very first day we met on college move-in day as young, naïve first-year students.

"You're right." I nod. "I'm not a negative person."

"That's right. You're not."

"I see the glass half full."

She raises her glass to me. "Damn right you do."

"Fuck his Lucky Charms."

"Yeah!" she cheers. "Fuck 'em!"

"I'm gonna be his lucky charm. He won't even see it comin'."

"Yes, queen! Do it naked and someone will be comin' when he tastes how magically delicious you are!"

Enter screeching record here

Wait.

What?

I tilt my head, giving my best friend a curious glance.

She cringes. "Too much?"

I bust out laughing once again, holding my thumb and forefinger close together. "Yes. Just a little."

"Oh, damn. Well, he's probably just pissed because you're hot and now he can't have you because, you know..." She shrugs. "One, you work together, and two, he supposedly hates you, so he shot himself in the foot. Now he can't turn back and be all like, 'hey, hot stuff,'" she says in a low, not nearly sexy enough voice for a true Colby Nelson impression. "'You look magically delicious. Want to jump my bones?'"

More giggles...and a big, fake gag from me. "Yeah, that won't be happening. Sorry to disappoint. He might be easy on the eyes, but his personality needs a complete overhaul."

"Meh. Maybe he's just going through something. Things can always change. You'll work your Carissa magic, and things will be fine in no time."

Always the optimist, this one.

I swallow the last drops of my beer and take a deep breath, releasing it as I look around Pringle's Pub. It's not the fanciest bar in Chicago, and not the biggest, but the atmosphere isn't bad, the appetizers are good, and the servers are quick. So, I guess it's not all bad.

"It's hard to believe the guys on the team come here. It doesn't seem... I don't know, big enough for all of them. It must get pretty cramped in here on game days."

Chelsea nods. "I imagine you're right. How have we never come here before?"

"I don't know." I shrug. "Probably because it's not close to campus and until now I have been living in a bubble. I just figured it would be a good idea to scope it out, so if I'm here with the team, I can come up with a few social media ideas."

"See? Always working, you are. I'm so proud of you."

"Thanks, friend. That means a lot."

"Have you told your parents about your job change?"

"Hell no!" I shake my head adamantly. "And please don't say

a word if they come asking about me."

She holds up a hand and crosses her heart. "I would never. You know that."

"The last thing I need is them knowing I'm now working amongst a group of millionaires. There's no telling what they might do."

God knows they've done enough.

Even with a nearly doubled salary from my last job, it'll still take me years to clean up their messes.

"I try not to talk to them unless I absolutely have to. I just can't trust them anymore."

Chelsea nods. "I totally get that. I'm sorry you have to deal with it at all."

"Yeah...me too. But that's the hand I was dealt."

Even though I never asked to play.

"So, you've survived your first few weeks. You've gotten your bearings around the arena and with the team, and you've gotten your feet wet," Valerie states. "You've made several solid posts to social media, all beautifully done and hilarious by the way."

I return her energetic smile. "Thank you! Yeah, I wanted to put out a few videos of them practicing, studying, working out. Things like that so the fans can feel like they're part of what goes on backstage while I'm still feeling out the players. And when the right background music hits..."

"It's perfect." She nods. "The fans are really taking to it. Speaking of that, I spoke a while back with a man by the name of Aaron Strongfield. He's an agent who represents a few on the team as well as a few players from other teams, but he brought up a few concerns about Colby Nelson, as did Coach Denovah."

Ugh. Of all the guys on the team.

Though it comes as no surprise.

Nobody likes a grinch.

"They both think some positive attention on him might help lift him from his funk. We don't tend to like it when chatter gets too loud on different media platforms about one or more of our players not pulling his weight. And the fans don't like it when a popular player such as Colby, who has a multi-million-dollar contract, isn't 'earning his keep,' as they like to lovingly put it."

I chuckle lightly. "Leave it to the fans to be blunt, huh?"

Though he kind of deserves it when he carries around that salty attitude.

"Exactly." She nods. "Think you can help him out?"

Out the door? Hell yeah.

"I can certainly do my best."

"Perfect. If I were you, I would spend a few minutes this morning behind your laptop watching a few post-game interviews and conversations. It might give you a little insight into where Colby's head is at and how you might be able to help him turn things around."

"All right. I'll get right on it."

"Do you guys get annoyed with how many times you're sitting in the penalty box?" a reporter asks Colby after one of their losses last week. The internet has been a plethora of help when it comes to Colby Nelson interviews. Everyone always wants to talk to the captain and quite frankly, given the sexy, sweaty look he has after a game, I don't mind watching these videos one bit.

"Of course, I'm annoyed. What kind of question is that?" Colby asks with a twist to his lip. "Yeah. I'm annoyed. We want to win, you know? We have integrity out there too, you know? Hell yeah, I'm annoyed. Like I'm annoyed with you for even asking that question."

I cringe at Colby's attitude in this video. "Whoa. Slow your roll, Captain."

Does he even enjoy the sport?

Why is he still doing it if he's in such a sour mood all the time?

The reporter continues, "How frustrating is this for you? You've lost four in a row after a strong winning streak. It's now a crucial point in the year when you're about halfway through the season. Are you feeling discouraged at all?"

"Oh, God." I roll my eyes. What does he expect Colby to say? I understand it's their job, but sometimes reporters ask the most ridiculous questions.

"Discouraged? God. I mean, when you go through stretches like this, of course...you... I don't... I don't even understand your question.

"Well, what's morale been like?"

"What's the morale been? It fucking sucks, man. That's how it is. Nobody likes to lose, Mike."

"Is this the team consciously—or—subconsciously trying to get your coach fired?"

"What? Hell no!"

I press the pause button and wipe my hand across my forehead.

"So, this is why they want to clean up his reputation. God, he's a perpetual crankpot."

Coach Den was right. I do have my work cut out for me.

This morning's practice is a special one because it's open to one hundred people, all of whom were winners of an online contest giving them the opportunity to watch the Red Tails practice. That means today, there are several young kids and their parents, as well as a few super fans lining the rink watching the team as they work. It's a great opportunity for the Red Tails community to be a little more up close and personal with the players and lets them see that the team is working hard for them.

I make my way around the rink, snapping pictures and

videos of the players and fans, as well as their interactions in between practice runs. Many of the children have signs with them in support of their favorite players that they hold up along the plexiglass in hopes they'll get acknowledged. Some of them are cute and sweet, and some are downright funny.

One group of what look to be college-aged girls holds up a sign that reads:

I WISH I ONLY GOT TWO MINUTES FOR HOOKING!

Another one, which made me laugh—and I most definitely took a picture—reads:

MILO LANDRIC GIVES GREAT SCOREGASMS!

But my favorite of them all so far though is a red poster board with large yellow letters held up by a young boy seated on his dad's shoulders. No older than seven or eight years old, he's dressed in a heavy coat and has a Red Tails fleece hat covering his head. The sign he holds against the glass says:

RED TAILS! YOU HELPED ME BEAT CANCER. THANK YOU!

He slaps the glass whenever the players skate by, but one player in particular stops right in front of him, reads his sign, and then motions for him to meet him at the opening of the rink, where the players come on and off the ice.

To my surprise, that player is number sixty-six, Colby Nelson.

"Shit," I murmur to myself and squeeze my eyes closed. "Don't be a dick to the kid, Nelson. For the love of God."

The need to catch whatever it is Colby says or does on camera overcomes me, and I scoot around the rink where I'm a few rows back to catch the moment with my phone. Colby asks one of the staffers something, and a moment later is handed a marker. He takes his gloves and helmet off, and then reaches behind him to pull off his jersey. The boy's jaw drops in surprise as Colby signs the back of it and hands it to him and his father. He says a few words that I can't possibly hear from where I'm standing and then gives the kid a fist bump. The dad shakes Colby's hand and is all smiles as he holds a short conversation with him. Finally, he skates away, but what happens next brings tears to my eyes.

Colby says something to the guys, and then the entire team skates over to this kid one at a time and gives him a part of their uniform. A signed jersey, a signed helmet, Zeke gives him his goalie gloves, and Dex hands him his stick. This kid is blessed with more hockey paraphernalia than he probably ever imagined he would receive today.

All because of Colby?

The rest of the crowd around the ice applauds and cheers for this brave young boy, and I have to suck in my emotions enough to continue doing my job, making sure to get this all on video because it will make a beautiful post for the team.

Regardless of what I think of him, or the impression he's left up until now, he has a soft spot in the rough-around-the-edges personality he portrays. Maybe Colby Nelson isn't the asshole I think he is. And the moments I caught on camera just now will surely show the fans who he really is.

A guy with a good heart.

With practice almost over, I grab the materials I brought down to the ice with me and make my way to the tunnel to film the other post I had planned for today. If I can get the guys to answer one simple question, I'll have something fun to put out to our fans this afternoon.

Setting up my phone stand in the tunnel just off the rink, I prepare to record each team member as they come off the ice from practice. Holding up my posterboard that reads:

WHICH TEAMMATE HAS THE BEST GAME DAY RITUAL?

One by one they start to trickle off the ice, and one by one they read the words on my poster board, brows pinched at first, but then most of them smirk and give their answer. One tells me Dex Foster listens to Taylor Swift before every game. Another tells me one of the other players has a little dance party with himself to get hyped up. But it's the starting lineup that surprises me the most.

Dex comes off the ice with a beaming smile, but after reading my sign, he nods with a more respectful expression. "Dude, it's Nelson and his Lucky Charms."

Quinton is next. "Uh...that's a toss-up between Foster singing some Tay-Tay or... well..." He seems to reconsider. "Probably Nelson and his Lucky Charms."

What is it with Colby and his cereal obsession?

"Hey, Carissa!" Milo smiles as he comes off the ice and spots me in the tunnel. I point to my sign without speaking since I'm recording, and he reads. What I don't expect though, is the slip in his expression. His smile falters a bit, changing to one of...pride? "Definitely Nelson. Eats a bowl of Lucky Charms before every game."

Narrowing my eyes, I quietly ask, "Why does he do that?"

Milo gently shakes his head, dismissing my question. "Not my story to tell."

My smile also falls, and suddenly, I'm questioning this entire idea. Why is everyone answering with Colby's Lucky Charms, yet nobody says why?

Hawken comes off the ice just before Colby and answers the same way, but when Colby enters the tunnel, I'm no longer smiling. And neither is he.

I hold my breath as he takes one look at my sign and frowns and lets out a huff, rolling his eyes before walking past me, nearly knocking me over in the process.

My stomach twists.

"Colby, wait!" I shout after him as he passes me by. He takes a few more steps and then stops, releasing an irritated sigh and turning around with a scowl.

"What do you want?"

"Uh, I just..." I rub my now sweaty palm on my hip. "What you did earlier, for that little boy..."

He shrugs. "What about it?"

"That was incredible of you. Almost like you have a soft spot inside that..." I gesture to his body. "Rough exterior."

He stares at me for a moment, and I second-guess even bringing it up in the first place.

Why does he look at me like that?

Like he wants to eat me but doesn't want to be bothered with me at the same time.

"Uh...anyway. I got some great shots, so umm, I'll make sure to post them and tag you. It'll definitely score you some points with the fans."

"I don't need help with fans," he clips. "Especially not from you."

"Well, according to Coach Den and your agent, you do. So, this is me doing my job to—how did you put it?" I raise my quote fingers into the air. "Make you look good."

"Are we done here?"

What the fuck?

I'm trying here!

With a heavy huff, I try to change the subject. "Your teammates all said you have a cereal obsession before every game. Maybe you could tell me why you—"

"Is that what they said?" His mouth curls and his nostrils flare. "I have an obsession?"

"Well, they didn't use the word obsession. I just figured—"

"Right," he snaps. "I didn't think so."

For a moment, I wonder if his cold glare might turn into

him invading my space and trying to intimidate me like he's done before, but he doesn't. Instead, his eyes fall to my shoes. He looks me up and down, and then rolls his eyes, leaving me, and continuing down the hall to the locker room. I immediately look down at my shoes —red pumps —and my outfit, wondering if something is out of place. But as far as I know, I look as put together as I should be for a normal workday.

Ugh.

What gives with him?

I'm not sure at this point if any kind of working relationship with Colby can be salvaged or not, but I can't admit defeat just yet. I've got to figure out the importance of his pregame routine and why everyone on his team gave the same answer. There has to be more to it than what he's letting on. If I'm being honest with myself, I'm starting to feel guilty that our very first fight was over the exact same cereal.

He was desperate for it.

Why did he need it that night?

The game was over.

Something flutters inside my chest and my eyes shoot up to watch Colby as he stalks down the hallway.

Oh no...did he not...

Did I...

I know I'm not the reason they've lost the last four games. There's no way it's because of a box of cereal. But why do I feel like I somehow played a part in how he's been handling it lately?

Crap.

I have to fix this.

Somehow.

CHAPTER 5

Colby

"I have an obsession." I scowl at Carissa's words as I trudge down the hall to the locker room. "She has a lot of nerve."

It's the oddest sensation to come off the ice after a strong practice, feeling good with a positive outlook, and then immediately spot Carissa Smallson standing in the tunnel. For a split second, I felt a hammering in my chest and a flutter in my stomach and then, just like that, it was gone. One look at her with her sign and the question she was asking, and I knew I wouldn't appease her with an answer.

She doesn't deserve to know why I do what I do.

And it pisses me off that she was making light of a part of me I'm proud of.

A part of me I know doesn't change anything.

A part of me that helps me remember.

I push through the locker room doors, and it feels like the air in the room is sucked out as the guys all stop to stare at me, waiting for me to say something. Do something.

"What?" I stop midway through the room, shifting to look at all of them. Some go back to changing and others continue to watch me.

"We didn't tell her, Nelson," Zeke is the first to say. "None of us did."

"Yeah, she doesn't know why, man." Quinton claps me on the shoulder with a swift nod and then sits to untie his skates.

"Whatever." I lay my stick against my stall, having forgotten to store it in the bin outside, and plop down on my bench. "Tell her whatever the hell you want. I don't care."

Milo shakes his head. "Not our story to tell, Colb. We always have your back. You know that, right?"

"If you don't want us to like her," Hawken starts.

Dex beams. "Even though she's a fine piece of ass with a rack like—"

My head snaps up from untying my skate. "Hey. A little respect, all right?"

Silently, the guys stare me down, brows raised.

"Ooh, so it's like that, eh?" Dex teases.

"Like what?"

Dex winks at Milo who lets out a light chuckle and then asks gently, "You attracted to her, Colb?"

"What? No."

None of them seem to believe my answer as they all silently smirk, lower their heads back down, and untie their skates.

"Look guys, she's part of the franchise now, all right? Like it or not —and right now I'm not particularly happy about it — she's on our team, and the very least we can do is show her a little respect. I don't always like you assholes either, but I put up with you and try to treat you with a modicum of respect."

Zeke throws his worn stinky sock right at my face. "You big, lying ass piece of shit," he laughs. "You love us. Don't deny it. You'd be lonely without us."

He might be right about that.

But I'll deny it to anyone who asks.

"Bullshit."

Zeke's sock-throwing breaks the tension, and we all get in a good laugh.

And a nice round of sweaty sock ball toss.

We're nothing if not a bunch of middle school boys in adult-sized bodies.

I like to be the first one at the arena on game day. Not just because I feel like it's the leader-like thing to do —first to arrive and last to leave—but because it helps put me in the right headspace for what I know will be a full-energy day. It's nice to be alone on the ice in the peace and quiet. It's reminiscent of my childhood, skating on the pond on my family's farm in Wisconsin when all you could hear outside was the crunch of your boots in the snow as you walked, and the soft sounds of the wind carrying snowflakes through the air. I'm not even sure I'm technically permitted on the ice this early in the morning, but Bruno, the only staff person around at this time of the day, never seems to mind and always wishes me a good, clean skate.

In about an hour, I can get a good feel for the ice under my skates, and then shoot a few pucks into the net from more angles than I probably ever actually shoot from in one game. It's good practice, and it feels good to channel my energy that way to start my day.

I'm mid-shoot when I notice movement in one of the offices a few floors up. Walking past an office lamp causes the light to flicker on the rink, which draws my eyes up —and it's then that I spot her.

What is she doing here so early?

She doesn't know that I've seen her, as she has her eyes trained on her desk. She pushes a bit of her hair behind her ear as she studies whatever is on her computer. I shake my head, trying to get the fact I think she's relatively pretty out of my mind, so I can get back to my skate —until she stands up and walks across her office to get something out of her coat pocket.

Oh, my God.

She's wearing a jersey.

The oversized jersey hangs just below her ass which is clothed in a pair of tight black leggings. I want to hate the look, but I can't.

She looks... Shit.

She looks good.

Part of me is dying for her to turn enough that I can see whose name is on that jersey. And for a split second, I question what I might feel like if I were to see my name on the back.

Would I like it?

Would I hate it?

Would I ask her to take it off?

Hell no, I wouldn't ask her to take it off.

But I would want to take it off her...slow and steady...while I—

Get a grip, Nelson!

You're not interested in her.

You told her you don't want to be friends.

And she hates you anyway.

End of story.

I take one last look at the exact same moment she happens to turn and look out her window, her eyes connecting with mine immediately. I'm the only one here for her to see.

She stares for a minute, and then raises her hand slowly to wave at me, but I don't return the gesture. Instead, I swallow the knot in my throat and ignore her, reminding myself I don't want to give her the time of day. I may have told the guys to be respectful, but I didn't say they had to be her friend. And friend is one thing I don't have the time, energy, or interest for. I have a job to do.

My phone dings where I have it sitting on the rink wall with my water bottle and towel. Already knowing who the message will be from, I finish out my skate before I skid to a halt next to my belongings.

> **Elias:** Hey! Good luck tonight! Eyes on the puck. Hustle, hit, and never quit.

My brother's message is the same every game day and one we

used to hear as kids all the time. There was a time when I thought Elias would also end up in the NHL and that we might one day play together on the same team, but he chose a different path, and I respect him for it. He's my biggest fan, and has been for years, and he's the only one who truly understands where my mind can go at any given time. He never judges me. Just lends his ear, kicks me in the balls sometimes, and tells me what I need to hear —even if it's not what I want to hear. In several ways, he's a better coach for me than Denovah is, and I appreciate him more than he knows.

> **Me: Thanks Bro. You coming tonight?**

> **Elias: Wouldn't miss it! Beckham and I will be in the suite with a few of the other guys from work.**

> **Me: What? No date tonight? *Smirk emoji***

> **Elias: That's what Pringle's is for asshat. *Smiley face***

> **Me: LOL. Right. How could I have forgotten?**

Ever since my brother has been on the accounting team for the Red Tails, he takes no shame in taking advantage of the puck bunnies who flaunt themselves in and around Pringle's Pub, hoping to score a professional athlete's adrenaline-filled dick for the night. When they can't find it, they'll leave with anyone if they're desperate enough. At least that's what I always tell Elias. It's a younger brother's job to be the pain in the ass, right?

I'm just doin' my job.

I make a quick stop in the locker room to trade out my skates for tennis shoes so I can hit the gym, but when I reach my stall, there's a gift waiting for me that wasn't there when I got here this morning.

Wrapped tightly with a red bow are five full-sized boxes of Lucky Charms. A small white envelope rests on top of the boxes with my name scrolled across it in what I can only assume is a woman's handwriting. I pull the small card out of the envelope and open it, reading the message inside.

Colby,

I really am sorry.

Good luck tonight. You've got this.

-Carissa

"Fuck." I drop down on the bench in front of my stall and reread her handwritten note three more times, each time my chest tightening a little more than the last. How am I supposed to be pissed at her when she goes and does something like this? I didn't see this coming. Didn't think she was that kind of person, honestly.

The kind of woman who does nice things for douchey guys.

The kind of woman who asks for forgiveness.

What am I supposed to do now?

This is obviously her way of calling a truce I was never going to give.

She's caught me off guard, and I don't know how to respond. My insides begin to quiver. A feeling I've experienced a few times over the past couple weeks, so I blow out a series of short breaths to regain control of myself and make the decision to not respond to Carissa right away. I have more important things to focus on.

Like winning tonight's game.

I push the gift into my stall and quickly change out my

footwear, and then high tail it to the gym for my next workout.

Lucky for me, I don't see Carissa for the entire day after this morning's skate, so I'm able to keep my head in the game and feel confident that we can pull out a win tonight. The energy is high in the arena as the team takes to the ice against the Vancouver Wolves. Once Landric starts the game with a faceoff against their center player, the puck never stops.

It's all hands on deck as we move around the ice like a well-oiled machine.

At the beginning of the third period, we're up by two points when the Wolves shoot a puck past Zeke Miller, bringing our lead down to one point.

"Shit!" Zeke shouts across the ice when he realizes he let a puck through. Nobody is harder on Miller than Miller, so we let him have his angry moment. It usually fuels him to finish strong. With Milo on top, he passes to Dex who makes a strong move to the net, but the shot bounces off the outside and is rebounded by Vancouver. Fighting back and forth for control of the puck, there's a battle along the wall including me, Quinton Shay, and three of their players. The crowd is on their feet, fans pounding on the glass next to us as we battle for the puck. It's finally released and shot across the ice, where Foster and Landric pass between each other. I race to the net as fast as my legs will carry me and spin around just in time for Landric to pass the puck to me.

Out in front, my adrenaline spikes as I shoot, watching the puck bank off their goalie's leg. Milo, Dex, Hawken, and Quinton are now with me, fighting for rebounds but unable to make any direct shot. When possession comes back to me, I race around the ice, driving the puck with the control of my stick until the very last moment I can possibly hold off. Bringing my stick back to near shoulder height, I slap it forward so that it hits the ice and bends slightly, acting as a spring against the puck, giving it immense speed. I watch with bated breath as it hits their goalie's shoulder and sails into the net, the red light and sirens going off signaling our third goal of the game.

"Motherfucking Yes!" I shout with a beaming smile and a raise of my stick as the crowd goes wild celebrating our lead. My teammates jump me, one after another, in heavily padded hugs and helmet slaps, some of us slipping and falling onto the ice.

Those are totally the bruises worth having.

"That is how it's *done*, Nelson!"

"Kick Ass Colby!"

"Beast Mode!"

Milo claps me on the shoulder. "Welcome back, motherfucker."

I can't help but smile and hug my best friend as we skate off the ice and onto the bench, the second string taking over for the next few plays.

Yeah. That felt good. Haven't scored a damn goal in the last four games, but tonight is my night. It feels good to be back. I drain my water bottle into my mouth, the cool water a refreshing treat as sweat drips from my face.

I catch Milo's eye as I wipe my face with my towel.

"What?"

With a smirk, he half shrugs and then leans over as close to me as he can get with our gear and helmets on. "Must've been those Lucky Charms."

I eye him curiously and his smile grows. "Don't think for a second I don't know about them, asshole. She played nice."

"Yeah, yeah."

"And we're going to win this fucking game."

I look up at the game clock —one minute left —and nod.

"Looks that way."

"Maybe you could play nice, too."

With that, he winks and scoots over to grab his water bottle, never saying another word about the gift left for me in the locker room, or the person who left it. As soon as the buzzer sounds, the entire team is on the ice celebrating our first win in the last five games. The deafening roar of the crowd coupled with the contagious excitement of the team puts me in a euphoric state.

And as I'm showering off the day's hard work and throwing

on my clothes for a celebration at Pringle's Pub, I actually consider thanking Carissa in the morning for her kind gesture.

CHAPTER 6

Carissa

As someone who hasn't been to many professional hockey games, I wouldn't know what constitutes a good game. But what those guys just left out on that rink tonight was nothing short of amazing. When I thought Vancouver might overthrow their lead, it was all I could do not to vomit from anxiety. And for Colby's sake, I just wanted him to have a good game. I wanted him to get back to whatever happy place he would usually be in when he's playing, instead of the slump he's been in.

He didn't say a word to me all day about the gift I left him, and that's okay. He doesn't ever have to say anything. I hope I didn't embarrass him. I hope he knows I was being sincere and not trying to make light of his special game day rituals. And I hope one day he can let go of our first couple confrontations and learn that I'm not such a bad person to work with. I mean, as far as I know, I'm delightful.

Ha! I should put that on a shirt.

I'm just making my way out of the press conference, and editing a quick TikTok, when Milo spots me.

"Carissa!"

"Hey! Congratulations on the win, Milo! You must be pumped!"

"Hell yeah we are!" He beams. "We're celebrating at Pringle's in a little under an hour. You should come."

"Erm...uh..." I cringe. "I don't know if I—"

"Have you ever been there?"

"Yeah, I—"

"Smallson!" My name is shouted from down the hall, and a very happy Dex Foster and Hawken Malone grab me for a hug, much to Milo's amusement. "Pringle's! Tonight! You're coming, right?"

"Uh..."

"That's what I was just telling her," Milo says with a nudge. "She thinks she's going to weasel out."

"No can do." Hawken shakes his head.

"Nope." Dex points at me. "You're coming. No questions asked. Be there."

My eyes narrow as I consider using this invitation to my advantage. "All right, if I show up, does that mean you three will let me make a TikTok of you doing something fun and silly?"

Milo starts, "Depends on what it—"

"Fuck yeah, we'll do it." Dex chuckles. "Whatever you need. Tonight is for celebrating."

I laugh along with them. "All right then. It's a deal. I'll see ya there."

All three guys smirk at one another and raise their fists in the air, shouting, "Yaaassss!"

Pringle's Pub is a hopping place, and nearly wall-to-wall with people as fans celebrate tonight's win. Music plays loudly overhead, the party-like beat creating an urge to dance. A few girls are already at it, but there isn't much room for dancing as I work my way through the bar.

"Carissa! Back here!" I see a hand go up in the air and wave as Dex and Hawken gesture for me to join them and the rest of the team. Wading through the crowd to get back to them, I take notice of how many women in short skirts and dresses are hanging around, hoping to snag one of these athletes.

What did Valerie call them again?

Puck bunnies?

"Hey guys!" I smile at the group of them, including two men I don't know, as I tear off my coat and hang it on the hook just behind their booth. It's a little funny to see eight large men sardined into what seems like a tight pub booth. And somehow, they've left room for me, which makes this even funnier in my mind. It's a big booth, but still.

When I turn back around, they're all staring at me with silly, heated expressions. Well, except for Colby who looks like he's about to devour me.

"What?"

My cheeks warm with embarrassment, wondering if this shirt also shows my goddamn nipples. I swear to God, Chicago must be one of the hardened nipple capitals of the world with its blustery winters.

"Shut your mouths, gentlemen," Zeke cackles. "It's just a jersey."

"It's not just a jersey," Dex murmurs.

"It's a woman like Carissa Smallson wearing our jersey." Hawken nods, approving of my outfit.

Zeke shakes his head, amused. He meets my eyes and explains, "It's not every day a hot chick wearing our team jersey is hanging out with us after a game." He shrugs, gesturing to the women mulling around the place with his head. "Well, not unless they're one of those—"

"Puck bunnies? Is that what they're called?"

That seems to break the tension and most of the men chuckle. All of them but Colby, who goes back and forth between staring me down and not meeting my eye.

"Puck bunnies, indeed," Dex confirms with a heated nod. "Zeke's just jealous because he's already spoken for, so no puck bunnies for him. I bet those girls would all like to be you right now though, Carissa."

"Well, you can have any one of them you want, Foster," I tell him. "Because I'm just here to do a job." I gesture to the two extra men sitting at the table and tilt my head with a friendly smile.

"I'm sorry, we haven't met. I'm Carissa Smallson. Social media marketing." I offer my hand to the first gentleman seated next to Colby.

"Elias Nelson." He smiles. "Pleasure to meet you, Carissa."

My brows peak. "Nelson, huh? Does that mean you're related to this grump?" I nod my head in Colby's direction in hopes the grumpy gene doesn't run rampant in the Nelson family. Elias laughs.

Thank God.

"Older, much wiser brother and accountant for the team. And whatever he's said, don't let him fool ya. He may have a rough, hardened exterior, but this one's nothing but a big-ass teddy bear on the inside."

Colby holds his glass mid-sip and flips off his brother. "Fuck you, bro."

"Love you too, Co-Co."

Co-Co... Wonder what that's about.

Not that I'll ever ask. Colby might skin me alive or feed me to a pool of piranhas.

"Good to know." I nod approvingly.

Elias introduces the guy next to him. "Carissa, this is my friend and colleague, Beckham Fox."

Beckham offers his hand, which I shake happily.

"Nice to meet you, Beckham."

"Pleasure's mine, Carissa."

"All right, gentlemen, I suppose we should get to work, huh?"

"Nooope." Hawken shakes his head, sliding me a beer. "We celebrate first. Got this for you. Drink up."

I wrap my hand around the glass and Hawken stops me. "By the way, never accept an open drink from anyone in this bar, got it?"

Eyeing him with a raised brow, I slowly push the glass he offered me back toward him. "Ooookay."

He laughs. "I don't mean me. We're safe. You can trust us. No offense, and I know this sounds crass, but we don't need to drug women to get them to sleep with us." He points at me as if I'm being scolded. "But nobody else buys you a drink unless you're watching that drink be made and immediately handed to you. You can't trust the crazies in this place, and there are enough women around lookin' for a good time. You have to keep your guard up."

"Awww, you lookin' out for me, Malone?" I'm finally getting their last names seared into my brain enough to use them.

"You seem like too nice of a girl to watch you get into some trouble."

I lift a brow. "You think I'm one of those good-girl types?"

Dex chuckles and hell, if I don't see Colby take notice across the table.

Hawken nods. "I absolutely fuckin' do. Yeah."

I shake my head. "Oooh, you have a lot to learn then, buddy."

"Oh yeah?"

I don't answer him. I merely give him a half shrug.

Quinton gestures to my drink on the table. "Think you can chug that beer?"

I scoff because uh, duh. With a tilt to my head, I ask him, "Would this be a good time to let you know I won every drink chugging competition in college I ever participated in?"

Dex guffaws with a shake of his head. "You're bluffing."

I raise a brow. "Am I?"

"No fuckin' way can you chug that whole glass faster than me."

I narrow my eyes playfully at the broad-shouldered man sitting across from me.

"Are you throwing down the gauntlet, Foster?"

He leans on the table, his face close to mine. "Are you picking it up, Smallson?"

I wrap my hand around my glass, lift it in the air, and wait for Dex to do the same. I also hand Milo my phone and ask him to record our little competition for my next TikTok.

"You're going down, Dex."

"In your dreams, Carissa."

"All right, all right. On the count of three," Hawken says. "One...two...three!"

We clink our glasses together, and then Dex begins to chug his beer. I give him about a three second advantage before I tilt my head back, open my throat, and pour my entire glass down the hatch, wiping my mouth with the back of my hand when I'm done and giggling at Dex who is still chugging.

"Holy shit, Carissa!" Zeke's eyes grow huge. "How the fuck did you do that?"

I meet Colby's eyes and watch his Adam's apple move up and down as he swallows. His stare moves between my eyes and my lips, though he never says a word.

How is he not having a good time?

He just won his game for Pete's sake.

I wonder if he doesn't want me here.

I'm sure he didn't want me to meet his family.

He's seriously not accepting my apology.

"Secret talent, I guess." A giggle erupts from my mouth, and I stop it with my hands over my lips. Turning to Milo, I ask, "Did you get all that on video?"

He hands me back my phone, a goofy smile on his face. "Sure did. That was seriously impressive."

Dex slams his glass down and shakes his head. "Woman!" He points at me. "Never do that in front of me again or I'll be forced to endure an uncomfortable ride home." He jimmies himself in his seat, giving the impression that he's sporting a nice boner. "Fuck me, that was hot!"

What a goofball.

"I need another drink. Be right back, fellas."

"Hey, I can get it for you," Hawken offers, but I'm already up out of my seat.

"I'm sorry, but I can't take an open drink from a man unless I watch it being made and immediately handed to me." Hawken smiles when I wink, tossing his instruction right back at him. "I'll just be a minute. Anybody want anything?" I wave my hand. "Wait. Forget I asked. Next round is on me."

You know...because the six or eight multi-millionaires at this table can't possibly afford their own drinks.

Five beers later, and I am more than happy I chose to say yes to the guys' invitation to join them tonight. They are the most fun group of men I think I've ever hung out with and surprisingly, not one of them has tried to hit on me. They've done no less than five TikTok videos for me, and they've let me take numerous pictures of them for social media. Even Colby glared at me for a quick snap. Dex took several pictures of himself while I was away from the table dancing and then lectured me about not having a password protected phone.

"Meh. I don't have anything to hide."

"You do now, Smallson. I just took about a hundred selfies for you."

"Well, in that case, you deserve to have your shit spread all over the internet. You better watch it, buddy. You know I get paid to put you guys all over social media."

The guys laugh with me, but they know I would never do anything to harm them. They're such a supportive group of guys. So down to earth and just plain fun, and it's been an absolute pleasure getting to know them all.

Colby's personality isn't at all like that of Hawken or Dex, who are clearly the partiers of the group. He's been much more reserved than I expected him to be tonight, and I can't help but wonder if it's because of me. He was in such a great mood at the end of the game. I watched him celebrate their win on the ice. I saw his genuine beaming smile. I watched him hug his friends. But, I also know I'm not his favorite person, and perhaps letting his guard down and relaxing around me is a hard limit for him.

For a moment, I start to feel bad.

And then I remember his emotions aren't my fault.

The only person who can control Colby's thoughts and actions is Colby.

Well, his loss.

Because I'm goddamn delightful!

CHAPTER 7

Colby

In the past three hours, I've watched Carissa Smallson waltz into this bar like she owns the place, not feeling at all uncomfortable. I've watched her tip her head back and pour an entire beer down her throat, eliciting more physical reactions from me than I was ready for. She's gotten my teammates to do crazy dance moves for social media —twerking, grinding, and stripper moves reminiscent of that *Magic Mike* movie —and she's snapped picture after picture of all of us, myself included, just by batting her eyes and saying please. Now she's dancing with a few other ladies, and I can't keep my eyes off her. Well, to be honest, I haven't let her out of my sight because she's had five or six beers tonight without eating much. Someone should be keeping an eye out for her, and that someone is going to be me.

I can't say it's a hard job.

The way she moves her body.

Her confidence.

Her goddamn smile.

Carissa Smallson is a breath of fresh air and not at all the stuffy bitch I mistook her for. I'm not just now coming to that conclusion, but I am just now openly admitting it. She's easily made friends with everyone here, except for me. Thanks to our unpleasant first encounter, I didn't want to be her friend. She doesn't deserve the attitude I've been giving her, I know, but I'm struggling to let down my walls where she's concerned. Mostly because I know where my focus wants to be when I take the time to really notice her, but I also know where my focus needs to be.

Where it's always been.

I'm the team captain.

I have a job to do.

And that job does not include Carissa Smallson.

No matter how good she might look in that jersey tonight.

"Did Zeke leave already?" Dex asks, with some blonde girl hanging on his shoulder, his arm wrapped around her waist.

"Over an hour ago," I answer him. "Lori was waiting up for him."

Dex shakes his head with a laugh. "That boy is whipped!"

Milo, Quinton, and I all nod.

He squeezes the girl on his arm.

"Well, Nila and I are—"

"Nora."

"Huh?" Dex turns to her.

"My name is Nora."

"Oh right. Nora. Nora and I are heading out for the night, fellas. You have yourselves a safe night." With one hand cupping his mouth, he loudly whispers, "Don't forget to use your rubbers!" then salutes us before escorting the blonde from the bar.

"Where's Hawken?" Quinton asks.

Elias lifts his chin, gesturing to the corner on the opposite side of the pub. "Sucking face with some chick over there."

The music changes, and I watch as Carissa waves to her new friends and weaves herself through the crowd over to the bar. I hold my breath, wondering just how much more she's going to drink tonight on top of the several beers she's already had. She's a bit tipsy. I don't want to have to step in and put a stop to it for her own sake, but I will if I have to. As it is, I've already decided to offer her a ride home tonight. Thankfully, she's handed a bottle of water.

"You all right over there?" Milo asks with a grin.

"Yep." I nod, not making eye contact with him. "Why wouldn't I be?"

Elias nudges me. "Did she move six inches? Scratch her nose? Pick a wedgie?"

Okay, that odd set of questions gets me to avert my eyes from Carissa to meet the amused faces of Milo, Quinton, Elias, and Beckham around the table.

"What?"

Milo swallows his laughter. "You haven't taken your eyes off her all night. Do you know that?"

"She's had at least five beers, Milo. Someone should be looking out for her."

"Uh-huh," he says. "And so that falls to you?"

I roll my eyes. "Doesn't everything?"

"What's that supposed to mean?" Quinton asks.

"Nothing. I'm just making sure she's safe."

"You haven't said much to her tonight," Elias reminds me. "Is this a thing? The two of you?"

At the very moment I say, "No," Milo and Quinton are nodding yes.

Taking a breath, ready to defend myself, I see one of the biggest sleazeballs I know approach Carissa at the bar. He's someone we see here often, picking up women every goddamn time he comes in. The two of them strike up a conversation, and my chest tightens. When he touches her hand, and then her arm, I want to yank his testicles right off of his body.

Quinton takes notice, sitting next to me and watching the same scene play out at the bar.

"Shit. That guy?"

I shake my head. "No way is she leaving with that douche."

Milo turns his body around to see who we're talking about. "Who?"

"Sir Fucksalot. Remember him?"

"Of course I remember. The guy who has a different woman in here every time we see him?"

"Yep." I nod, my eyes focused on the only important person in the bar right now.

The minute he touches her waist and she steps back, rage fuels me right out of my seat. It only takes me a few steps to get to the bar, because hell if I care who's in my way, words of caution from my brother and friends be damned. I step up behind Carissa and wrap my arm around her waist, my palm resting on her hip.

"She's with me, pal. You might want to back off."

Every single one of my muscles tenses when Carissa looks up at me. I practically pin her into submission with my eyes.

She flips around in my hold but doesn't step away from me.

"Oh, now you're talking to me?"

"What?"

Does she not get what I'm doing here?

Sir Fucksalot butts in, leaning up to Carissa again. I can smell his whiskey breath from here. "Hey, is this guy bothering you?"

I puff my chest and glare at him, nostrils flaring, brows knitted. "Fuck off right now, or so help me God, I'll tell every woman in this joint what a sleaze you really are. You think I don't see you picking up different women every goddamn time you're here?"

He lifts his shoulder in a half-assed shrug. "I ain't breaking no laws. Some of us can't afford to pay top dollar for a random whore like you can, rich boy."

I step toward the asshole, nearly pinning him to the bar, clench my fist and raise my arm preparing for the punch I'm about to land. "Listen here, you piece of shit!"

"Colby!"

Carissa steps between me and the guy I want to beat to a pulp, both of her hands flying to my chest to steady herself. The warmth that flows through me, straight to my groin, is an unimaginable shock, and suddenly I want her hands everywhere.

What the fuck is happening right now?

Her hazy, pleading eyes peer up at me. "Take me home. Please, Colby."

Milo, Quinton, Elias, and Beckham show up beside me, but all I have eyes for now is the girl who just sucked out all my rage with three little words.

Take me home.

"Let's get out of here, okay?" she breathes against me, her hands clutching my shirt and her eyes barely blinking. "Will you help me get home? Please?"

I gaze down at her. My pulse thrums, yet her touch oddly calms the storm inside me. I can't explain my body's reaction to Carissa's gentle touch. My mind is fucking with me, and I don't like it. Without letting go of my hold on her, I take a deep breath and shift my focus for just a second to the asshole I have pinned to the bar. "Leave. Find another bar to fuck around in."

The guy swallows hard and quickly exits the bar when I release my hold. An awkward silence surrounds us as Carissa smooths her hands down my chest. Once I know the guy has left completely, I return my gaze to the brown eyes staring up at me.

"That was completely unnecessary, don't you think?" she says, pushing on my chest. There's no oomph to her movement, so I know she doesn't really mean it.

"What?"

"I could've handled that guy."

I scoff. "Like hell, you could. Do you even know who that guy is?"

"Does it matter?"

"Yes, Smalls. It matters. Spoiler alert, he wasn't Ryan Reynolds either, but he sure did want in your pants."

"So, what's wrong with that?" Her arms flail. "A girl's allowed to have a good time, you know."

What the fuck?

She has to be toasted.

"Carissa, he would've taken advantage of you or worse. He's done it many times before, and it was written all over his face. He called you a fucking whore. Did you not get that?"

"I..." She freezes, speechless, and I wonder what just bit her tongue.

Milo leans into our conversation. "Hey, I don't mean to

interrupt here, but people are starting to stare. We don't need this all over the internet, all right?"

"Shit," Carissa murmurs, stepping back from me. "I need my coat."

"I have it right here." Quinton hands it to her. "Let's get out of here."

The six of us make our way out of the bar, Quinton and Milo turning right with Elias and Beckham, their keys at the ready, and Carissa turning left.

"Where do you think you're going?" I ask, watching her turn away from us.

She stops and zips up her coat. "To the L Station."

"You don't have a car?" I don't know why I assumed she did.

"No," she huffs. "We can't all afford luxury vehicles in the city, rich boy," she says, imitating Sir Fucksalot.

Was that seriously her way of throwing shade? The guys unsuccessfully hide their smirks as I wipe a frustrated hand down my face.

"Good. I wouldn't let you drive anyway in your condition. Let's go. I'll take you home."

She shakes her head, nearly swaying where she stands. "What condition? I'm perfectly fine, and the L will get me home. It always does."

"Carissa, you've had several beers tonight, and that little body of yours can only hold so much alcohol. Please let me take you home so we know you're safe."

"I'm a big girl, Colby. I can handle it."

Jesus fucking Christ.

"Let's get one thing straight here, Smalls," I say, barging into her personal space. "There's no way in hell you're walking by yourself at night in downtown Chicago to find the L station. And there's also no way in hell you're riding a fucking train home, drunk and alone."

"I'm not drunk, Colby! I'm tipsy. There's a fucking difference, and it's nothing I haven't done bef—"

"For fuck's sake, Smalls, would you just take my goddamn hand and let me drive you home safely, please?"

I hold my hand out to her, and she stares at it for a good fifteen seconds. She even looks to Milo, Quinton, and my brother for help, but they all shrug and tell her I'm right. It's the safer way to go.

At least they agree with me.

"We can do this the easy way or the hard way, but either way, you're coming with me, so the choice is yours."

She blinks several times, and I have half a mind to throw her over my shoulder and toss her in my car, not that I want that all over the internet either.

Her eyes narrow. "What's the hard way?"

She's really trying to challenge me right now?

"The hard way is I throw you over my goddamn shoulder and toss you in my trunk."

She scoffs and rolls her eyes, assuming I'm kidding, but then I move toward her as if I'm about to pick her up, and she finally relents.

"Fine. I'll go with you."

Her hand slips into my protective grasp, and I walk her carefully across the snowy sidewalk to my car, opening the door for her and helping her inside. Relief slowly calms the unrest in my chest.

From outside his car, Elias gives me that look —saying all the things I already know but don't want to admit or hear right now. So, instead, he simply raises his chin and tells me to be careful. I say goodbye to the guys and lower myself into the driver's seat of my car, now alone with the one girl whose effect on me is different, unnerving, exciting, and fucking scary all at the same time.

At my request, she enters her address into my GPS, and I bite my tongue when I see where she lives. It's not the safest part of town by any means, and I have half a mind to refuse to take her there and take her to my place instead. It's not like I don't have enough room for her.

But would I be doing that for her or for me?

We drive in silence for several minutes while I navigate the snowy streets. I can't tell if she's mad, sad, or half asleep, but I think her eyes are closed. She finally lets out a soft sigh, and I try to break the awkward tension.

"Are you comfortable?"

As if she forgot we were arguing just a few minutes ago, she replies, "My buns are definitely toasty, if that's what you're asking. Seat warmers, huh? That's high class."

Her comment makes me chuckle, but only because she really is a bit tipsy, and her satisfied grin is fucking cute. She seems so down-to-earth right now. It's an odd change from where we were just outside the bar.

Not that I'm complaining.

I guess, in all honesty, I would rather laugh with her than say mean things to her that she doesn't deserve.

"You can turn it off right here if you want to." I reach over and show her where the button is to turn off her seat, but she slaps my hand away.

"Not a chance, rich boy! My nether regions haven't felt this warm in a long time." She giggles. "Gotta take my kicks where I can get them."

My grip tightens around the steering wheel. "Uh..."

"Sorry." She snickers. "Too much information. That's the beer talking."

"Right."

Hell, the things I could do to warm up her nether regions.

That is definitely something I should not be thinking about.

She turns her head. "What about you?"

"What about me?"

"Is it 'goodness gracious great balls of fire' over there?"

I bite my cheek so I don't laugh aloud at her, but my brows shoot up. "Are you seriously asking about the temperature of my balls?"

"Pbbbffft!" She giggles, covering her mouth. "You're right.

Sorry. Your balls are none of my business."

I mean, if you want them to be your business...

"Jesus, you must've had more to drink tonight than I thought."

"Nah." She turns her head away from me. "Just trying to get you to lighten up a little and pull the stick out of your ass."

Ouch.

"You think I'm uptight?"

Why did I even ask? I don't have to be looking at her to know her eyes are rolling.

"Is the Pope Catholic? Yes. Yes, he is. So, yes. Yes, I do think you're uptight."

"Why do you think that?"

"Oh, my God," she quips. "Did you even enjoy tonight? Because if you did, it would be news to me. You won your game today, even scored a damn goal, but you had the personality of a turnip all night."

I sit with that for a minute because she's actually caught me off guard. "What do you mean?"

"Let me count the ways, shall I?" She lifts her hand up, counting on her fingers. "You didn't say two words to me all night until right before we left. You just gave me the stink eye, which is basically what you've been doing since my very first day, so no surprise there. I can't remember you even cracking a smile when Dex was twerking to that Lizzo song, and it was funny as hell..."

That was damn funny.

"You maybe drank one whole beer the whole night, not that I was keeping track because after my third beer I didn't give a shit anymore."

But she gave a shit before that?

"I just don't understand why you even went if you weren't going to have a good time. Nobody likes a party pooper. All I can come up with is that you were pissed that I was there."

What?

"You think I didn't want you there?"

She scoffs. "Dude, I'm not stupid. I know you didn't want

me there. You seem to hate my guts for some godforsaken reason. You're an asshole every time you're around me. It doesn't take a genius to figure out I'm the common denominator."

"You're right."

"Duh."

"I am an asshole."

"What?"

"I mean, I've been an asshole. To you. You're right about that." I push my hand through my hair. "I don't really even have a good reason. You've been nothing but... nice, I guess, but I took my frustrations out on you anyway."

She's not saying anything.

Why isn't she saying anything?

She's just staring out her window where I can't see her face.

Shit.

Now I feel even worse.

"I'm sorry I've been an asshole. And for what it's worth, thank you for the gift. It was...nice."

"You're welcome."

"But in my defense, tonight I am the team captain."

"What does that have to do with anything?"

"Someone has to be the responsible one. Those guys are my life."

Finally, she turns her head back toward me. "Okay. I get that. But they're also adults. You didn't see the owner of the team with you making sure you were safe and being good little boys tonight, did you? You didn't stop Hawken from sucking face with that redhead, did you? You didn't stop Dex from hooking up with... whoever that girl was he left with. They're all fully capable of adulting themselves. You're allowed to have a little fun. You won that game tonight just as much as they did. You should've been celebrating."

"Jesus, you're making it sound like I'm a shell of a person. You know, contrary to what you might think, I can be a fun guy."

She scoffs out a laugh. "Oh, really?"

"Yes. Really."

"Well then, please tell me more about how you're a fun guy, because the only guy I've seen since we've met is one who literally argues with women over his Lucky Charms...or lack thereof."

Tension begins to slither its way back through my body.

"Watch it, Smalls." I shake my head, my jaw clenched.

"Tells me we're not friends and we'll never be friends..." she rattles off a little louder.

"For fuck's sake. Here we go." I bite the inside of my cheek to keep myself from saying anything more, my fingers curling tightly around the steering wheel as she continues.

"And then flips into alpha mode and basically pisses all over me in the bar just because some guy tries to talk to me... "

"Oh, for the love of—" I curse under my breath and run a hand through my hair. My body temperature is definitely rising, and it's more than just my seat warmer.

She raises her voice this time. "So please, tell me again how you're such a—"

"Son of a bitch, Carissa. The Lucky Charms are for my brother, all right?" I shout over her. "Fuck!"

How do I let her bring the emotions out of me like this?

What is it about her? Like I want to spit out all my feelings but keep them from her at the same time.

Chewing on the inside of my cheek, I try to take a deep breath and settle my nerves, my frustrations, my irritations before I explain.

"I eat Lucky Charms before every game because it was his favorite cereal, and that day when we lost, I hadn't had any because I was fresh out. That's why I was so fucking irritated with you, all right? I just wanted to feel close to my fucking brother."

Yep. That does the trick.

I've rendered Carissa Smallson speechless, her stare making me even more uncomfortable than her incessant whining about my stellar personality.

"Why aren't you saying any words?"

She's backed herself against the door, her body turned toward me but staring at me like she's frightened I'll hit her.

I would never do that, by the way.

"Because you said 'was,'" she finally murmurs, her eyes big and round.

"What?"

"Was," she repeats. "You said it was his favorite cereal. Past tense."

"Yeah." I pull up beside what looks like a small convenience store, baffled as to why my GPS directed me here, and ignore her questioning glance. "Is this where you live?"

She nods. "Upstairs apartment." She continues to watch me as I stare out the window, taking in the shithole next to us.

Why here?

Of all the places in Chicago.

"Colby..."

"What?"

"Your brother. Did he..."

I squeeze my eyes closed, trying to push down the feeling of unease in my chest. It's not that I don't like talking about it...but I don't like talking about it.

"He died twenty years ago," I sigh. "So yeah. I said 'was.' Past tense."

She turns away from me, righting herself in her seat, and within seconds I hear her light sniffles.

Shit.

Is she crying?

"Hey." I reach over and take her chin between my fingers, directing her to look at me, and when I do, my chest tightens. "I'm sorry, Carissa." I sigh. "I didn't mean to shout at you."

"No. It's okay. I deserved it." Her tears flow a little quicker now.

I comb my fingers through her hair and bring my hand forward to cup her cheek.

"Nobody deserves it. Well, except for the guy in the bar. He fuckin' deserved it for touching you. I didn't like seeing his hands on you like that."

Her eyes snap to mine, and it's in this moment that I feel like she's seeing me. Seeing more of me than I was ready to show. Like she's seeing all the way down into my soul. It's uncomfortable as hell, but I can't take my words back now. So, if she's capable of reading between the lines, then she has a pretty good idea of how I feel.

Trying to lighten the moment so we don't have to talk about this anymore, I offer her a gentle smile.

"Why are you crying, Smalls?"

Her frown and light sniffles grow exponentially, and she starts to sob, her words coming out a blubbery mess.

"Because..." She sniffles. "Because you just wanted your lucky cereal so you could remember your brother, and I took that away from you, and I'm so freaking sorry! I was a complete bitch to you that night, but that's not who I am."

She shakes her head.

"It's not." She sniffles again. "I just didn't understand why this hot guy was out shopping for kid cereal that late at night—alone—so I figured you were either there trying to steal something, or you must just be an asshole... because all the good-looking guys are assholes." Her hands flapping in front of her, she tries to take a breath. "But you're not an asshole, and now I understand where you were coming from, and I just feel so terrible for doing that to you and I'm sorry Colby."

She buries her head in her hands and cries, and all I can do is push my lips tightly together and try to hide my smile, thankful she's not looking at me. This sob fest has to be the alcohol talking, and it's kind of humorous. She's cute when she's drunk.

"Hey, it's okay. My brother doesn't even know I missed a bowl. No harm, no foul."

"I should've been nicer to you that night." She cries.

"I certainly could've been a hell of a lot nicer to you, too."

"I'm so sorry."

"Me too." I swipe my thumbs gently across her cheeks, drying her tears, and then we sit in silence for a few seconds before my eyes glance behind her, out the window and take in the neighborhood. "You really live here?"

"Mmm-hmm." She nods.

I'm not sure how that's even possible.

"I'll walk you in."

"It's fine," she says with a shake of her head. "I can handle it."

"Yeah, that wasn't a suggestion. Hold tight, I'll open your door."

I walk her inside and up a set of narrow stairs until she's unlocking an old door at the top. When she swings it open, she steps inside and turns on a lamp, and that's when I'm able to take in her living space.

And it's fucking tiny.

The door opens to a kitchenette space with a refrigerator to the right, next to the sink. To our left, a microwave hangs over an oven and stovetop. Each of her appliances look to be older than me. There's no way in hell they all work well.

This setup has to be a fire hazard.

A few more steps inside, and the room turns into a living-room-type space with a loveseat, a folding chair, and a small beat-up coffee table. I look like a giant standing in the middle of this room.

"No TV?" I ask, looking around and wondering if maybe it's in her bedroom.

She shakes her head, still slightly sniffling. "Uh, there's no cable here. Or Wi-Fi for that matter." I give her a dumbfounded look —who doesn't have Wi-Fi anymore? —and she says, "It's fine though. I don't watch much television anyway. I work a lot. Would you like a glass of water?"

From that tap? Hell no.

"Uh, no thank you. I'm good. Is that why you were at work early?"

She walks back into the kitchen area and reaches into the

fridge, pulling out a bottle of water, and I instantly feel guilty for judging her living environment. Housing in the city isn't cheap. It's easy for me to forget that sometimes. Still, she should be able to afford more than this on the salary she's making now.

"Yeah. I, uh... I had some studying to do. Valerie encouraged me to watch some of your recent post-game interviews so I could understand your headspace a little better. You know, so I could try to help brighten your reputation."

I shake my head. "Nobody can understand my headspace, Smalls. Don't bother trying." She's already learned more tonight than I ever intended to tell her. I don't share my feelings about my brother with just anyone, and as much as I've thought about my attraction to the feisty woman standing in front of me, I'm not so sure she reciprocates those feelings.

Why would she? It's not like I've given her any reason to.

"How did you find this place?" I ask, genuinely curious.

She gives me a half-hearted shrug. "I found it online, and it fit my budget. The kitchenette is crap, and there's a continuous leak in the bathroom sink, but as long as I empty the bucket once a week, I'm good."

Good God.

This is her budget?

"Your parents aren't helping you?"

She huffs, rolling her eyes. "Are you crazy? My parents don't know where I live, and I hope to keep it that way."

"Oh." My face falls. "I take it you don't have a relationship with them?"

"Nope." She pops the P between her lips and shakes her head. "Not anymore."

"Hmm." I nod and narrow my eyes. "I guess there's a lot I don't know about you, Smalls."

She chugs her water and then wipes her mouth with the back of her hand. The unladylike move makes me smile.

Because tipsy Carissa is kind of cute.

She steps closer to me and has to raise her head to look me

in the eye. "Well, since you shared a secret with me, how about I share one with you?"

My chest flutters a bit, and I'm all of a sudden nervous about what she might say.

"All right. Let's hear it."

She lifts up on her tippy toes, her hand resting on my chest to leverage herself, and that warm feeling shoots through me again. I breathe in her proximity, a faint vanilla scent filling my nose, and bring a hand to her hip, steadying her. For a quick second, she pauses, her mouth in this perfect little O as her eyes flash to my lips before settling back on my gaze.

Shit. Does she want me to kiss her?

Does she want to kiss me?

Why am I not making a move?

I would usually make a damn move.

We're in the perfect position.

So, why am I pussying out?

She leans in close to my ear so that her cheek is against mine and whispers, "I don't know shit about hockey."

CHAPTER 8

Carissa

"Riss, I miss you so much!" Chelsea grabs my hand across the table, her coffee in her other hand. "Ugh, Gretchen just isn't you. Are you sure you want that nice, cushy job with the Red Tails? I'm sure it's a rotten experience hanging out with hunky hockey players, right? Seriously, let me save you. You can always come back to me!"

I laugh at her desperate attempt. "I'm sorry, friend. Is Gretchen really that bad?"

She takes a sip of her coffee and frowns. "What do you think?"

"Uh-oh." I cringe. "Tell me more."

"Ugh. She's annoying as fuck! She keeps mentioning you in the projects she does, like she thinks she does them better than you ever did..." She raises her hand up. "And I'm like, girl, that's why Dr. Sweeny recommended Rissa for a job and not you. Seriously, I kinda want to bitch-slap her. It's so obvious she's jealous of you."

Serves the girl right. She was a whiny bitch in and out of college. She deserves to not get the leg up for once. As much as I like to see people succeed and reach for their dreams, I'm not the least bit upset that she's where she is and I'm where I am. I couldn't be more appreciative to be given the opportunity to make a better living for myself. I realize it still means living in a shithole and doing without for a few more years, but it's a sacrifice I'm willing to make to finally live my own dreams instead of the desperate attempt my parents made to live theirs.

"Hmm, well... I don't know what to say about that except

sorry-not-sorry." I grin into my mug.

Chelsea giggles. "That's right, babe. You do you, girl! She can suck on a hairy dick for all I care."

I nearly spit out my coffee. "Ew. Chels! Just...ew."

She puts her mug down and leans on the table. "So, speaking of dick..." She wags her brows.

I watch her, waiting for the end of that sentence, but it doesn't come.

"You want to finish that statement?"

She bows her head with a laugh. "You're horrible. Come on, you have to have snagged yourself a hot hockey player by now. Spill all the tea!"

Colby's face pops into my mind, but I shut that thought down just as quickly as it comes.

"Nope." I shake my head. "Why would I do that?"

She scoffs. "Uh, why wouldn't you is the bigger question."

"What? Why? What do you mean?"

"Rissa! You're literally working with an entire team of hot guys who probably like to fuck...a lot—if they're anything like the ones I read about in books."

"Your smut books, you mean."

She points at me. "Hey, don't you knock 'em till you try 'em!"

"No judgment here," I chuckle. "Just facts."

"You mean to tell me none have hit on you yet?"

Several of the guys enter my mind as I recall jokes we've told, laughs we've shared, silly videos we've made. And then I think about the conversation I had with Colby the other night in his car.

"I didn't like seeing his hands on you like that."

"A-ha!" Chelsea points at me with a goofy smile.

"What?"

"You're blushing..."

"I am not."

"You so totally are. Spill it right fucking now. We're not leaving until you do."

I sigh. "There's really not much to tell, I don't think."

"Which one? Wait!" She spreads her hands out on the table. "Let me guess..."

Her eyes narrow, and she stares at me and then says, "Hawken Malone."

I shake my head with a laugh. "No way. Hawken is great, but a little too...umm...pretty for my taste."

"Too pretty, okay...umm..." She rubs her chin. "How about Dex? Dex Foster?"

I laugh aloud this time. "No way. I have a feeling he'll fuck anything that moves. Again, great guy, but it's a no from me."

"Okay, okay, just tell me."

Knowing she can read me too well and I'll never be able to hide it, I let the cat out of the bag. "Remember the argument I had with Colby Nelson?"

She gasps. "Oh, my God! You slept with Colby Nelson?"

I shush her quickly, not wanting anyone to have heard what she just said because, "No! No, I didn't sleep with him! God it's not like that!"

"Okay, but what then?"

"So, that home game last week against Vancouver, afterwards we all went out to celebrate at Pringle's. The guys on the team—well, all the guys except Colby—asked me to join them, and I made a deal that if I went, they had to help me make a few videos."

She nods. "Right. Gotcha."

"Well, I went. We all had a great time. I drank...probably more than I should have..."

Chelsea's eyes grow. "Oh no."

"And then this guy...kinda sleezy-looking, was hitting on me at the bar. He put his hands on my hip and the next thing I know, Colby's behind me, his arm wrapped around me, telling the guy I was with him."

"Fuck, that's kinda hot!" Chelsea grins. "He was protecting you and claiming you! Oh, my God! Please tell me he kissed you!"

I shake my head. "Nope. First of all, I was pissed. He hadn't said two words to me all night, but then he thought he could lay claim to me? No, dude. Doesn't work that way. You don't claim me. You earn me."

"Ooh!" She nods. "That's a good one."

"So anyway, he wouldn't let me walk to the L by myself and insisted on driving me home."

Chelsea smirks. "Did he do the whole put his hand on your thigh thing? Gah! I love that feeling. Did you make out in his car? Also, was it nice? Like, a rich guy's car?"

"It had heated seats, so my lady bits were getting a nice spa experience, but no. There was no thigh holding or kissing of any kind. We sort of joked around and then sort of argued." I opt not to tell her about our Lucky Charms conversation out of respect and privacy for Colby's feelings, and because I don't want to tell her how sappy I became because I drank too much.

"And then I told him I don't know shit about hockey, and he laughed his ass off, and that's where we are now."

"He likes you."

I give her a half shrug. "I don't know."

"I think he does. You just wait."

"I'll admit that a few times after he tried to, you know, lay claim to me, I thought I felt this spark between us, but I could be so totally off base. He's grumpy a lot of the time, and I get it. He has a job to do. He makes a shit ton of money to do it, but his attitude can be a lot, you know? I might be doing myself a favor by keeping my distance."

Chelsea sips from her mug and then lowers it back to the table, her shoulder lifting. "Or you could be just the change he needs in his life."

CHAPTER 9

Colby

"Nelson! What the fuck is wrong with you today?" Coach yells across the ice. "You should've had that puck in the net four different times!"

Shit.

That's the third time he's yelled at me today, and for some strange reason I just want to laugh about it. Usually, I'm laser-focused during a practice, but today, it seems I'm anything but. A stupid grin crosses my face when I turn away from Coach, and some of the guys are quick to catch it.

"What are you grinning at, butthead?" Milo asks, skating up beside me in our afternoon practice session. "Did you not hear him?"

I steal another glance at the big window a few floors up with its lights on. "Yeah, I heard him."

I try to fire another puck into the net, but it banks off Zeke's pads and is rebounded by Quinton, who shoots it back to me. Milo's eyes narrow, and he tilts his head.

"And that doesn't bother you?"

"Not today." I chuckle to myself and shoot another puck toward Zeke, who blocks it with his stick. Milo drives one down the ice as well, and once again, Zeke intercepts it and sends it flying around the net for someone to rebound.

"What's so different about today?"

Just as he asks, Carissa's silhouette appears in her office window as she bends over the counter behind her desk to retrieve something. When I glance up, Milo's eyes follow me.

Fuck me.

Bent over in her office.

That's a position I could get used to seeing her in.

Milo coughs out a laugh. "Dude, you've got it bad."

My head snaps toward him. "What?"

"Smallson." He smirks. "I take it that's her office?"

"Did you know she doesn't know shit about hockey? She told me that."

"When?"

"The other night when I took her home from Pringle's."

"Right." He nods. "I forgot to ask you how that went."

Four more pucks slide toward us, and we hurl them one after the other down the ice. Finally, one of mine makes it past Zeke and into the net much to his dismay.

"It was...interesting." For lack of a better word. Not wanting to go into detail about our conversations, I keep it at that.

"Interesting..." Milo repeats with a laugh. "So, you either argued the entire way home or..." He considers his thought and then shakes his head. "Nah, you argued."

"She told me I'm not fun. 'Personality of a turnip' I believe is how she put it."

"You?" Dex snorts as he skates by. "Accurate!"

"That's it, gentlemen!" Coach blows his whistle. "Be ready for our team meeting in thirty."

Milo scratches the back of his neck, and I have to do a double take. "What? You think she's right? I'm not fun?"

"No, it's not that."

"Then what?"

He bobs his head. "You're fun, Colb, but...I don't know," he says, lifting a shoulder. "Sometimes you get into these moods, making yourself so ridiculously busy, and you seem to forget there's a life to live out there...outside of hockey, I mean."

I roll my eyes. "Hockey is my life."

"It has been, yeah," he says as we slowly glide off the ice.

Gesturing back toward Carissa's window, he continues, "But then Smallson came along, and whatever's going on between you two, it's caused you to spend more time gazing up at her window during practice today than staring at the damn puck."

"So, what are you saying?"

"He's trying to say you have the hots for Smallson," Hawken says from behind us. "So just do something about it already."

"I don't have the hots for—"

"Save it, Colb." Quinton shakes his head, wiping the sweat from his brow. "We were all there, man. We all saw how you acted toward her."

"What is that supposed to mean?"

"You wanted to jump her bones," Dex snickers. "Can't say I blame you, though. Not gonna lie. She looked hot as sin in that jersey."

That she did.

If only my name had been on the back.

That's my new wet dream. Carissa Smallson wearing my name on her jersey and nothing else.

Milo pushes through the locker room door, the rest of us following behind him.

"Yeah, she's hot. I'll admit that. Who wouldn't? But that doesn't mean I'm interested. Sure, she's not bad to look at, but I'm a little busy with the season and don't really have the time to spend—"

"Bullshit." Milo turns and faces me, arms crossed. "Did you kiss her that night? When you dropped her off? Is that why your brain is mush today?"

"What? No."

"But did you want to?" He lifts a brow.

"I..." Fuck. I'm going to lose this fight. I may as well be honest. "I thought about it, yeah."

"Then you're interested." He smiles. "So do something about it. Scratch the itch."

"She's not an itch I need to scratch." *Even though I bet it would feel oh so good.* "And besides, what the hell would I do about it? She thinks I'm a dud to hang out with. She's clearly not interested, and I have a team to lead."

Zeke sits down next to me. "Okay, first of all, you're no good to us when you're not focused and happy, and you said yourself a couple weeks ago that something's off with you. Maybe this is the thing, Colby. Maybe this is what you need. A little time spent with someone who pushes your buttons and doesn't take your shit. Secondly," he continues, "when has a woman's interest or lack thereof ever stopped you before?"

"Yeah." Milo nudges my arm. "Look at you, man. You're Colby fuckin' Nelson, Captain of the Chicago Red Tails hockey team, and I promise you, whether she wants to admit it or not, she's interested. If you want the girl, go get the girl...before someone else does."

Dex wraps his towel around his naked ass.

"I mean if you don't want to give her a shot, I'll be more than happy t—"

"Back the fuck off, Foster." I glare at Dex, but he just points at me with a grin.

"And that's how you know you're interested." He winks with a laugh as the rest of the guys quietly chuckle with him. "Can't believe you fell for that one."

I'm seriously fucked.

Six a.m. on a Saturday and where am I? Where else? Walking into the arena to skate, lift, ride the bike, and grab a few notes to go over on a few new plays. After the guys encouraged me to go after Carissa, we had a day packed full of meetings and workouts, and by the time I had the nerve to find her, she had left for the day. I don't have her cell number, so I couldn't text her. I suppose I could've shown up at her apartment, but I didn't want to come across as a stalker, so I allowed her absence from the arena to be my excuse to not do anything about it yesterday. Little did I know that would also backfire. She was on my mind all damn day. I couldn't think straight and got no sleep last night trying to think up the right things to say to her if and when the time comes.

I'm not great at dating. I'm great at fucking, but other than that...the emotions and shit, I'm not great at those. I've never allowed myself to really get to know someone. I had relationships in high school and college, so I'm no virgin when it comes to feeling the nervous butterflies, or asking a girl out, but as an adult...yeah, I got nothin'. With no time for relationships when the season is in full swing, my idea of a good time has been grabbing a puck bunny in whatever town we're in, showing her a good time, and forgetting her name by morning...if I even ask her name in the first place.

But I can't get Carissa out of my damn head.

It would be one thing if I didn't see her that often, but she's everywhere.

She shows up at practices to take pictures and make videos.

She's in the hallway with the media before and after games.

She sits in the back of the room during press conferences.

She has yet to show up in the locker room, but I figure it's only a matter of time.

And when she does show up in all those places, she's dressed in some form of flawless outfit that makes me want to pull her against me and do dirty things to her. I don't even want to think about what she looks like in a sexy piece of lingerie or a little black dress. Even in her normal state, without having to try very hard, she's attractive as fuck.

And I don't think she knows it.

Since the day we met, she's never come across as someone who is easily intimidated, and even though she's pushed all of my buttons lately, and I have every reason to find her annoying and irritating, I don't.

The truth is, I'm attracted to all of her.

Her feisty take-no-prisoners attitude, her bold confidence,

her cute drunk sobs, all of it.

But knowing how I feel and acting on how I feel are two totally different things. For the first time in a while, I find myself out of my element where Carissa is concerned. I have thoughts about her I probably shouldn't be having, and my conscience warns me against allowing myself to do anything about it because hockey is my life.

But Pinocchio didn't always listen to Jiminy Cricket, and he became a real boy in the end, so maybe just a taste wouldn't be so bad.

After a quick three miles on the bike, I take to the ice for my morning skate. Just me and the rink. Time to clear my head, center myself.

And that's when I notice the light on upstairs.

What's she doing here on a Saturday morning?

"Free Wi-Fi," I murmur to myself, recalling her comment about not having internet or cable at her apartment.

Remembering something else she told me that night, an idea sparks in my brain that has me hustling off the ice, grabbing my cellphone, and calling the arena menu to get Carissa's office number.

I watch in her window as she continues working instead of picking up her ringing phone.

Dammit.

I guess I can't blame her. It's technically her day off. I wouldn't want to answer the work phone either.

I've got to get her cell number.

I'll do this another way. Heading back to the dressing room, I unlace my skates and step into my Crocs — *yes, I'm a big burly man who wears Crocs in between lacing up my skates because why not* —and then head up a few floors to Carissa's office.

"Uh, come in," she states, when I knock on her door. When I push the door open and step inside, I can already tell I'm not the person she expected to see, if she expected to see anyone.

"Colby. What are you doing here?"

"I could say the same, Smalls. It's Saturday. Don't you ever take a day off?"

Her brow shoots up. "Do you?"

"Touché."

I take a minute to look her over as she sits at her desk. Her hair is in a messy knot at the top of her head, several loose strands hanging down around her face. She literally looks like she rolled out of bed, knotted the bed head, and came to work, but it works for her and is damn cute. Her light blue sweater hangs delicately off her shoulder and is loose around her wrists. I'm always taken aback by how normal she looks.

Natural.

Beautiful.

"What are you working on this morning?" I ask her.

"Uh," she says, looking around her desk, piling up a few papers and envelopes. It almost looks like she's paying bills, and I feel bad for even asking in the first place. "Nothing of great importance. Is there... uh...is there something you needed?"

I force myself to smile, remembering that sometimes I'm not good at that. This is the new-and-improved fun Colby I need her to see.

"You have a few minutes?"

She nods. "Yeah. Sure."

"Great." I offer her my hand and gesture out of the office with my head. "Come with me."

She stands up from her desk and my eyes fall to the bit of skin on her abdomen peeking out from her sweater.

Good God, her sweater is cropped.

Fuck me.

This might be harder than I thought.

Correction.

I might be harder than I thought.

"Those are some interesting shoes you're sporting, Mr. Pro hockey player." She grins at my Crocs as she takes my hand, letting me lead her back downstairs. "Please tell me you sit in the locker room before games and trade charms like kids."

"Fuck no. I would never," I say with a laugh, squeezing her hand in mine. "But not because I wouldn't want to. You should see Zeke's though. He has some sweet ones."

"Is that so?"

"Yeah. All our charms are given to us by kids, so we don't trade them for anything."

"Specific kids?"

I shake my head. "No. A lot of them come from meet and greets or clinics we do with kids from time to time. Every once in a while, a young fan will toss one at us on the ice before a game, and we'll have someone save it for us. As silly as it seems, it's turned into something we all kind of take great pride in."

"You really do well with kids, huh?"

"What do you mean?"

"I mean you just recently handed a kid the jersey literally right off your back, and then the entire team followed suit. And now here you are wearing the charms on your shoes that kids pick out for you."

Giving her a half shrug, I answer, "It's simple, isn't it? Kids are the future and all that."

"Is that really the reason?"

"Part of it, sure. I had good role models growing up. I've always seen it as my job to be that for others as long as I'm able."

"Do you think you'll have kids of your own one day? Little hockey players?"

"Honestly? I try to tell myself it's not worth it. That kids are too much responsibility when my life has me busy as fuck nearly every day, but the reality is, I know this hockey playing life will end for me eventually. I'll get too old or too injured and then what will I have? No family tying me down. No kids? Nah, I don't want to end up like that. Besides, I come from a strong family and would like to have something like that of my own someday."

We step into the elevator, the doors closing in front of us, and she gazes up at me. Her eyes flicker with amusement, and her mouth curves into a lopsided grin. "Wow. There really is a human in this big hockey body somewhere."

"Well, I'm not all good looks and strong body, Smalls. I have other fine attributes."

"Yeah?" Her brows quirk up. "Like what?"

I pass her my best ornery grin as we walk down the hallway toward the ice. "You're about to find out. What's your shoe size?"

"If I tell you, am I contributing to some sort of perverted foot fetish?"

I almost choke on a laugh. "Nah. Feet really aren't my kink."

"What is your kink?"

My head turns her direction, a brow raised, my mind reeling over her question and wondering just how exactly I should answer her, but then she starts to backpedal.

"I... Wow. I said that aloud. I didn't...you know. Don't answer that. I mean...you know, unless you want to, but I didn't mean... Everybody has kinks. It's not like it's shameful or embarrassing...I didn't mean that." She shakes her head, her nerves besting her. "Shit. I'm sorry. I should never have asked in th—"

Gently, I step toward her in the hallway until her back is against the wall and my body is pressed against hers. She gasps lightly, and fuck if I don't want to hear that over and over and over again in the very near future. She releases my hand and grabs hold of my biceps when I bring my arms up to clear away the wisps of hair from her face. I've never wanted to flex so hard in my life. Her mouth falls open, her eyes flitting between my eyes and my lips, and I automatically know what she wants.

What she expects.

I want it, too.

"You want to know my kink, Smalls?" I rasp, encroaching entirely too close into her space and shifting a hand down and around the back of her neck, my thumb poised at her chin.

She swallows hard, and I feel it in my grasp. She looks me square in the eye and with all the confidence I know she has, murmurs, "You tell me, Nelson. Do I want to know?"

A deep chuckle emerges from my throat.

"Stick around. You might just find out."

I press a kiss to her forehead, squeezing my eyes closed and willing myself to calm the desire building inside me, yet inhaling every bit of her I can in case I'm not given the opportunity I so badly want later. Stepping back from her, I pat her ass and then tug her along. "Come on. Let's have some fun."

CHAPTER 10

Colby

Searching through the skates typically worn by members of the ice scrapers team, I find a pair that should fit Carissa and then grab my own.

"Have you ever skated before?"

She smiles. "I'm no NHL pro, but I can skate, yeah."

"Good. Put these on."

She sits next to me and pushes off her shoe. "What are we doing exactly?"

Lacing up my skate, I turn to her with a grin. "It's time to learn some shit about hockey."

She lets out a laugh. "Oh God, this ought to be good. Did you bring bubble wrap? I should check my life insurance policy first."

"I won't let you get hurt. I promise. It's just you and me out there. Now, if Dex were here, this would be a whole other story."

"A little rough around the edges, I take it? I could see that about him."

"Oh, Dex loves to choose violence when he can. You'll have to ask him sometime about the game against Pittsburgh two years ago. He loves telling that story."

"I'll try to remember that."

I escort Carissa carefully to the ice and watch as she takes in the massive room around us. I forget sometimes what it's like to be down here looking up at all the seats when you usually spend your time looking down at the ice. The ice is my home. It's always been my home. I've rarely been a seat dweller except for those few times

I would watch my brothers play when I was young. The arena is an impressive place when you take time to soak it all in.

"Damn," Carissa murmurs. "How do you not practically shit yourself every time you come out here?"

Her question makes me laugh. Totally not what I was expecting to come out of her mouth. She's always surprising me.

"I don't get the nervous shits, so it's never been a problem for me. Plus, when it's game time, your adrenaline spikes, and you're focused on getting the puck in the net and winning the game. There's no time for nerves."

"Did you ever get nervous? Even when you were learning to play?" she turns on her skates. I'm impressed with her maneuverability on the ice. "I mean not only is hockey a dangerous sport, but, my God, there are literally thousands of people watching your every move. Some wishing and waiting for you to mess up, fall, or get hurt. I mean, seriously, some fans specifically come to watch the violence."

I nod. "You're correct on all counts. And sure, I used to get nervous all the time when I was a little kid. I had the hardest time learning to just remain upright on my skates, let alone push a little black rock around on the ice. And don't get me started on being checked for the very first time." I laugh as the fleeting memory pops into my head. "I was having the best practice day and then my brother came along and checked me right in the hip. I slid sideways on the ice and cracked my lip. Cried forever. That motherfucker hurt."

"Aww, you poor thing."

"Yeah, but it ended up being the best thing for me. Taught me not to be scared the next time it happened. I just needed to be prepared. I needed to be stronger. So, I got stronger and with that came more confidence."

"And now here you are, huh?" She smirks.

"Yeah." I grin back at her. "Yeah, I guess so."

"All right then. Teach me Obi-Wan Colby. You're my only hope."

My mouth falls open and my eyes bulge. "Fuck me, did you just Star Wars me?"

She laughs, bending at the waist. "Yeah. I think I did."

"Who knew you were adorable with a side of nerd?" I shake my head, trying to wipe the ridiculous smile off my face that I can't seem to get rid of when she's around. For as much as she pissed me off in the beginning, everything about her is setting my insides on fire now. Everything about her makes me want to know more. Everything about her makes me feel... happy.

"All right, basic rules of hockey." I take her hand and lead her to the center line. "This line is where the puck is dropped at the start of each period and after a goal is scored. Only one player from each team can be in this circle until that puck is dropped."

She nods. "And then all hell breaks loose?"

"Pretty much. That's when the dance begins. There are six players on the ice at any given time and that includes the goalie. Each of us has a specific job to do in order to make sure the puck gets down the ice and into the net. Basically, the offensive team works on scoring the goals, and the defensive teams protect our net."

"Right." She smiles. "Puck in their net good. Puck in our net bad."

With a raised brow, I point to her. "You're bright, Smalls. You'll be a pro in no time."

"Thank you." She does a little curtsy, and I stop myself from peeking right down her sweater. "And you're a defenseman?"

My brows lift in amusement. "Doin' your research on me?"

"It's my job and all, so yeah. You could say that."

"Yeah, I'm a defenseman. I try hard to rebound or intercept pucks and get them back down the ice, though every now and then we get to see some net action."

"Got it."

"You feel like shootin' some pucks?"

She smiles. "Can that net stretch the entire width of the rink? 'Cause that would be most helpful."

Beaming at her as I hand her a stick, I shake my head. "Sorry, Charlie. The net stays right where it is. Don't worry though. You've got this."

We spend the next half hour or so skating around and playfully shooting a bucket of pucks down the ice. Most of the time, I can get mine to go in the net, but I tell Carissa not to quit her day job no less than twelve times. Watching her try to hit them though is all kinds of a turn-on as she pushes her ass out like she's putt-putt golfing every time. What I wouldn't give to be a cliché and stand behind her, showing her how to grasp my stick.

"Maybe you should get your eyes checked," I tease.

"Maybe you're a sucky-ass teacher, Nelson."

I shake my head with a goofy smile. "I think you just pronounced spectacular wrong."

"Har har." She smiles. "I think I'm just too far from the net. Who shoots from all the way back here? Y'all are always up each other's asses at the net trying to get it in."

"All right, let's do that then. We'll see if it helps your game."

We move up to the net, and I round up all the pucks. "I'll be your goalie. You just try to shoot them in the net one by one. Let's see how many you can get and how many I can keep out."

"Deal." She nods, her greatest focus face at the ready. She steadies herself with her stick, and at the count of three, begins to shoot her pucks in and around my net, but fails to get one in.

"Son of a bitch!" She flies forward on her skates, moving a puck between her stick and shooting hard, but I see it coming and block it, tossing it back to her. She giggles. "This fucker is going in if it's the last thing I do."

"Not on my watch, Smalls."

We slap pucks back and forth to each other in our haste to win, and she's nothing but grins, giggles, and cuteness.

I can't stop smiling.

God, this is so much fun.

She sends two at me and I hit them right back to her.

Who knew she would be such a good sport hanging out with

me on the ice?

Fuck, she's great.

And she smells good.

We go round and round a few more times until I shoot a puck a little too hard her way and she screams.

"Ah! Fuck!"

My smile fades, and I drop my stick immediately when I see her grab her shin.

"Carissa?"

Shit.

"Carissa? You okay? Did I hit you?"

Way to go Nelson.

Play too hard and hurt the one good thing you had going.

She'll never want to do this again.

I'm on my knees in front of her, my hands smoothing down her leg. "Hey. Talk to me. Let me see. Where does it hurt?"

She stands up, swings her stick, and sinks a puck into my net.

"Yaaaaaas!" She turns swiftly with a hearty laugh and points at me with both hands. "Told you I would get one in!"

For the love of...

This girl.

I shake my head with a huge smile watching her celebrate, mentally kicking myself for letting her get one over on me. She moves to skate toward me, but my stick is in the way, and she fails to see it. In one quick movement, she's tripping over the stick, sliding on the ice, and about to fall on her face, so I swoop in. Neither one of us wearing any padding, I wrap my arms around her and allow her momentum to push us both down, my body cradling hers.

I can take it.

I've fallen many times before, padding or not.

But if she actually got hurt on my watch, I would never forgive myself.

We both crash to the ice with an "oomph!"

Her head pops up and she looks down at me, her eyes wide

with concern.

"Oh, my God, are you okay?"

I gaze up at her soft brown eyes, noting the pinkness in her cheeks from the chill of the ice and the spread of freckles across her nose. I'm also keenly aware that one of my hands is resting on the skin of her back, her sweater having shifted in the fall.

I'm not mad about it.

And so far, she doesn't seem to be either.

But I keep my hands still all the same...just in case.

"I'm perfectly fine." I brush her hair back behind her head, holding it there with my other hand. "Are you okay?"

She gives me a few small nods. "Yeah. I'm good." Then she giggles. "I got one in. That's all that matters."

The corner of my mouth curves. "You totally cheated."

Her tongue peeks out of her mouth as she quickly moistens her lips and then she pulls the corner of her bottom lip between her teeth.

Fuck, she looks sexy from this angle.

She's sexy from any angle but on top of me is most definitely a front runner.

"It's an unfair advantage playing against you. I had to do something."

Watching her lips the entire time she speaks, I gently tug her bottom one free and then swipe my thumb over her mouth. She gasps again, like she did in the hallway earlier, and my dick twitches between my legs. My eyes move between her hooded brown orbs and her soft pink lips.

"Cheaters never win, you know..."

Her chest rises and falls on top of mine, her breasts resting against me. With my hand on her back, I can feel her pulse rising. Like mine.

I feather my fingers across the smoothness of her back. I can't help myself. I want to touch her. Any part of her.

She takes one last look at my lips and whispers, "I beg to differ." And then her mouth is on mine, my hand sifting through her soft hair, holding her head in place so I can get a good long taste of her.

Her lips are warm as she moves them against mine in a slow magnificent kiss. How she remains in such sweet control is beyond me because just one taste and I would do anything to strip her bare and have my way with her right here on this goddamn ice. Forgetting to ask permission, I push my tongue through her lips, and she captures it with her teeth eliciting a hungry moan from my throat.

My hand on her back stretches out over her exposed skin, caressing the side of her velvety soft body as I kiss her, lick her, taste her. Goosebumps erupt all over her skin and somewhere in the back of my mind—okay, okay it's totally at the front of my mind—I just know her nipples are hard and now I'm aching to touch them.

This might very well be the first kiss where I've actually felt something.

Desire, want, interest, curiosity, passion, whatever it is...it feels nice.

It feels good.

And I want more.

So much more.

I like kissing Carissa Smallson.

And I want to do it again, and again, and again.

I let her decide when our connection ends because fuck if I don't want to lay here all day and let her nibble on my tongue. Among other things...

When she pulls back, there's a new blush to her cheeks that I'm happy to have put there.

"Is this how you kiss all the girls you bring out here?"

My chest flutters with a weird feeling as I take in her natural beauty.

"Well, first of all, let's not forget who kissed whom here. I'm pretty sure you kissed me, not the other way around."

Her eyes widen. "Right. I'm sorry. I shouldn't ha—"

"If you even think of saying you shouldn't have kissed me, I'm going to drop you on this ice right now because it was a fucking good kiss, and I liked it very much."

She bites her lip again, unsuccessfully hiding her grin.

"Secondly, you might find this hard to believe, Smalls, but you're the first girl I've ever brought out to the ice."

Her brow crinkles. She's speechless. I must've shocked her with that little confession.

"And I really fuckin' enjoyed it."

She smiles down at me. "Me too."

"And now I'm famished." I pat her gorgeous ass a few times. "Grab lunch with me?"

Anything so I don't have to let her go.

"Yeah. That sounds nice." She blinks her beautiful doe eyes at me, and I swear a large chink in my proverbial armor falls right off.

Maybe the guys are right.

Maybe life isn't so bad when you have someone to enjoy it with.

And maybe, just maybe, Carissa Smallson is my someone.

CHAPTER 11

Carissa

Holy shit! I just kissed Colby Nelson.

Me.

I didn't second guess it. I simply saw the opportunity for what it was and went for it.

And damn, he can kiss.

When I came to work this morning, on my day off, I certainly didn't do so with any expectation of seeing Colby today, let alone spending hours playing hockey with him.

Or having lunch with him.

Or kissing him.

Truth be told, I came in to pay bills because work equals free Wi-Fi. I made sure to make a few social media posts in between bills to curb me of my guilt for using the company internet. Anyway, Colby showing up in my office was a surprise. Even more, he hasn't been a dick once. Instead, he's been...engaging, kind, and fun to hang out with. Add a whole lot of sexy on the side and dang, I may have just had the best morning I've had in a very long time.

"I've got to watch what I eat when we have games coming up. Soup and salad okay with you?"

"Of course," I tell him as he holds the car door open for me. "I'm game for wherever you want to go."

"Great. I know the perfect place."

Within minutes, we're parking in a side lot and heading into a small family-owned deli whose menu looks similar to that of a Panera.

"Do you come here often?" I ask as we wait in line, perusing the menu so we can order when we get up to the counter.

Colby smirks. "Is that the line you use on all the guys you meet?"

"Did I say it to you the first time we met?"

He huffs a quick chuckle. "If you had, Smalls, our interaction probably would've gone much differently."

I jut my hip out, looking up at him as he tries to hide his smirk. "Oh yeah? How so?"

He slips his hands into his pockets. "Well, I probably would've turned on my sexy charm, and you would've fallen for me hook, line, and sinker."

"Sexy charm," I repeat, raising a curious brow.

He nods. "Yep. And this would be our third or fourth date by now. And if I hadn't already, I would most definitely be wondering when I would get to put my hands on you." He leans in a little closer and murmurs in my ear. "And looking forward to having the opportunity to hear you screaming my name, in all the best ways."

I swear I catch a sparkle in his eye before he winks at me.

Yep. My lady bits are all a-tingle.

That's all it took.

Now I'm all hot and bothered just thinking of how that first interaction could've gone.

But hell if I'm going to admit that to him.

"And you really think I would've just fallen for your good-guy charm and jumped your bones?"

Spoiler alert, I totally would've fallen for the good-guy charm and jumped his bones.

He shrugs with a swift lift of the corner of his mouth. "I guess we'll never know, will we?"

Before I can respond, we reach the counter, and he places his order for a large bowl of minestrone soup, garlic bread, and a side salad, and then with his hand on the small of my back, asks me what I would like.

"Uh, can I please have a bowl of broccoli cheese soup with a breadstick and side salad?"

The girl behind the counter smiles and finishes our order.

"Let me get this," I tell Colby, but he scowls with a laugh.

"Not a chance, Smalls. I asked you out. It's on me."

Inside I'm relieved, as penny pinching is the name of my game right now, but I would've made the sacrifice had he allowed me to pay. I never want to assume someone is paying my way. Even if I'm hanging out with one of the richest hockey players in the league. It's obscene how much money professional athletes make. I don't know what I would do with that kind of money.

Besides pay off debt.

"Well, I just mean, it's not like this is a date," I mention. "It's just us having..." His cheek twitches, and I'm pretty sure he just scowled. "Lunch."

Colby shakes his head, his lip twisting into a half grin. "Whatever helps you sleep at night, Smalls."

I kinda wish you would help me sleep at night.

I follow Colby when he grabs our table number placard and heads to a table in the back corner of the room, a little out of the way from other customers. I suppose it would be hard for someone of his stature and fame to find much privacy in a public restaurant like this one, so I don't mind at all finding a spot where he might not be recognized.

"So, have you lived in Chicago all your life?" he asks me once we're seated and waiting for our food.

"Not Chicago, no, but mostly Illinois, yes."

"Mostly Illinois?"

"I was born in New Orleans and lived there for a few years before moving to Illinois. I actually grew up in Decatur."

"Ah, so you're a small-town girl."

"Livin' in a lonely world," I murmur.

One of the deli staff places a tray with our food on the table between us.

"What's that?" He tilts his head, having not heard me.

I shake my head with a soft chuckle. "Nothing."

"What brought your family to Illinois from New Orleans?"

"Hurricanes."

About to take a spoonful of his soup, Colby pauses. "Really?"

"Mmm-hmm. Some started hitting a little too close to home, and Mom didn't want to keep retreating inland every summer, so they decided to leave. I think I was eleven when we finally moved."

"Wow. That must've been hard as a kid. To just pick up and leave."

I give him a shrug. "Yes and no. My parents told me we were going on an adventure, and I went with it. I stayed in touch with a few friends and actually still talk to them thanks to social media, but once we got to Decatur, I fell in with a whole new group of friends."

"So, what brought you to the city then? This job?"

"Nope. I went to school at DePaul and then worked my first job on campus for several years after graduation. It was great but..."

I need a lot more money, so I can get my life back.

"I knew I wanted more." I take a breath, not wanting to dive too deep into this conversation. "And then the job with the Red Tails opened up, and my boss encouraged me, so I went for it." Not wanting to talk about my past, I turn the table on Colby. "How about you? Have you always played for the Red Tails?"

"I played for Denver for a few early years, and then the Red Tails offered me a deal I couldn't refuse."

"Are you from Colorado?"

He shakes his head. "Nope. Appleton, Wisconsin."

"Wow!" My brows shoot up. "That's quite the jump you've made then. Small town farm life to the NHL. In Chicago, no less."

Colby laughs. "Well, when you put it that way, you're right. I guess I've become accustomed to it now, though. It's almost hard to think about what life was like on the farm." His smile fades, and his eyes drift, and I wonder what thoughts are floating through his mind right now.

Is he thinking about his brother?

"Sorry." I touch his arm softly. "I didn't mean to pry."

He shakes his head. "No, no. You didn't. It's fine." Our eyes connect, and he holds my gaze, his lips forming a decadent smile. "You're good on the ice, Smalls. Better than I expected."

I shrug. "Six years of ice-skating lessons. Did I forget to mention that?"

Colby's outright belly laugh gives me all the warm fuzzies. "Yes, you did. Had I known that, I might not have gone so easy on you."

"To be fair, that was years ago, and I haven't skated much since, so don't act like I didn't beat you fair and square."

"I think your idea of fair and square is quite skewed."

I shrug playfully. "Po-tay-to, po-tah-to."

"So, were you one of those chicks with dreams of being an ice princess?"

"Doesn't every girl have that dream for a good solid six months of her life?"

"Probably at least every four years when the Olympics are televised, eh?" He chuckles.

Resting my cheek on my fist, I let out a sigh. "Yeah. I so wanted to be the next Michelle Kwan. God, she was so graceful. I thought I could spend my days being as bendy as her, but then I never grew taller." I gesture to my whole self. "What you see is what you get. I felt more like a spunky klutz than a graceful swan, so I gave it up when I got to high school. Used my long nights of homework as an excuse to find something new."

"And did you?"

"Find something new?" An ornery smirk spreads across my face. "Sure."

He quirks a brow. "Why does that smirk make me think you were nothing but trouble?"

"Let's just say, when a good little ice princess hangs up her skates, she hangs up the good-girl persona right along with them."

"Ah, the rebellious teenager, huh?" He smooths a hand down his short beard and leans across the table. "Carissa Smallson, did you become a bad girl?"

The way he says "bad girl" with the slight growl to his voice makes me wet in places I shouldn't be thinking about in public. His brandy-colored stare is so intense, the words "yes, sir" almost tumble right off my lips. Instead, I steel myself to match his gaze, lick my lips, and say, "Wouldn't you like to know?"

"Yes," he says with absolute seriousness. "I absolutely would."

"You know you don't have to keep driving me here. I've been taking the L for years. I even have my very own pass."

He reaches over and rests his hand on my thigh, and oh my God, it's the best feeling in the world. "Humor me, will you? I like to make sure you get home safely. Besides, riding the L as a single female isn't necessarily the safest of situations. Not in my book anyway, so if I can keep you a little safer by taking you home myself, it's the least I can do."

Sometimes the protective side of a man can be a huge turn-on. I've had to learn to be extremely independent since my parents ruined any chance of a relationship with them. Every once in a while, I suppose it's nice to have someone else in the world looking out for my well-being.

It's comforting.

Makes me feel safer.

"Well, thank you then," I tell Colby as I reach for the door handle. "Do you umm..." I eye my apartment above the small general store on the corner. "Do you want to come up?"

I don't really know what I'm asking or what he might be expecting.

He kissed me this morning. Does that mean he wants more?

Does he want to make out in my apartment?

Does he want to spend the night?

Would that be weird on our first non-but-maybe-semi-date?

Yes, yes it would.

But would that thought stop me from doing it anyway?

No. No it would not.

Colby takes one look at the hole-in-the wall I call my apartment building, and his brows pinch. He nods his head and turns to me. "Yeah. I do."

Cocking my head, I narrow my eyes. "What was that look for? Do you think I can't make it upstairs to my own apartment?" I wink so he knows I'm only teasing, but he doesn't return the smirk. Instead, he opens his car door, lifts himself out, and comes around to my side, offering me his hand.

"You couldn't score a goal today without tripping over your own skates, Smalls. So yeah, someone needs to make sure you can walk those rickety stairs and still be in one piece when you reach the top."

Stepping out of the car, I give him my best playful scoff. "I didn't trip over my skate. I tripped over your stick, which you dropped!"

"Yeah. When I thought you had actually hurt yourself, or worse, that I had hurt you."

Something in my chest tightens and my stomach flips upside down.

Or worse...that I had hurt you.

"You really thought that? You thought you hurt me?"

He stares at me, his expression befuddled. "Of course. I promised I wouldn't let anything happen to you."

"Shit." I cringe. "I'm really sorry about that. I shouldn't have done it."

"Nah." He takes my hand and leads me across the street. "It was a good move. I needed the ego check...and a reminder my heart still works." He murmurs that last part, and I'm not sure if I was meant to hear it or not.

But I did.

And now I'm biting my cheek to keep myself from smiling too big.

Who is this Colby, and what happened to the pompous

asshole he used to be?

When we reach the door to my apartment, there's an envelope taped to it. It's addressed to me, but with a handwritten note on the front that reads, "This got mixed in with the store's mail. Sorry about that, Carissa."

Great. Another bill, most likely.

"Everything okay?" Colby asks from behind me.

"Hmm? Oh, yeah. It's fine. Everything's...fine." I unlock my apartment, squeezing my eyes closed tightly and praying I didn't leave my unmentionables lying around. Not that I do that on the regular, but drying them over the shower curtain is cheaper than paying for a load at the laundromat.

"How do you breathe in here?" Colby asks, eyeing the space once again as I turn on a few lamps.

"What do you mean?" I sniff several times. "Is there a smell? Because I can't control the stale frozen food or the wet cardboard box scent that wafts up here sometimes from the back room of the store downstairs. I would get one of those nice smelly plug-in things, but I only have so many outlets in this place so I—"

"No." He chuckles. "I just mean it's so small. Cramped, even for one person."

I cock my head and raise a brow at him. "Have you taken a look in the mirror lately, Nelson? You're a giant of a man."

He stands tall. "Is that how you see me? A giant?"

"Well, let's look at you..." I grin, gesturing to him. "And then let's look at me."

He inhales a deep slow breath as his eyes rake over me from head to toe and back again enough to make me blush. "If you're giving me explicit permission, I will gladly look at you, Smalls." His expression is heated and hungry. "But maybe I should see the whole package. When do I get to do that?"

Shaking my head at his audacity—even though I don't really mind it—I reply, "I just mean this place fits me. I'm small. It's small. It works for now."

"Mmm-hmm. But you didn't answer my question." He steps

toward me like a lion on the prowl, and my cheeks heat. There's only so far I can go before I'll run into a wall. Clearing my throat, I try to find my voice.

"And, uh, what question would that be?"

Stepping toward me again he doesn't smirk, doesn't grin, doesn't smile. His body now within inches of mine, his breath warm against my neck. "When do I get to see more of you?"

Now.

Right now.

Right fucking now.

"Presumptuous, don't you think?"

So, we're not saying what we're thinking now?

Nice going, Carissa.

"Let's go with confident." He boxes me in with his arms, though I know I could slip away if I really wanted to.

But I don't.

Instead, I raise my chin and match him stare for stare as our chests rise and fall together.

"You know what else I like?" he mumbles.

"Hmm?"

Finally, his lips curve up as he gazes at me, his nose rubbing against mine. "I like how your nose blushes when you're turned on."

"Wh-who said I'm turned on?" I argue with a breathless stutter. "I never said a thing about being turned on."

"You don't have to. Your cute little nose gives you away."

"I beg to differ."

Why am I arguing with him?

"Yeah?"

"Yeah."

He shifts his weight just enough that I can feel his bulge between us, and then he pushes a hand through my hair at the base of my skull, our foreheads nearly connected. My pulse quickens, and my breath catches in my throat. The closeness of him making me hypersensitive to his deliciously clean scent. My eyes close for a quick moment while I breathe him in.

"Are you telling me you haven't been turned on since the moment we kissed on that ice this morning?"

So hella turned on.

"Are you telling me you have been?"

He strokes my cheek with his thumb. "Since the very moment we met."

A tingling pleasure floods my body, but I try my best to remain calm instead of becoming putty in his hands. If he wants me, he needs to work for it.

"That's a lie." I laugh. "You hated me that night."

He shrugs with a smile. "Semantics. Your feisty attitude wasn't my favorite, but only because I'm not used to being told no. Didn't change the fact I thought you were hot as sin."

"Hmm. I see. And is this some of that good-guy charm you mentioned earlier?"

Why. Am. I. Still. Arguing?

For the love of Christ, Carissa!

Push your tongue down his throat!

He chuckles. "Depends. Is it working?"

"Have you gotten into my pants yet?"

God, have mercy.

I clearly can't control the words coming out of my damn mouth.

"Sweetheart, that can most definitely be arranged."

Yes please!

"Oooh, promises, promises. Do tell, Nelson." I use his last name to get under his skin. "Just how, pray tell, do you see this going?"

"Are you really asking me what sex together would be like?"

I scrunch my nose, fully aware I'm about to provoke him to the point I might just piss him off. "That bad at it, huh? Can't even describe it to me?"

He gives me a wicked laugh that has me almost throbbing between my legs.

"You want to know what I would do to you, Smalls? How I

could make you feel?"

Sweet little baby Jesus, yes.

I wet my lips, his eyes on my tongue as it swipes across my mouth.

"Tell me."

He takes a long breath, inhaling my scent as his nose traces my collarbone. "I would start with a kiss," he says. "I would kiss you like I've wanted to kiss you all damn day, ever since you gave me a tiny taste on that ice this morning."

Oh God.

Who am I torturing?

Me?

Or him?

"I would part your lips and suck that delightful little tongue of yours into my mouth," he explains and then lightly trails his tongue across my lips inviting himself in.

My head tips back as one of his hands wraps lightly around my throat.

Fuck, this is hot!

He continues to murmur against my lips. "And all the while, my fingers would be working their way across your smooth skin, just like this." His eyes never leave mine as he sneaks his fingers beneath my sweater, first gripping my waist and then feathering up my side, causing my nipples to harden.

Hell, his hands.

I might have a crush on his hands.

I want his hands to feel what he does to me.

"I would tease this sweet little body at first. Make you want. Make you hungry." His hand glides lazily up my body until his thumb swipes softly just underneath my breast. Aching for his touch on the hardened peaks just above, I gasp a breath.

"And what makes you think it's you I want?"

This time he chuckles against my ear. "Don't think I don't notice the way your body responds to me, Smalls. The way it has responded to me every time we're near each other."

"That's... That's not...true." God, I can barely say the words. He knows I'm lying. He has to know.

Colby runs his tongue lightly along my ear and then nibbles my earlobe between his teeth, making my knees weak. "Keep telling yourself that, Carissa, but you and I both know damn well if I slid my hand between your legs right now, you would be deliciously wet for me."

I close my eyes, feeling him touch me in my mind.

Fuck, why doesn't he just do it already?

Rip my pants off and have your way with me.

At least let me fuck your hand.

I'm throbbing here!

"Tell me," he whispers, kissing my temple, down my cheek to my jaw. "Tell me you're wet for me."

So very wet.

"Colby..." His name is a heated whisper. A breathless gasp on my lips.

"Show me," he says. He takes my hand that was resting on his sculpted chest and guides it down my body. "Touch yourself, Smalls. Show me just how wet you are."

He guides my hand right to the waistband of my pants, and before I can even think of stopping myself, I push them further down into my satin panties until I'm sliding a few fingers through my own drenching arousal.

My eyes close and my head falls back against the wall.

Fuck.

I bite my bottom lip when I circle my clit, and that's when I feel his hand around my wrist.

"Christ." He pulls my hand from between my legs, holds my wet fingers up to his nose, inhales like it's the best thing he's ever smelled, and then slips them into his warm mouth, his tongue circling them once, twice, three times.

Oh. My. God.

"Fucking delicious."

My jaw hangs open as I watch him in complete awe, my body

throbbing from the inside. My need for relief surging through me. Knowing he's hooked me one hundred percent, he tips my chin with his finger.

Finally.

Bring on the kiss.

Please, God. I need some relief.

He leans in close enough that I close my eyes, anticipation running over me. His lips brush mine, and he whispers against my mouth. "Next time, Carissa Smallson. Next time, you'll taste yourself on my tongue after I enjoy every last drop your sweet cunt will give up for me."

I nearly moan out loud as I revel in that thought, and then suddenly, the air is cooler, Colby's body no longer pressed against mine. My eyes pop open just in time for me to see the door to my apartment close.

And I'm alone.

My hand on my chest as my heart pounds underneath, I take in a huge breath, releasing it slowly.

"What the fuck just happened?"

CHAPTER 12

Colby

Sometimes I want to kick myself for the decisions I make, and hanging out with Carissa for the day was clearly one of them. Not because I didn't enjoy myself. On the contrary, I had such a good time I haven't been able to get it out of my mind. It's been a long time since I felt that relaxed, that carefree —like I could have a little fun, and nobody was judging me or telling me where I needed to be next. Though I skipped out on an afternoon of watching videos and studying our plays in preparation for this weekend's game to spend time with her, I made up the work later. I pulled a few late nights studying with Milo at home, when what I really wanted was Carissa snuggled between my legs on the couch while I worked. Something about having her nearby calms me, and I can't quite figure out why —because she's anything but calm sometimes.

She's feisty and opinionated, she's outspoken and energetic, and she's so fucking pretty. And dammit! Why I walked out that night, leaving her clearly wanting what I wanted, is beyond me, and I've been pissed about it ever since. I had her right where I wanted her. Wet and willing, and I totally walked instead of taking what I could've had. For the first time ever, instead of acting on my impulses, on my carnal desires, I denied myself a happy ending for the night. I had to drive home fast so I could take care of the uncomfortable chub I had just thinking about her.

I came twice in the shower that night.

And it's not that I didn't want to sleep with Carissa, because fuck, did I want to.

I still want to.

I just didn't want to treat her like every other woman I've dated in the past.

Like a puck bunny.

A one-and-done.

A pump-and-dump.

Carissa is no puck bunny. She's more than that.

She's the girl you want to come home to at the end of a long day. The one you want by your side when life throws you a fucking bucket of lemons. She's a relationship kind of girl.

A forever girl.

And I don't have time in my life for forever girls.

I don't have time for what she wants.

What she deserves.

But hell, do I want her.

I should've called her the next day. Texted her. Anything. But I didn't. I couldn't, because I'm the idiot who didn't ask for her number. Could I have used my resources in the main office to find her contact info? Yes, but instead, I convinced myself not to bother her. Assured myself I'm doing right by her by leaving her alone and not stringing her along for something she thinks will be more than it can ever be. So, rather than allowing myself the mental break from my job responsibilities —and the physical pleasure of wrapping myself around the one girl I've shown any real interest in —I'm diving back into work. The only world I truly know.

But I haven't seen Carissa in three days.

And it's pissing me off.

Her office light hasn't been on, and I haven't seen her lurking around the locker room area where she usually does her thing. I don't want to make a big deal of her absence in front of the other guys, but knowing where she lives, it does worry me a little that it doesn't seem like she's been to work.

Maybe I should drive by and check on her.

Right, because that wouldn't make me look like a stalker.

Or a pathetic teenager.

But what if she's hurt?

Or sick?

She doesn't have a relationship with her parents.

Does she have anyone?

What if she's alone?

Fuck.

She's an adult.

She can handle herself.

Don't get involved.

"Okay, what's going on with you?" Milo slams his locker shut and leans up against it, his father-like stare boring holes into the side of my head as I pull my sweatshirt on.

"What? Nothing's going on. What are you talking about?"

He huffs and moves in a little closer. "I'm not an idiot, Nelson. Do I need to call your brother to find out what your problem is?"

"Nope. He wouldn't know anyway."

"A-ha." He points with a smirk. "So, there is a problem."

I shut my locker with a little less slam than Milo. "Motherfucker."

"I just don't get it, man," he says, his voice lowered so the entire room doesn't hear us. "Last week you were a completely different person. This week...you're the Hulk. What gives?"

"We have a big game, Milo. If we want the Cup, we have to win, and someone has to lead the team. That's on me."

I grab my coat and push through the locker room door, Milo practically on my heels. "That's complete bullshit, and you know it. Whether we win or lose is not all on you. It's on all of us. Plus, I know your game mode. You don't let anything bother you when you're in the zone, so what else is it? Are you out of Lucky Charms again because Carissa—"

"No. It's not about Lucky Charms. And leave Carissa out of it."

He's quiet for a second, and then I hear a soft chuckle behind me followed by, "Oooh. Got it. Okay. Say no more."

That makes me freeze in my step and sharply turn around.

"What is that supposed to mean?"

Milo stares at me before he speaks. Like, fucking stares at my eyes, the corners of his mouth turning up. "You sly dog."

"What the fuck, Mi—"

"You slept with Smallson, didn't you?"

"What? Fuck you." I turn back to walk to my car. "I did no such thing."

Even though I really wanted to.

"You did!" he sings. "You like her!"

"That doesn't mean I fucking slept with her."

"So, it's true then. You do like her."

I stop in my tracks, inhale, and breathe out a heavy breath.

He's not going to let this go.

"All right, if I tell you, will you just let it go?"

"Not a chance." He beams, shaking his head.

I give him a dramatic eye roll. "You know, sometimes I hate that you're one of my best friends."

"Whatever," he laughs. "You love me, and you'd do me in a heartbeat. Spill it."

Fuck, he's right again.

He's been a third brother for longer than I can remember.

And if I had to swivel dicks with any one man on this earth, I guess it would be him.

"All right, listen. Last Saturday, I came in to study some gameplay videos, and she was here."

"On a Saturday morning?"

"Yeah. She was in her office. I didn't expect to see her, but once I did, I remembered her telling me she didn't know shit about hockey and thought it might be fun to bring her down on the ice and show her a few things. Teach her the game."

"Smooth." He smiles and crosses his arms over his chest, listening intently.

"She was a better skater than I thought, and we actually had a lot of fun, and then she tripped over my stick, and I thought she was going to fall flat on her face, so I caught her, and fell first to ease her blow."

"And they say chivalry is dead."

"And then she kissed me."

"Wait. She kissed you?"

I nod. "Yeah."

The corner of his mouth curves up. "How was it?"

"What do you mean, how was it? It was a kiss."

It wasn't just a kiss.

It was an amazing tongue fuck.

"But you kissed her back, right?"

"Fuckin' right I did. And then I asked her to lunch."

"Where did you go?"

"Parker's Deli. I didn't want to eat heavy before a game."

"So, did lunch not go well?"

"No, lunch was fantastic. Talking to her was a breath of fresh air. I haven't felt that relaxed in a fucking long time."

"I'm not catching the problem here."

"The problem came when I went to take her home. I walked her into her apartment, came on to her like a nut job, had her right where I wanted her, and then I bailed."

Milo's brows shoot up. "You bailed?"

"I..." My shoulders fall and my head drops. "I didn't want her to be just another jump in the sack. She's not a bunny. She's not like them. She's...Carissa."

"You wanted it to mean something."

"It did...mean... I don't know," I tell him, shaking my head. Why is this so hard to explain? "Yeah. I guess to me it would've meant more than just a one-night stand."

Milo purses his lips. "So, again, not sure I see the problem. Who cares if it would've meant more? If she wanted it, and you wanted it, I don't see why—"

"Because she's a you type girl, Milo. Not a me type."

"I don't follow."

"You do relationships. You pick and choose, and you don't sleep around all the time like Dex or Hawken. You've had a couple girlfriends in your days. But me? It's not me. I'm busy. I can't give her the kind of attention she deserves."

"So, you just decided to bail on her?"

Fuck. Hearing that question makes me cringe. "Yeah. I did. I'm not proud of it, if that makes you feel any better."

"Let me ask you something, Colby. Did Carissa tell you she wanted a relationship?"

I shake my head. "No."

"Did she tell you she wanted more than sex?"

"No."

"So, you're making those judgments and assumptions for her?"

"I...hell, I don't know. Yeah. I guess I am."

"Mmm-hmm." This time, it's Milo that walks away toward his car parked right next to mine. And it's me on his heels.

"So, you're saying I should've gone for it."

He lifts a shoulder. "Well, I suppose there's something to be said for holding out on her. Having a little flirty fun. In the long run, I think that's a question only you or Carissa can answer."

"That doesn't help me for shit."

He opens his car door and turns. "What do you want me to say?"

"I want you to tell me what you would do."

"That's easy for me, Colby. If I thought she might actually mean something in the long run, I would give her the time of day. I would...you know, woo her."

"Woo her?"

"Yeah. Woo her. Spend time with her. Get to know her. Build the relationship slowly. If she's interested, she'll let you know it. Or just fuck her and get on with it."

I cringe again at his words. Even the thought of a one-time hookup with Carissa makes me uncomfortable.

"But I'll tell you this, Colby. And I'm not saying it because I've heard it around the locker room—though we both know Dex would sleep with anything that breathes—if you don't show her how you feel, if you don't show her even the slightest bit of interest, I guarantee you someone else will."

He's not wrong.

She's a beautiful girl with a great personality.

Any guy would be lucky to have her.

But I just don't know if that guy can be me right now.

"Yeah. Thanks, Milo."

"Sure thing. See ya tomorrow."

Four days.

Finally, after four days, I get to lay eyes on the one person I can't stop thinking about. She stands at the top of the steps inside the plane, recording our entrance as each of us climbs aboard.

"Good morning, Hawken."

Hawken grunts in response. He's not exactly a morning person, but Dex is hot on his heels and the most awake of all of us.

"Mornin' sweet pea," he says to her. My insides tense up, and I'm instantly in a sour mood. "Missed ya these last couple of days. Where ya been?"

Exactly what I want to know.

Carissa pats Dex's cheek. "Aww, how sweet to know you missed me, Dex. Just needed to handle a few things before this long stretch of away games."

A few things?

What could've taken three days?

Is she okay?

"Well, we're glad you're back." He smiles at her, lifts his coffee in her direction, and boards the plane.

"Thank you, Dex." She points her phone at Quinton and Zeke. "Good morning, fellas."

"Morning, Carissa," they greet her in tandem.

"You ready for New England snow?" Milo asks her as he boards in front of me.

She laughs. "Can't be too much worse than a Chicago blustery bitch-slap to the face."

Milo gives her a high-five. "True that. One hundred percent."

It's my turn now, and I have no idea how I want to greet the girl I came on to just a few days ago. I mean I know what I want to do, but it's not like I can lift her up in my arms, kiss her senseless, and fuck her all the way to Boston on a plane filled with teammates. Hell, I would settle for a peck on the cheek or tip of her chin with my finger. Anything just to touch her again, but when her eyes catch mine behind Milo, her smile fades.

"Colby."

What? No fun greeting?

No smile?

No blush to her cheeks?

No nothing?

I want to wrap her up in a hug and ask if she's okay. I'm itching to kiss her again.

But I can't.

I shouldn't.

Besides Milo, the rest of the guys have no idea anything ever happened between us, and from her demeanor right now, it doesn't look like she wants to make it known to anyone. I thought we had something going, but maybe that's just my ego talking.

I deserve that.

I'm the one who didn't call her.

I'm the one who left her wanting... and alone.

"Smalls."

I open my mouth to say something...anything...but nothing of any value comes out.

Instead, I hitch my thumb over my shoulder. "I should..."

"Yeah. Me too," she murmurs. She pockets her phone and finds her seat in the front part of the plane. Several rows in front of where Milo and I always sit.

Fuck.

"Uh, that was awkward, no?" Milo whispers when I finally

take a seat next to him. "Or did you just pussy out?"

"What the fuck ever."

If that's the way she wants to be...if she's not interested, fine.

That's a lie. I'm totally not fine with this. I don't like to be told no, and I don't like not getting what I want, and what I want is Carissa on her back writhing underneath me. I want to taste more of her. One small taste will never be enough. I want my tongue all over her body. I want to lick every inch of her until she comes unhinged.

I want to claim her.

But right now, I need to stop thinking about her. It's not like I don't have a million things to take care of for the team when we get to Boston anyway. She'll talk when she's ready. Once we're in the air, I pull my headphones over my ears, close my eyes, and try my best to sleep off my mood.

We have a game to play.

CHAPTER 13

Carissa

Well, this isn't awkward at all.

Several hours on a plane where Colby sits just a few rows behind me, and I'm supposed to pretend nothing happened between us just a few days ago? I guess I should've seen it coming though. He didn't contact me at all in the past three days. I don't know why I thought maybe he would.

No, that's a lie.

I really thought he would. I expected a text the very night he left me hanging in my apartment, my panties wet and my body throbbing with need. Never in my life has any man come on to me the way Colby Nelson did, only to walk away rather than follow through.

I spent the entire night wanting him after he left. Touching myself until my eyes rolled back in my head as I thought about the scandalous things he could do to me. And then I didn't hear from him for three days. Three long fucking days.

What turned him off?

Why did he leave?

Does he not want me now?

Did he ever really want me?

Or did I fall prey to his womanizing antics?

Either way, I feel ridiculously stupid for showing him my cards and giving him the power over me that night. I would've done anything for him. I would've submitted to his every whim if he had tried to take things to the next level. I would've stripped myself bare for him, and for what? So I could be another notch on his puck bunny belt? So he could tell the team how I willingly let him into my pants?

No, thank you.

Maybe I dodged a huge bullet where Colby is concerned.

Maybe it was good to put a few days between us so we could cool off and reset ourselves.

Maybe he's not the kind of guy I thought he was deep down.

Maybe he's exactly the guy I met in the grocery store.

God knows I've been wrong about people before.

I want to convince myself of all these things, but there's still that tiny little part of me that's both pissed and saddened that I'm, for whatever reason, not enough for him.

No.

Fuck that.

He's not enough for me.

Yeah. That's it.

He doesn't deserve me.

We're an hour into our flight, and I can't just sit still in my seat and allow myself to wallow in my feelings. Not when there's easy work I could be doing.

"All right Zeke, what's that one item you absolutely can't travel without when you're on the road for games?"

"Can't go anywhere without this." Zeke holds up his cell phone, beaming at me with hearts in his eyes. "Gotta be able to call my girl before I go to bed and when I wake up."

"Aww, that's so sweet! How long have you and Lori been together?"

"Three years, four months, and seventeen days."

"But who's counting, right?" I giggle and he nods with a smile. "Exactly."

"Quinton? How about you? What's that one special item you always want to have on the road?"

He tilts his head back so I can see him from where he's seated, and says, "Gotta go with my phone as well. It's the best way to keep in touch with my sister when I'm on the road."

"Oh, you have a sister? Where does she live?"

"Manhattan," he answers. "She'll be at the game actually. It's not every day we play on the East Coast, so she comes to all the close games she can get to."

"That's awesome, Quinton. And what does your sister do?"

"She works for a news network in the city, and she runs a podcast. It's called *TJ on Par: Practical Adult Relationships.*"

"Practical Adult Relationships," I repeat. "I've never spent much time with podcasts before, but that sounds...interesting."

He chuckles. "Nah. Interesting is when she fought publicly with the Love Guru this past Christmas. You've heard of him, right? That guy from New York?"

"Oh yeah! Wait..." My brows shoot up, and I drop my phone, forgetting I was recording. "Are you telling me...?"

Quinton smiles, obviously knowing what I'm about to ask.

"Are you seriously telling me your sister is that girl? The one who went to Hawaii with a guy she had never met?"

He nods. "Yep. Her name is Tenley Shay. Tenley Jane Shay to be exact...hence the *TJ on Par.*"

"Holy shit! That was quite a story back in December! Aww, and now they're in love?"

How's that for dreamy?

"Yep." He shrugs. "And moving back to Hawaii to take over the resort they stayed in while they were there. It's this big story, but yeah. This will be her last week on the mainland before they fly out, so she wanted to come watch me play."

"That's incredible!" My smile is as sincere as the warmth in my heart. "I'm really happy for her and for you that you get to see her before she flies out. I certainly hope you get a win tonight just for her."

"Me too."

I gesture quickly to the team. "You all better move your asses so Quinton can score at least one goal tonight. For his sister."

The guys all murmur among themselves, teasing Quinton

and laughing together. I go back to my video, interviewing Hawken and Dex next, but when it's time to turn around and talk to the last two, I nearly chicken out.

Gesturing to the device in Milo's hand, I ask, "What are you reading, Milo?"

He looks up from his e-reader but doesn't get the chance to answer my question before Dex and Hawken start giving him a hard time.

"Yeah, Milo. Tell Carissa what you're reading this time," Hawken teases.

"Milo's a hopeless romantic, Smallson," Dex explains with humor in his voice. "He's always reading some smutty romance book. Aren't ya, Milo?"

With wide eyes, I turn from Dex's direction back to Milo. "Is that true? You like romance books?"

He nods. "Guilty."

"You mean guilty pleasure," Zeke snickers. "We like to call him the President of the Smut Club."

"Call me whatever you want, gentlemen. But my mama didn't raise no dummy."

"I think that's great, Milo. I wish every guy would sit and read a few romances now and then."

"Precisely," he says. "My mom always told me if I wanted to find out what women really want, what they wish for, what they fantasize about, I just need to open a damn book. Romance books are like tutorials for men." He bobs his head. "And women, I suppose. If they didn't want the fantasies they read about in books, they wouldn't read them. Did you know the romance book industry alone is a billion-dollar industry?"

I suck in a quick breath. "Really? That large, huh?"

"Yep." He raises his e-reader a bit. "Just playing my part, I guess. Plus, it's a fun way to pass the time. Better than dealing with this brooding teenager over here." He elbows Colby, who rolls his eyes and grunts, his headphones hugging the sides of his head. I know this is Milo giving me the green light to finally say words to Colby, but I really can't think of anything I want to say. Plus, it doesn't look as though he's really interested in conversation given the headphones and all.

"I hear you," I tell him. "Maybe one of these days this big lug will be able to pull the huge stick out of his ass and be a little more human."

No sooner than I speak the words do Colby's eyes lock onto mine like he heard everything I just said.

Maybe he did and maybe he didn't, but regardless, he doesn't respond audibly. He only gives me a narrow-eyed stare and an expression that could read two different ways. Like what I said either irritates him or hurts his feelings. Either way, if he's giving me the silent treatment now, what am I supposed to do? I raise a shoulder in response like I don't give two shits what he's thinking and then turn back to my seat.

Except I do give two shits what he's thinking. Leaning my head back on the seat, I close my eyes and take a deep breath, exhaling slowly.

I wish it didn't bother me so much that he's not speaking to me, but it does. What the hell happened between three days ago and today?

And why am I the bad guy?

The crowd goes wild at the final buzzer, and every fan dressed in red and black is on their feet, celebrating a Red Tails win. I record a few seconds of the team hugging one another on the ice, and then pocket my phone and cheer them on along with the crowd. It doesn't take long for the players to disperse, with some heading straight to the locker room and some being interviewed by members of the press.

"Nice game out there, Colby, and congratulations on the win, but if you don't mind my saying so, you looked kind of angry out there today."

Colby's eyes find mine as I stand along the back wall.

What the hell? Is he implying I'm the reason he's in a bad mood? Not my fault he was a dick on the plane and didn't talk to me.

Also, not my fault that he wasn't talkative before the game either, though I was trying to be respectful of his Lucky Charms time. I know how important that is.

"Yeah. Where's the question?"

"Oh, well, um, you just looked angry sitting in the penalty box. Talk to us about the emotion you were feeling at the time."

Colby huffs out a laugh. "What the hell am I supposed to do, Tom? Smile? You want me to smile more while I'm sitting there wanting to get back in the game?"

I have to hide my smirk at his answer. Sometimes reporters are so dense.

"Is that what you think about in there? Just wanting to get back in the game?"

He gives them a shrug. "Nah. Sometimes I run down my grocery list, or I work on my times tables." He rolls his eyes. "Dude, what do you think? Hell yeah. I just want to play hockey, man. That's my job, isn't it?"

Yikes.

My brows pinch as I watch and listen. I get that reporters can sometimes ask ridiculous questions, but I don't understand why Colby looks so annoyed up there.

They won their game for Pete's sake. He should be over the moon right now.

"Did you do something different with your team this time around to pull out such a strong win?"

He cocks his head. "Nah. In the end we got more goals than they did. That's it. Boston's a great team with a lot of great guys. I'd be honored to play with anyone of them any time, but we had a good day today. We played like the team I know. That's it."

The press manager raises his hand and announces, "All right, we have time for one last question..." He points to one of the reporters in the far corner of the room.

"Mr. Nelson, do you think your brother would be proud of your performance today?"

The room goes silent as Colby stares down the reporter, and I wonder for a moment if everyone is as uncomfortable as I feel standing in here right now. I watch as Colby swallows and bows his head, his jaw pinching as he contemplates how to answer the reporter's question. Though the tension in the room grows thick, it's not lost on me that every single cell phone owned by a member of the press is in the air right now, recording his every move.

What the fuck, guys?

Finally, Colby raises his head and stares down the reporter who asked the question.

"You know what? If my brother were here, he would tell me I played like shit and should get out of my own head, because he would've been able to tell that even our team's winning game wasn't my best personal performance," he says, holding the reporter's eye. "He would probably remind me that I'm letting my team down when I'm not at my very best, and then he would tell me to pull the stick out of my ass." He locks eyes with me, and I gulp in response, feeling like the smallest person in the room.

And not just because I am physically the smallest person in here.

Shit. I guess he did hear me on the plane.

"And enjoy playing the game instead of making everything seem like it's a do-or-die situation," he continues, his face reddening.

Several of the press are nodding their heads as Colby swallows again, his head bowed. He licks his lips and then his cold, hard eyes are on them once more, his hands in fists on the table in front of him.

"But then, my brother's not here, is he?" He shakes his head. "No. He's not. Because he died. Twenty years ago. But for some sick, fucked up reason, you all feel like it's your duty to mention him in every interview I do, as if I'm going to sit here and cry you all a river..." His Adam's apple bobs and his nostrils flare. His voice booming the more agitated he gets.

Oh no.

Stay cool, Colby.

He stands, making himself the giant in the room, his lips curled into a sneer. "When what I wish would happen is that you would all focus on the goddamn team and the fact that we did our fuckin' jobs tonight to pull out a win instead of always making my performance, good or bad, in one way or another, about my dead brother."

Fuck.

I cringe as Colby exits the press room and then sneak out my door to catch up with him.

I'm going to have to do damage control on that one.

"Colby!" I shout down the hall, and he comes to a halt outside the locker room. I just reach him at a jog as he turns around.

"What do you want?"

My brows narrow. "Whoa. I was coming to make sure you're all right." I gesture back toward the press room. "It was a little... rough in th—"

"I'm fine."

I tilt my head, studying his hardened expression. "Are you though? Because you don't seem fine. You didn't seem fine on the plane, and you don't seem fine now. Did I..." I try to reach out, but he steps away from me. My eyes widen, and I recoil as well. "Did I do something to upset you because it seems—"

"It's a game day, Smallson."

He doesn't call me Smallson.

He's never called me Smallson.

He always calls me Smalls.

He lifts his arms, gesturing to himself still dressed in most of his uniform. "I'm busy, all right? I have a job to do."

Somewhere in that bullshit of an excuse, I find a little confidence and stand up a little straighter. "Oh. Yeah. Right. I'm sorry. I wasn't aware being a dick to the girl whose wet fingers were in your mouth just a few short days ago was part of your job description." His face contorts, and I can tell I've made him uncomfortable, so do I stop there?

Hell no.

"Of course, you walked away from me that night too, so I guess this," I say, gesturing to him, "should come as no surprise." I clench my jaw so hard I'm surprised I don't break a tooth. I'm so angry, and admittedly hurt, I don't even want to look at him right now, so giving him my most dramatic eye roll, I turn on my heel and march myself down the hallway. "See you around, Nelson."

I hear him sigh loudly before he shouts, "Carissa, wait." But it's too late. You don't get to be a dick to me and then think I'm just going to bend over and ask for more. I may have a small crush, but I also have dignity and a heaping ton of self-respect. I lift my hand in the air and toss up my middle finger, walking away from Colby without looking back.

Serves you right, asshole.

CHAPTER 14

Colby

"She's in room eight fourteen, Mr. Nelson."

Sliding a crisp fifty-dollar bill across the counter along with the hat I was wearing that now has my signature on it, I smile at the hotel attendant, grateful that he's a Red Tails fan. Sometimes, and I mean sometimes, it's good to be famous.

"Thank you very much."

"My pleasure, sir."

The elevator drops me off on the eighth floor, and I jog down the hall only a short way until room eight fourteen is right in front of me.

"Smalls?" I knock three times lightly on her door, but she doesn't answer.

"Carissa, can we talk?" I knock a few more times to no avail.

Resting my head against her door, I murmur, "I'm sorry, okay? I really want to talk to you."

I know I'm a little late getting back to the hotel. After the press conference and then Carissa putting me in my place, I took an extra-long shower, pouting over the fact I should be celebrating a great win tonight, but instead, I'm both pissed off at the media and irritated with myself over how I treated her.

How I've been treating her.

She looked good tonight. Tight jeans. Team jersey. And a pair of red fuck-me heels that were calling my name. Her hair pulled up in a ponytail. By the time I was finally packed and ready to go, the team was gone, so I grabbed an Uber back to the hotel.

Now here I am trying to make amends, hoping maybe Carissa will forgive and forget my asshole-ishness.

I don't know what I'm expecting, really.

I know I'm the one who hasn't followed up with her in days.

I'm the one who ghosted her.

I'm the one who has been nothing but a grump in front of her.

But I still want her.

Even more now than before.

As the tension inside me boils, my need to be around her grows, too. Did I want to wrap myself up in her after that press conference tonight? I sure as hell did. So, why I gave her the cold shoulder, I wish I knew.

I'm not very good at this.

Because the last thing I want to do is upset her.

I know, I'm doing a great fucking job so far.

Not wanting to look like a desperate teenager, I give up knocking on Carissa's door and head down to the bar where I know the guys are probably three or four drinks in by now. Thank God we don't have to be on a bus or a plane tonight.

When I don't see Carissa hanging out with the guys, my entire body slumps in disappointment. "Tequila," I mumble to the bartender as I take a seat. "And keep 'em coming."

He hands me the first shot, and I down it immediately, hoping to God it'll kick in fast. My phone dings in my pocket, and I'm quick to toss it on the bar in front of me, hoping it's Carissa, except it's then I realize we still haven't traded phone numbers.

Dammit!

I'm such an idiot!

> **Elias: Great game tonight, bro!!**
> **Drink a few for me! Wish I could've**
> **been there!**

> **Me: Yeah. Thanks! Feels good to win.**

> **Elias: Maybe stay outta the sin bin next time eh? *wink emoji***

> **Me: Maybe I like it there.**

> **Elias: LOL I bet you do. At least get a good punch in next time. No more weak-ass penalties.**

> **Me: Yeah yeah. I'll see what I can do.**

"Where's your girl?" Milo takes a seat next to me at the bar as I'm handed my second shot. It slides down my throat with ease.

"Who?"

"Smallson. She's not with you?"

I shake my head. "She's not my girl, asshat. And why the fuck would she be with me?"

"I just thought...you know."

"You thought what?" I knock back my third shot and notice the bartender places a glass of water in front of me as well. "That I would find her somewhere and profess my undying love for her and then make her mine right there in the arena? Is that what you thought? Sorry. I'm not one of your mushy romance books."

"All right, asshole. You don't have to be a dick. I was just asking because I haven't seen her. Hadn't seen you either so thought maybe you two finally got together."

"Yeah, well, you're wrong. She wants nothing to do with me." I hang my head like the desperate motherfucker I am.

He scoffs out a quiet chuckle. "Mkay."

"What?"

"I find that hard to believe."

"Yeah, well, she flipped me off and walked away from me tonight, so what does that tell you?"

"That tells me you probably deserved it." He laughs but, I'm not smiling. "Dude, you need to blow off all this steam that's been building in you for weeks. Clear your head, you know? Relax for once. You do so much for the team. We all know it, but damn," he says, elbowing me. "We pulled out a hell of a win tonight, and that deserves to be celebrated. So, fucking live a little, huh?" He slides my next shot in front of me, the side of my mouth pulling up in a smirk as I shake my head. "Stop being a shithead for one night."

"You're a horrible influence on me, you know that?"

He's right though.

I just need to relax.

However I do that.

Get Carissa off my mind.

Yeah right.

"And you love me for it." He smirks. "Always have."

"Fucker." A laugh finally escapes my mouth, and I must admit it feels good to smile a little.

"My pleasure, bro." He lifts his fist and bumps it against mine and then gestures beside me with his chin. "Bunnies nine-o-clock."

The tequila setting in and dissolving my anxiety, I turn to the two girls seated next to me, martinis in hand. One of them is the typical blonde-haired, blue-eyed bunny always hanging around the team wherever we go. The other woman, though, catches my attention, but only because she bears a striking resemblance to Carissa. Brown wavy hair, deep brown eyes. A few freckles across her face.

"Ladies." I nod, lifting my shot of tequila in their direction. I swallow it back. My head is fuzzy as the alcohol does its job, but at least I still have my faculties about me enough to flirt with the walking pussies. "What's your name?"

The blonde smiles at me and answers, "I'm Lauren. This is

my friend Marissa."

My brows shoot up. "Marissa?"

What are the fucking odds?

That's almost laughable.

"That's me." The girl waves with a mischievous grin, and already I know she's nowhere near the woman Carissa is, but her pussy will be warm, and if I say Carissa's name as I plow into her, she'll never know the difference.

Yeah. She'll do.

In the past hour, I've chatted with Marissa and Lauren about the jobs they don't love, their dream of becoming flight attendants, their bra sizes —impressive by the way —and their excitement over sharing my cock when I take them both upstairs to my room. I mean, what guy wouldn't take them up on that offer?

Milo, that's who.

He's always the good guy.

And Zeke 'cause he's already pussy whipped.

But that's not me.

Not tonight.

Tonight, I want to fuck my feelings away until I have nothing left to feel.

"You ready to get out of here?" I ask them, kissing the side of Marissa's neck, and smoothing a hand up Lauren's leg as she giggles.

Marissa licks her lips. "I was ready an hour ago." They grab their drinks and head out of the bar, my hand on the small of their backs, leading them.

Lauren turns to ask, "What floo—"

I stop dead in my tracks when we nearly collide. Standing just outside the bar, the color drains from her face, though her eyes are a bit puffy, as if she's been crying. Her mouth falls open in shock.

"Carissa."

"It's MAR-issa." The girl next to me tries to correct me, but I push away from both women, my eyes on the girl I've been trying to forget.

Carissa's eyes shift to Marissa and Lauren, and then back to me, and I see the hurt in her expression. Her chin trembles for a moment, and then she's increasing her distance. Shaking her head as she backs up, creating more space between us.

"Carissa, please..." I step toward her, but she raises her chin, her lip curling in disgust as she speaks in an unsteady tone.

"This?" she fumes. "This is your kink?" She laughs, but there's an edge to it that is not funny at all. "One's never enough for you, huh? Is that it?" She rolls her eyes. "God, you're such an asshole." She starts to walk away, but then turns back. "But you know what? You deserve this..." She gestures to Lauren and Marissa. "This, and every bit of syphilis, gonorrhea, or herpes you end up with after tonight."

And then she walks away, leaving me boiling hot on the inside.

She doesn't get to judge me.

She didn't lay claim to me.

I fuck who I want, when I want.

Yeah, keep telling yourself that, Colby.

"Who the hell was that?" Lauren scoffs. "What a bi—"

"Shut your mouth." I turn on her with a finger in her face. "That woman means...something to me." Though I'm not sure what exactly. "I have to go."

I don't even bother to see them out before I stomp off to find Carissa. It's time to figure out this shit once and for all. Jogging toward the elevators, I make it just in time to see the doors closing on Carissa as she's punching the button furiously. Once she sees me, she flips me off and the door closes.

"Shit."

Ding!

The elevator next to hers opens, and I jump on and punch

the eight button. She thinks she's so sly running from me, but little does she know, I know exactly what room she's in. When I reach her floor, I see her briskly walking down the hall toward her door. Her hands shake as she tries to put her keycard in the lock. Thank God it doesn't work on her first try.

Walking up behind her, I cover her fragile little hand with my giant one, and nearly flatten her body against the door. She yelps, but I don't give two shits. I wrap an arm around her waist, my hand splayed over her stomach, and growl into her ear.

"Where the absolute fuck do you get off judging me like that, Smalls?"

I feel her gasp under my touch. "Get your filthy hands off me," she says the words, but her body is speaking another language. Her mouth opens, and her head falls back against my shoulder. Her tight little ass grinds into my growing bulge.

"You want to know my kink, Carissa?" I bite her earlobe, and she groans. "Is that what you want?"

"I know your kink, you disgusting man-whore."

"You don't know shit about anything." I sneak my hand underneath her untucked jersey, my fingers feathering her skin, and her breath hitches.

"You're an asshole."

"Open the damn door, Smalls," I growl in her ear.

"Fuck you."

Grabbing her hips, I turn her around, so she has no choice but to look at me. Leaning down, my lips are mere centimeters from hers as I angrily whisper, "No, Smalls. Fuck you. That's my kink. You are my kink. Everything about you turns me the fuck on, even when I don't want it to, and right now I don't want it to because God knows you've been a complete—"

WHAM!

She slaps my face.

"Don't you dare even think of finishing that sentence, Colby Nelson," she hisses. "I have been nothing but nice to you. In fact, I've bent over backwards to be nice to you. We shared a kiss on the ice literally four days ago. And dammit, it was a good fucking kiss. I thought..." She doesn't finish her sentence. Her eyes dart one way and then another as her cheeks heat.

"You thought what?"

She shakes her head, confounded. "And then I... I... I touched myself for you." She whisper-shouts, her voice quivering, blowing hair out of her face. "Because you asked me to and then you left me, remember? You left me." She pushes against my chest, but I don't budge. "So, don't you stand here and try to tell me that I'm the one who—"

"I didn't see or hear from you for three days after that!" I push away from her, irritated and overwhelmed, sliding my hand through my mussed hair. "You could've been hurt or worse, and I wouldn't have ever known. We never exchanged numbers, so I couldn't contact you. Instead, I spent three days worrying about you. How do you think that made me feel?"

Her eyes narrow. "What? I don't answer to you. You're not my father, you—"

"Thank God for that," I sneer with an eye roll. "Though I hear you don't talk to him either so..."

She huffs to the point that I'm pretty sure she's about to slap me again, so I grab her keycard out of her hand and plunge it into the lock. The light turns green, and I push the door open. My arm wrapped around Carissa's waist, I lift her with one arm and walk us into her room, kicking the door shut behind me.

"What the fuck are you—"

I pin her against the wall just inside, her arms up over her head, our hands now intertwined against the wall. Her chest heaves against me as I lean my weight on her, my stiff cock evident between us. Her chestnut eyes pierce mine and then fall to my lips.

"Do you feel that?" I murmur, pushing my pelvis against her a little more. "This is how you make me feel, Carissa. You've been driving me absolutely fucking crazy since the day we met, so tell me you don't want this, and I'll walk away and never bother you again." I huff. "But, you better fuckin' know what you want because I swear to God I will not chase you. This ends here. If you tell me to walk, I'll walk, and I won't come back. Not tomorrow, not the next day, and not the day after that. So, which is it, Smalls? Yes or no? You need to say it."

Say yes.

Just fucking say yes.

Her eyes widen at first, and she bites her bottom lip.

"It's not that easy," she argues.

"The fuck it isn't," I breathe against her lips, and slide a hand down her torso, my thumb brushing against her breast.

She whimpers. "You could've had this a couple of days ago. You could've had me. I wanted you that night."

"I wanted you, too, Smalls. Believe me, I did."

She clenches her jaw in a huff as she glares at me. "I was right there, Colby. I was right fucking there. Putty in your hands and you walked aw—"

"I know I did," I blurt out, squeezing my eyes closed.

"What the fuck?" she shouts. "Why? Why would you do that to me?" Her chin lifts, and she sneers at me when I don't answer right away. "What's the matter? You didn't think you could satisfy me?"

That makes me chuckle. "Oh Smalls, I think we both know how much I can satisfy you. Don't pretend you haven't fantasized about my cock in your—"

"But you didn't satisfy me, did you? You fucking walked aw—"

"Because I didn't want you to be one of those random women like the ones downstairs!" I finally shout back. "Don't you see? It wouldn't have been just a random fuck for... Dammit!"

I pinch the bridge of my nose. I'm letting my emotions get the best of me, I know, but she's driving me crazy.

Her face falls, and I think I've stunned her into silence.

That's a first.

Trying to rein in my irritation, I open my mouth to speak my mind, but the words just aren't coming out the way I need them to.

"It would've..."

Breathe...

"Fuck! It would've..."

Breathe.

My forehead falls against hers, and I count to five in my head, my eyes closed. "It..."

I wish she would see how vulnerable she makes me, but she's just not seeing me.

"Let go of me."

My eyes pop open as my heart shatters into tiny pieces inside me. My chest constricts, making it hard to catch a breath. My shoulders slump, and I pull my hand away from the wall, dropping her arms. I try to come to terms quickly with the fact she just rejected me, but without warning, she grabs my face and smashes her mouth against mine.

Wait, what?

She's kissing me?

Holy hell.

Her lips are warm. Fierce. Strong as she kisses me with all the fire she has in her petite, sexy body.

Time stops.

The earth stops moving beneath my feet.

Nothing else in the world exists.

Not hockey. Not my teammates downstairs. Not the people walking down the hall outside the door. Not the traffic outside.

It's just the two of us.

With ease, I lift her up and wrap her legs around my waist, my tongue plunging into her mouth, taking everything she's willing to give me, because I want her.

Need her.

Crave her.

"Tell me you want me, Smalls. I need to hear you say it."

She yanks on my hair, and holy fucking shit, I almost come on the spot.

"If you don't claim me right fucking now and finish what you started days ago, I'll never speak to you again, Colby Nelson. This is your last chance. Take me or leave me, and if you choose to leave, don't even think of coming back."

Fuck, I've never had a woman who tops me from the bottom the way she does, and I am fucking here for it.

Turning with her in my arms, I carry her to the bed, where I sit down on the edge of the mattress and deposit her in front of me. "I need to look at you. Touch you. Taste you."

With Carissa standing between my legs, I lift her jersey up and over her head, a black satin bra greeting me.

Beautiful.

Her breasts aligning perfectly with my face, I waste no time palming them, rubbing them, my thumbs caressing her nipples. Her mouth falls open, her head tips back, and she arches her back.

"God, yes."

I gently pull the cup of her bra down, revealing her darkened taught nipple and pull it into my mouth, sucking, nibbling, enjoying, while I unzip her jeans and push them down as far as I can. She slides her hand through my hair, grabbing it and holding my head in place as I suck on her tits, one nipple and then the other.

"Harder, Colby. I'm not a porcelain doll. You won't break me."

I slip my hands down the back of her matching black satin panties, grabbing her ass, kneading it in my hands, and slipping a finger as low as I can from behind. She gasps in pleasure when I slip one inside her and bite down on her nipple at the same time.

When she whimpers, I murmur against her breast, "I tend to play rough, Smalls. Hope you can handle that."

"Give it your best shot, Nelson," she pants as my finger slides in and out of her. "If you can't satisfy me, I'll have no problem letting your buddies know what a slacker you are in bed."

Her smart mouth makes me smile.

"Sweetheart, if you can even walk out of here tomorrow morning, I'll be impressed. Spread your legs. Now."

CHAPTER 15

Carissa

Without hesitation or warning, Colby rips my panties from my body and brings them to his nose, inhaling my scent. He pushes them into the pocket of his pants and then reaches behind me to unhook my bra. With a rugged breath, I stand in front of him completely naked, and oh my God, hornier than I think I've ever been.

I need his fingers to go back where they were.

I need his fingers everywhere.

"You're making my mouth water, Smalls." He shakes his head. "You're incredibly beautiful."

Taking his head in my hands, I lick the inside of his mouth and then rip the buttons on his dress shirt until it falls open and I'm gazing upon his sculpted chest. "I'm even better looking when I'm coming, Colby," I breathe against his mouth as his warm hands roam my body. "Make me come."

"Baby, you'll be coming several times tonight whether you want to or not."

His promise sends shivers down my spine. I've never had multiple orgasms before. Only ever one in a night, but who would I be if I simply submitted to the one person who enjoys a little smack talk?

"You assume my body will simply bend to your will."

The corner of his mouth pulls up, and his hands smooth up my thighs. He grabs me between my legs, his fingers moving through my arousal, and flattens his tongue against my nipple.

My mouth falls open and I almost scream. "Oh, God!"

He merely chuckles and pushes two fingers inside me, dragging them forward and back, forward and back, rolling my nipple between his teeth. I have to grab onto his shoulders just to stay on my feet, and he doesn't stop. He accelerates the speed of his fingers inside me, curling inward against me as his thumb rubs quick circles on my clit. He moves his mouth to the other nipple and bites down, pulling it tight in his mouth as I pull his hair. His dark orbs watch my every expression.

He moans against my breast as I practically fuck his hand.

God, I need this relief.

"Colby!"

"I know, Smalls. Give it up for me. Feel me. Say my name again."

My head falls back as the tingle begins in my legs and moves through my chest up to my throat. "Colby... I'm almost there."

"You're fucking drenched for me, babe. So fucking sexy."

He pumps even faster, and a spiraling fury explodes inside me. Warmth spreading down my spine and in between my legs until I can't hold on anymore.

"Yes!" I smack his shoulders and then grab onto his shirt, holding on for dear life as my orgasm rips me apart from the inside. "Shit, that was," I pant trying to catch my breath. "That was—"

"Not done."

My eyes bulge when he lifts me and then tosses me on the mattress.

I gasp his name when he pushes my legs apart and buries his face at the apex of my thighs, licking me. Sucking me. Eating me. His tongue flicking my clit at every pass. Relentless in his tracking of another orgasm.

My back arches off the mattress at the overwhelming sensations going on in my body. Extreme pleasure. Heated desire. Mild soreness and an excitement I haven't felt in a long time.

"Colby," I cry out, shaking my head. "I can't..."

"Yes, you can, Smalls. You can and you will." He brings his head up and licks his lips like a lion eating his prey. "Fuck, you're delicious. I could eat you every day. Breakfast, lunch, dinner, and dessert."

The frenzy builds so quickly I grab whatever hair I can on his head and push him back down my body, writhing against his face. His beard burning my thighs but feeling marvelous at the same time.

"Eat it all, Nelson," I breathe. "And don't you leave one fucking drop."

"Fuck, Smalls." He sucks me even harder and within seconds my next climax is ripping through me. Colby doesn't say a thing after this one. Only wipes his hand over his beard with a hungry smirk on his face and then hastily unzips his pants, pushing them down with his boxer briefs and stepping out of them. His massively hard cock at the ready.

I think I've died and gone to Heaven.

CHAPTER 16

Colby

Fuck me, this woman is all I've ever wanted and more. Two orgasms within minutes and I want so much more from her. Reaching down into my pants pocket, I grab a couple condoms from my wallet and slide one on as Carissa watches.

I climb onto the bed with her and lift her leg, alternating between tender kisses and sharp bites up her inner thigh. A little pleasure, a little pain. Her sharp intake of breath on every bite fuels me to pleasure her in all the best ways. Once I reach the top of her thigh, I rub my hand quick and rough over her glistening pussy several times and then grab her hips and plunge inside her. She screams loud enough for people two doors down to hear her.

"Oh my...*Christ yes*!"

"Fuck me! You're incredible, Smalls." I pump in and out of her a few times in quick succession and then pull out entirely, holding her legs open and spanking her soaked pussy until her back arches off the mattress and her mouth falls open. Her eyes roll back in her head.

"Absolutely incredible."

And then I thrust back inside her, pumping harder, faster. Refusing to slow down because fuck if I don't need this release as bad as she does. Our bodies slap together as I lift her legs and rest them on my shoulders. I reach up and palm her breasts, giving them a tight squeeze and then a gentle knead.

"Colby! Jesus fuck. Yes! Don't stop!"

I'm slamming into Carissa at a furious pace, her cries and

147

moans growing louder and louder. Then she clenches around my cock, milking me until my body quivers, my balls tighten, and I erupt inside her, coming so hard I nearly collapse on top of her, assaulting her petite body with the full weight of me.

She wraps her arms around me and holds tight as we both catch our breath together.

"Are you okay?" It finally dawns on me that I just put her through three back-to-back orgasms. I lift from her body, tenderly kissing her neck, her shoulder, her chest, her breasts, and then her lips.

She gazes up at me with a satiated look that almost makes me chuckle.

"I couldn't be any better."

My eyes drop to her lips and then her body lying open underneath me, and something in my chest flips or twists. It's a weird, foreign feeling that I brush out of my mind for now because I finally have the woman I want in my bed.

She's finally here.

She's finally mine.

I want more of her.

I want all I can get.

There's no way I'm done with her yet.

"Yeah, you could. You could be so much better."

Her brows narrow. "What do you mean?"

I give her a smirk and then bow my head to suck her nipple, popping off loudly when she gasps. "You have one more in you." Sitting back on my knees, I pull off my condom, tie it in a knot, and toss it into the trash can by the bed. Then I grab a new one, my cock excitedly ready for round two.

Carissa's eyes widen. "You're serious?"

"Do you think this cock would lie to you?" I gesture to my hardened shaft. "Now, be a good girl and get on your knees, Smalls."

She swallows with a hungry stare, and when she starts to flip herself over, I spank her sweet little ass cheek, rubbing it as

I smooth a hand down her back. "Chest on the bed, I want this pretty little ass in the air."

"Colby, I don't know if I can—*fuck*," she gasps when I nibble and lick her cheeks and then trail my tongue between them. "More. Oh, God, more."

I knew she wasn't done.

"So demanding, you dirty, sexy woman." I spank her right cheek, and then grab them both, kneading and spreading, kissing, sucking, and then I line myself up and slowly push inside her, her body reacting and squeezing me tight.

Carissa groans at the pleasure, and her head rises just enough for me to grab her hair and wrap it around my hand. "So goddamn gorgeous, Smalls. Now hold on tight because I'm about to fuck you to kingdom come."

"Yes, please," she begs. "I need more, Colby."

One hand pulling her hair and one hand grasping her hip, I thrust into her so deep my balls slap against her ass, and she's squealing with pleasure. I spank her a few times and then let go of her hip and hair, wrapping my hands around her until I'm palming her breasts. I tweak her nipples and listen as she screams out.

"Yes! Yes! Yes!"

Lifting her up so her back is to my chest, I continue to pump into her as hard and fast as I can, her body starting to quiver as she gets closer. Grazing her earlobe with my teeth, I lick around her ear and pull her as close to me as I can get her and murmur, "Your body is mine, Smalls."

God, it feels good to say that to her.

"Yes!"

"Say it," I demand. "I want to hear you say it."

She swallows, a sheen of sweat across her body. "I'm...oh, God, I'm yours, Colby."

"All mine, babe. And when you try to walk in the morning, I want you thinking of my cock. My cock that is made for you. Only you, Smalls."

"Oh God, Colby," she cries in a stuttering voice, our bodies thrust and bounce and move against each other. "I'm going to come."

"Me too, baby. Fuck, you are incredible."

Wrapping my arms around her, reminding myself not to crush her, I nuzzle into the side of her neck, sucking hard and fast until we both reach that moment when our worlds explode and she's screaming my name as I groan loudly behind her.

"Motherfucking fuck." We're kneeling together in the middle of the bed, my strength the only thing holding Carissa up as her body nearly collapses. I gently lower her to one of the pillows and rub her legs and back to relieve her muscles. She's turned away from me and looks to be almost asleep, so I pull off my condom, disposing of it in the trash can, and then sit up to grab her a washcloth.

"Stay," she murmurs softly. "Stay with me, Colby."

A reassured smile on my face, I lean over and kiss her cheek. "I wouldn't leave even if you wanted me to." That's a lie. I respect her enough to leave if she asked me to —but thank God she's not asking that of me, because it would be very hard to do. "Just getting you a warm washcloth."

I've never cared about taking care of my previous bedmates before. They know what they want when they approach me, and if they're accepted into my bed, they're on their own when I'm done with them. That's how it's always been. But Carissa Smallson is different.

Sharing this time with her tonight was unlike anything I've ever done. I found myself wanting to satisfy her. Instead of a one-and-done like most women, I couldn't get enough. I had to claim her. Make her mine. Make sure no one else could have her.

Is that a little sick and twisted? Maybe.

But her body, her mind, her personalit... She's like a bowl of nothing but Lucky Charms marshmallows.

Magically delicious.

CHAPTER 17

Carissa

Warmth and weight flutter into my consciousness as my dream-filled sleep comes to a disappointing end. Visions of his body and mine, becoming one in so many delicious ways. Colby Nelson, the man, the myth, the legend, in my bed, pleasuring me repeatedly, always wanting more. Never getting enough. My voice hoarse from screaming out in ecstasy.

There's a feather of movement on my stomach, and I open my eyes to see why. Two strong hands hold me in place, one of them resting on my abdomen, the other flattened underneath my neck. A warm breath beside me has me lifting my head to see the insanely gorgeous Colby Nelson nearly wrapped around me. His leg intertwined with mine. His head nestled into the crook of my neck and shoulder. His...

Oh, my God, is that his penis?

He's naked?

Wait...I'm naked.

Suddenly, the visions of my dream-filled sleep flood my mind.

Oh, my God.

It wasn't a dream.

It was all real.

His lips on my nipples.

His fingers inside me.

On my knees.

My legs in the air.

Against his chest.

And he stayed with me!

"*You're mine. Say it.*"

His words float through my mind, but as I lie here with his warm body clinging to me, I wonder if things aren't the other way around. Before last night, I would've described Colby as independent and self-sufficient, not needing anyone in his life. But the way he clings to me, holds me against him, and the way he wanted to hear me say I was his... Maybe he needs me.

And that thought makes me panic.

I don't know how to move forward after what we just did when I'm in the job I'm in. My boss didn't say that relationships with team members were forbidden. Just that it would be in my best interest to steer clear.

What would she say if she knew Colby and I were together?

What would the other team members say?

I'm still new in this job, and the last thing I want to do is ruffle anyone's feathers.

"Take a breath, Smalls." His raspy morning voice in my ear is a surprise. I thought he was sleeping.

"What?"

He chuckles softly beside me. "You've been holding your breath for a good thirty seconds. You okay?"

"Mmm-hmm."

He smooths his hand over my stomach and lifts his head from the crook of my neck enough to kiss my temple. "That doesn't sound very convincing." He rolls me over so we're facing each other, his sleepy hazel eyes watching me. How does someone wake up looking as gorgeous as he does? "What are you thinking about in that pretty little head of yours?"

"What do you think I'm thinking about?"

A cute, lazy grin spreads across his face. "You're thinking you don't know how you're going to get out of this bed because your body is unequivocally sore after all the fun we had last night."

"Hmm... Not quite what I was thinking, but now that you mention it, I am a little sore... good sore though."

"So, maybe you're thinking about how good it felt to have my cock inside you, and you're trying to figure out how to make that happen again?" He smiles and wags his brow.

I lift my hand to the side of his face. "It was amazing, Colby, and I loved every second of it, truly. But no, that's not what I was thinking."

He takes a deep breath, his eyes narrowing. "So, then you're thinking you don't know what this is now. Just two people fucking, or more than that? And if it's more than that, how much more and what does it all mean? What happens next? You're not sure what you want it to be?"

Bingo.

"Wow. That was spot on. What do you want it to be?" I ask timidly.

"If you're asking me whether I'm going to want to fuck you again, the answer is a resounding yes."

He's saying nice things, but it's what he's not saying that bothers me slightly. Not that I expect after one night of orgasms, Colby Nelson will want to spend the rest of his life with me. But after some of the things he said last night, I guess I expected he might have more of an attachment than just wanting a sex partner.

Sitting up in the bed, I wring my hands together, my nerves starting to get the best of me.

"My boss warned me about fraternizing with players."

His brow furrows. "Did Valerie forbid it?"

"No. She didn't forbid me. She just..." I lift a shoulder. "She strongly encouraged me not to." I turn toward him, his hand now on my thigh. I don't think he's taken a hand off my body in one way or another since last night. Admittedly, it's a nice feeling. But it's not helping my mind calm at all. "So now, just a month or so into the job, I went and slept with the captain of the team."

"Well, go big or go home, right?" Colby laughs.

I definitely went big, that's for sure.

"I guess. But now, I just don't know how to proceed. I mean, what will the guys think?"

"Who gives a damn what anyone thinks?"

"That's easy for you to say, Colby. You're paid millions to play hockey. I've only been an employee here for a month. I'm easily replaceable. I have to care what people think. At least to some extent."

He looks away, but huffs out a laugh. "Well, I can assure you nobody on the team is going to care. They'll all slap my ass and say it's about damn time."

"What?" His response catches me off guard.

"Well, Milo anyway. And Zeke. They know how I feel. I have no secrets with the guys. Zeke is my best friend, and Milo is like a brother to me."

Feeling a knot in my stomach, I bow my head and mumble, "And how do you...um, feel?"

Do I even want to know this answer?

The last thing I want is for him to tell me this was just another one-night stand. I know he mentioned last night that he doesn't view me as just another puck bunny, but, sitting here, naked, in front of him doesn't make me feel any less nervous about what he might say.

He takes a big breath and grabs me by the waist, lifting me until I'm straddling his lap.

His naked lap.

His hands run up and down my thighs. "I like you, Smalls," he confesses with a grin. "Your body is a fucking wet dream, and I thoroughly enjoyed you last night."

I'm about to ask him if that's all when he continues, "But more than that, there's something about you I'm drawn to." He absentmindedly reaches out a hand and traces circles around my nipple. It puckers at his touch. "I don't know what it is but...you calm me."

I have to laugh at his answer. "I calm you? How the heck do I calm you when all we do is argue?"

"We're not arguing right now." He laughs, and I feel it right between my legs.

Whoa!

Yes please!

"You're right. We do argue. But I like that about you. About us. You're feisty and confident. You don't take my shit. You're good at throwing it back in my face, and I need that. That day on the ice with you, it was..." His eyes find mine. "It was a breath of fresh air and a moment in time I didn't realize I needed. I was able to relax with you. You helped me have fun. You made me realize there could be more to life than hockey."

So, he wants more?

He wants this to be a thing?

"Now, tell me how you feel." He leans forward and takes my nipple into his mouth.

"Oh, my God, that is not fair of you."

He chuckles. "I know."

"I don't want to lose my job."

"Mmm," he moans against my skin. "If you do, you can live rent free in my bed."

"Colby!"

He laughs and leans back. "Kidding, but not. You know I would still want you even if you weren't working for the Red Tails, right?"

"Hardly." I scowl.

"What's that supposed to mean?"

"Colby, you have any number of women throwing themselves at you after every game. I'm sure you would have no problem making an arrangement with any one of them."

"So that's what you want this to be then?" He goes back to licking my nipple.

Good God, why does that have to feel so good?

"An arrangement?"

"I'm just...not sure I'm ready for everyone to know yet."

His lips move across my body and up my neck. "Okay."

"Is that bad?"

"No. Not bad. So, you're not saying no. To us." He kisses my lips and scoots my body forward on his warm, stiff cock. "To this."

"Definitely not saying no. Who in their right mind would say no to this?"

He chuckles against me and then grabs a condom lying on the bed stand, sheathes himself, and then guides me to sink down onto him. As I do so, my eyes close, and I inhale a pleasured breath as I focus on the fullness inside me.

"Tell me I'm yours, Smalls."

Lowering myself over him, my breasts brushing against his chest, his hands on my ass, I thrust forward and then push back over him. "You're mine, Nelson," I murmur into his ear, sucking on his neck. "All mine."

"Damn right, I am."

Finding my confidence, I think now is as good a time as any to lay down some rules after our brief conversation. "And that means you'll fuck nobody else but me. Do you understand?"

"There's no pussy like your pussy, babe. You've fucking ruined me for anyone else."

"Good. Now give me your hands because I need to ride this train until the steam blows."

"All aboard, babe. Take me for a ride."

Colby holds his arms out slightly to each side and I grip his hands to steady myself. Slowly at first, I move forward and back on his cock, creating a rhythm, building a friction so intense neither one of us can control ourselves. At one point, I let go of his hands and lean back, holding on to his thighs behind me, my chest pointed toward him. Our movements quickening.

"Stunning, Smalls. Absolutely breathtaking. You're so damn sexy." He runs his hands up my torso to my breasts, squeezing them, kneading them, pulling them, twisting my nipples between his fingers until we're both in such a frenzy, we become desperate for our release. I go first, letting my orgasm rip through me, and before I can come down from my high, Colby has lifted us and flipped me to my back where he plunges balls deep into me until his body stiffens and he explodes.

A relationship he's willing to keep on the down-low and all the hot sex I want? I think this is something I could get used to. A simple way to get what we both want. At least until I can feel out my boss.

Our next game is in Tampa tomorrow night, which means a late morning flight for the team followed by an evening practice. Colby was nice enough to order us room service, so we could eat breakfast together before I made him take the walk of shame back to his room to get dressed. Lucky for him, his room was only one floor up, but he refused to leave until I punched my number into his phone contacts. And then he proceeded to text me every step of his getting ready routine, as if I needed to know exactly what color socks he's wearing today.

Goofball.

I take a blissfully hot shower, the heat relieving my aching muscles, while trying to make sense of the last fourteen hours of my life.

I just slept with Colby Nelson.

I didn't just sleep with him.

I did all kinds of the nasty with him.

And I loved every minute of it.

I'm not usually one to find the alpha persona necessarily attractive, but with Colby, I found myself wanting more and more of it as the night went on. The way he spoke to me coupled with the roughness of his movements turned me on more than I ever thought possible.

His touch.

The way he grabbed me, spanked me, fucked me...like he was in complete control, and I could relax and focus on the pleasure he was giving me. A new kink unlocked.

What's more, after all is said and done, the way he looks at me and holds me against him like I'm everything he's ever needed...

damn. As scary as it might be, he makes me want to consider more of a relationship with him beyond the bedroom.

Except I'm not so sure Colby is the falling in love type, and the last thing I want to do is put myself in a situation where I could get hurt.

Once I step out of the shower, I give myself a few minutes of pampering before getting dressed, gathering my suitcase, and heading to the lobby where I meet my other marketing colleagues —Jasmine, Ricky, and Morgan —and head to the airport.

"Someone looks fresh-faced this morning," Jasmine says, eyeing me with a smirk. "What's your secret?"

Sex. Lots of sex.

Intense orgasms.

Hockey player dick.

"Uh, no secret." I shrug. "Just got a good night's sleep."

Morgan adjusts her seatbelt. "I don't know how you managed that with all that noise going on."

I nearly spit out my coffee.

Oh, fuck! They heard us?

"Right?" Ricky laughs. "I mean someone was havin' themselves a good night. That's for damn sure. I almost got off on them getting off."

Wait.

Maybe they don't know...

"Cody? Is that what she was screaming?"

Ricky shrugs. "Dunno. I couldn't tell for sure." He perks up and snaps his fingers.

"Actually, maybe it was Colby. I saw Nelson at the bar with a couple ladies last night. I suppose it could've been one or...maybe even both of them."

Stupid whores.

I can't believe he even gave them the time of day.

What would have happened had I not showed up?

Would he have fucked them?

"Seriously, Carissa, I can't believe you didn't hear them."

Morgan yawns. "They were so loud."

"Yeah. I'm a pretty deep sleeper, plus I usually use a sound app on my phone to help me stay asleep. White noise, you know?"

Jasmine giggles. "This was definitely not white noise. It was fucking hot though. If it was our Colby doing the deed in that room, that woman is hella lucky."

"And probably isn't walking very straight this morning," Ricky states. They all laugh, and I join them, because no way in hell am I telling them the woman in that room was me. I do, however, pull my sunglasses out of my purse and slide them on to protect my face from giving me away.

The team is already on board when I enter the plane, and I couldn't be happier that I decided to slip on my sunglasses. Though I'm sure they're not, it feels like all eyes are on me as I enter the plane and find my seat. I'm certain there is one pair of eyes watching my every move though, and I try like hell to remain neutral in case anybody else is watching us.

Nobody is watching you, Carissa.

Stop acting weird.

There's no need to feel guilty.

It was just sex.

Mind bending, toe-curling sex.

But just sex.

With the captain of the Red Tails hockey team.

Who just happens to be sitting four rows away.

"Morning, Smallson!" Zeke smiles and waves from his seat. "Good night last night?"

Fuck.

Does he know?

Colby said he tells them everything.

Do they all know?

I swallow and look over at Colby who smirks but merely quirks a brow with no indication whether they all know or not.

Damn him and his nonchalant-ness.

God, it's hot in here already.

I think I'm sweating.

"Uh, yeah." I clear my throat and pull off my coat and sweater to relax for the flight. "Restful night, yes. You?"

"FaceTime with my girl," he answers, beaming. "And she's flying to Tampa for tonight's game."

"That's great!"

"Hey! Smallson," Dex shouts at me from his seat across the aisle, and then gestures to my neck, his head tilted. "What's that on your neck?"

My brows furrow, and I flinch, swiping at my neck assuming it's a bug or something, but don't feel anything there. I pull my hand away to look. "What? I don't see anything. Is it a bug? Get it off!"

"Nah, it's no bug. Just a..." He grins. "It's like a..."

"Hickey," Hawken finishes his sentence. "He's trying to say you have a big old hickey on your neck."

My face falls in horror, and, thank God they can't see my eyes through my sunglasses right now, because this might be one of the most embarrassing things to ever happen to me.

"What? No." I shake my head. "It's not a hickey."

What the fuck do I tell them?

Lie!

Anything!

"It's probably just a mosquito bite."

"Except mosquitos don't fly in the wintertime, babe," Hawken argues with a grin. "So, that can't be it."

"You're right." I rub a hand over the side of my neck. "Must be an allergic reaction to... something."

"Yeah," Dex laughs. "Some guy's mouth from what it looks like."

I glance one more time at Colby, and this time, even though his head is bowed, he's all smiles, licking his lips like he just devoured a good meal.

"So, you had a good night last night, huh?" Hawken winks.

"More than a good night, I'd say." Dex jumps up for a closer inspection even as I try to shoo him away. "Whoever he is, he got ya pretty good there. Wonder if he's got a tutorial or something. That's impressive."

"Leave her alone, guys." Milo finally comes to my defense. "Carissa is an adult, and she's free to do whatever she wants. It's none of our business."

Swallowing back my fears, I give Dex a patronizing smirk. "You jealous, Dexter?"

Colby finally snorts a laugh, and the guys chuckle with me.

"A little, yeah," he finally admits, his eyes narrowing as he tries to get a better look at the red mark on my neck. "I mean, if you wanted a nice big smacker, all you had to do was ask."

Colby's smile fades, and for a hot second, I wonder if he might stand up and punch Dex for that comment, but he doesn't. Instead, he rolls his eyes and brings his headphones over his ears.

"Thanks for the offer, Dex." I pat his chest and then turn him around, pushing him back to his seat. "I'll keep that in mind."

Once I'm seated and we're taxiing down the runway, Jasmine bumps me with her elbow. "Good night's sleep, huh?"

I bow my head and pull in my lips to keep from smiling, but to no avail. Jasmine giggles. "You bitch. It was you last night, wasn't it? Oh, my God, it was you!"

"Shh. Keep your voice down."

She looks me over and shakes her head with a tsk. "Girl, I want to be you when I grow up. No wonder you slept so well. Who the hell was it?"

"Just some guy I met at the bar."

It's not a lie, right? I mean I met him outside the bar last night, but still.

"Did he have a friend? If so, I'm totally hanging with you next time."

Once we're up in the air and everyone has gone about their business, my phone dings. Every single time I get a text message on this plane, I'm startled because who the heck has Wi-Fi while flying?

The Red Tails, that's who.

> **Chelsea:** Hey! Checkin' in! How was your first away game travel experience? Heading to Florida today?

> **Me:** Hey! Was a GREAT night! And yeah, on our way to Florida now! Miss you!

> **Chelsea:** Just tell me you finally let loose and had some hot sex with one of those players so I can daydream about it while you're gone.

> **Me:** *wink emoji*

> **Chelsea:** *gasp emoji* OMG does that mean what I THINK it means??

> **Me:** Maaaaaybe *smiley face*

> **Colby:** Sorry not sorry. *heart eyes emoji*

My cheeks heat when I see Colby's text.
Did he mean to send the heart eyes?
Am I supposed to read into that? Gah!
These are the things I would be asking my best friend if she were next to me right now.

Me: You owe me.

Colby: Another night of orgasms. You got it.

Me: That's not what I meant.

Chelsea: OH. MY. God! DEETS. Right now!!!

Colby: Words do not compute. Revise and resubmit.

Me: Submit my ass.

Colby: Hey if that's your kink, I'm all in, Smalls. You can submit your ass to me anytime you want. I'm here for it.

Me: That's not my kink.

Chelsea: What's not your kink?

"Shit." I huff a quiet laugh at myself. Two conversations at once can be tricky.

Me (to Colby): Not my kink.

Colby: Dying to know what your kink really is. Will explore until I find it.

Me: It's furries. I totes have a furry kink.

Chelsea: WHAAAAT? You did the nasty furry style?

"Fuck!"

Me: No!

Colby: No what?

"Double fuck!"

Me (to Colby): Never mind. Two conversations at once is messing with me.

Me (To Chelsea): No! That was a joke and wasn't meant for you! Sorry! Two convos at once.

Colby: Are you talking to another lover?

Me: Very funny.

Chelsea: Penis size! Is it everything you might have thought it would be?

Me: His penis is perfect. In every way.

Colby: *growls* You had better be
talking about MY penis, Smalls.

"Oh, fuck me. I'm done," I whisper in frustration, turning my phone to airplane mode and tossing it in my bag. Time to take a breather and get my mind out of the gutter anyway. I have a job to do when we land, and I need to be prepared.

CHAPTER 18

Colby

"Lucky Charms. I should've guessed."

"It's game day, Smalls. What else would I be eating?" I shovel a heaping spoonful of my favorite sugared cereal into my mouth, watching as Carissa sits across the table from me between Milo and Zeke.

Almost at once, the guys at our table pause mid-bite, noticing the empty seat next to me-and that Carissa doesn't take it.

Yeah. They know.

We practically live together night and day, my teammates and I, and I don't like lying to them.

They know me better than anyone.

How could they not know?

But she doesn't know they know.

Which makes every outside-of-our-hotel-room encounter slightly humorous as Carissa tries to act chill when she's around me with the guys, like I didn't just have her sweet perky nipples in my mouth upstairs.

"What?" she asks, eyeing the guys as she forks her pancakes.

In tandem they answer, "Nothing," some of them clearing their throats, and continue with their breakfasts.

"Don't you also need your protein, Nelson? You wouldn't want to lose your stamina out there." She pops a bite into her mouth.

A slight chuckle erupts from deep within my chest as I eye her across the table. "You worried about my stamina, Smalls?"

Her eyes spring up, and her cheeks pinken. "No. I mean—"

"Pretty damn sure I can last longer than anyone at this table, and that includes Dexter over there."

Dex drops his fork harshly against his plate. "For fuck's sake it was one time, and you're never going to let me live it down!"

The guys at the table laugh at our inside joke of the time Dex blew his load his rookie year during a make-out session with a puck bunny. He said she smelled so much like the laundry detergent his mother used to use that all he could think about was wanking off in his teenage bedroom. Before he could get control of himself, his fireworks exploded. Didn't even get to see her boobs first.

So no, we never let him forget that moment.

After our laughter subsides, I bring my gaze back to the sexy woman across from me. "Anyway, I don't think anyone needs to worry about my stamina, but just to ease your mind, Mom..." I tease with a grin. "I ate my bowl of eggs first."

"All right, wise ass. I'm just making sure you're all prepared for another win tonight. No one wants to see Dex twerking in the locker room on social media if you guys don't win."

Dex gives me the stink eye. "I wholeheartedly beg to differ. Have you seen my ass?" He stands and smooths his hand over his rounded, and admittedly firm, butt cheek. "It's grade-A twerking material."

"Sit down, Dexter," I laugh. "Nobody needs to be looking at your ass this early in the morning."

He plops down in his seat with a grin, grasping his water bottle. "You're just jealous, Nelson, because Smallson isn't posting videos of your ass for the world to see. That means my ass is far superior."

"Whatever helps you sleep at night, big man." I eat the last spoonful of my Lucky Charms and then take a few gulps of my protein drink.

"Oh!" Carissa's eyes light up as they dart between Dexter and me. "Maybe we need to have an ass contest among all of you! Let the fans decide once and for all."

"Done!" Dex slaps the table. "I'm in. Give me the championship belt because this is an easy win."

"I don't know, man," Milo pipes in. "Zeke squats for a living. Have you seen his ass? He's a walking butt muscle."

Carissa nods with a chuckle. "Speaking of which, I can't believe I haven't put a video of you warming up on the ice, Zeke! A post of you doing the ice-hump set to some *Magic Mike* music would be killer with the ladies."

"Ice hump?" My brow quirks.

"Yeah. You know when he's stretching out his glutes and his adductor muscles? You have to know it looks like you're all humping the ice when you do that. Especially when you bounce a little."

Hawken laughs. "I'll never unsee it again. Zeke, I'm totally ice humping with you tonight."

"Me too, yo!" Dex adds. "My ass could use a good stretch."

"That's fine." Zeke's cheeks redden as he glances at Carissa. "But you better make sure to include the fact I'm taken in your post, or I'll have all sorts of riff-raff sliding into my DMs."

She winks at me and smiles at him. "It's a deal, but that might not keep them from trying anyway." She stands and grabs her now empty plate. "Gotta run, gentlemen. Marketing meetings wait for nobody. Good luck tonight!"

The guys say their goodbyes, and she shoots a quick glance my way, which I know is her way of saying goodbye to me without making a spectacle or rousing suspicion. Once she's out of earshot though, Dex leans forward smirking at me.

"She doesn't know we know, does she?"

"Nope." I chuckle.

"She still doesn't want anyone to know?"

"Nope."

Hawken chimes in. "She thinks we'll give her a hard time?"

"Oh, she's well aware you would all give her a shit time about it, but no. She's more concerned about Valerie."

"There's no set policy, though," Dex explains. "Believe me, I've checked."

"Yeah, I told her that, too, but apparently Valerie strongly encouraged her not to get involved with us because it can create sticky situations."

Dex giggles. *Yes, that's right. I said giggles, because he indeed giggles...like a thirteen-year-old boy.* "You said sticky. Damn right it can get sticky."

I whack him on the arm. "You know what I mean, dumbass. Anyway, it's just until she can have a conversation with Valerie. So, she feels comfortable I guess."

"We hear you, Colb." Milo nods. "Don't worry. We've got your back. It's good to see you happy. You've been on your game this week. Besides, we like Smallson too much to see anything happen to her."

Yeah. Me too.

Skating. Blissfully happy with her.

My arms wrapping around her as I show her how to shoot the puck down the ice into the net.

She hugs me in celebration when she gets her first goal.

And every goal after that.

And then we're speeding.

Speeding down the ice.

It's a race that I let her win because I'm a sucker for her.

I like to see her smile.

She makes me happy.

And then it happens again just as I knew it would.

The ice cracks beneath her feet and she falls through.

It's not a lake! It's an ice rink! This is impossible!

Yet, it's happening.

"Carissa!"

"Colby! Help her!"

"I know, Eli! I fucking know! Stay there!"

My heart races and my gut twists as I watch in horror. She thrashes through the icy water trying to pull herself up but to no avail.

The ice is taking her.

"Co...Colb..." She catches water in her mouth, and it takes her breath away. She coughs and reaches for me.

"Give me your hand, Smalls!" I shout, desperation clawing at my chest.

Her hands are too slippery. I can't hold on.

"Help me, Colb," she chokes out, her voice trembling with fear. She slips through and dips back under the water.

"Eli! Go get Dad!" I scream, my voice breaking.

"Please don't leave me, Smalls! Please...!"

"Dad! Did you take the last box of Lucky Charms?"

I wake up only when my body falls to the floor with a thud. My eyes open, and I try to spring up to my feet intent on saving Carissa from the icy hell from which she suffers, but my legs are twisted in my bedsheet. I kick and flail until I'm free and then stand, but she's not here.

And I'm not on the ice.

I'm in my bedroom.

Alone.

I blink several times and shake the nightmare from my head.

My eyes sting, and my chest hurts when I try to take a breath.

I sit down on the edge of the bed, my head in my hands, and try to calm my racing heart.

Breathe in. Breathe out.

Breathe in. Breathe out.

"Fuck."

I take a moment to use the restroom and get myself a drink of water, but when I eye a bottle of Scotch resting in the corner of the sink I opt for that instead and then return to my darkened bedroom. Tapping my phone, the clock on the screen flashes two o'clock which is too fucking early to start my day. I'll never have enough energy for tomorrow's workout if I don't go back to sleep. But I don't want to fall back asleep either. If I have another dream like that...God, it felt so real. Like my heart was actually shattering inside my chest watching Carissa slip from my grasp.

I wish I could call her right now.

Hear her voice.

Somewhere in the past couple of months or so since we first met, she's become a security blanket I want to wrap myself up in every day. Her smile, her laugh, the way she fits in with the guys, like she's one of the team, the way she can calm my inner storm with her touch, and she doesn't even know it. *Damn.*

She makes me feel good.

If she wasn't so darn stubborn, I could've fallen asleep with her nestled in my arms. I got a little too used to sleeping next to her during our away stretch, but now that we're home, she insisted on sleeping in her apartment. After all, we did agree we weren't a committed thing. Just two people enjoying each other's company. I'm trying to respect her space, but it's definitely harder than I thought it would be.

I'm not sure I can be someone who merely enjoys her company.

She's knocked me off my game.

And I'm not exactly sure what to do with that feeling.

She's surely sleeping, snuggled comfortably in her bed, but the urge to call her — to wake her, just to make sure she's okay— is overwhelming. Before I can stop myself, I'm scrolling to her number and tapping the green call button. On the third ring, she picks up, but it takes a minute for her to say anything. The sounds of muffled movement fill the other end of the line.

"Colby?" The scratchy, sleepy tone of her voice tells me I most definitely woke her up, but hearing her say my name helps my shoulders drop and my chest deflate.

"Smalls."

"Are you okay? What's wrong?" Her speech is clearer now, startled.

"Nothing's wrong. I just..." I hang my head in shame, embarrassed that I even called her in the first place. "I'm sorry I woke you."

"Don't be sorry. Don't ever be sorry."

I try to huff out a soft laugh in hopes she won't grow too concerned. "Just a bad dream."

"You want to talk about it?"

No.

Yes.

"Nah, it's okay. I shouldn't have bothered you."

"You can come here if you want."

I glance again at the clock, wishing it were even two hours earlier. "I shouldn't. By the time I get there..."

"I get it."

"Yeah."

I don't really have much to say. I didn't have a plan when I called her other than to just hear her, but I'm also finding it hard to hang up.

"Colb?"

"Yeah?"

"Now that I have you on the phone, do you think..." She pauses.

"Do I think what?"

"Would you be willing to stay on the line? While we fall back asleep, I mean?"

Thank Christ.

Maybe she senses it's what I need, or maybe she needs it too, but if I can't be next to her tonight, this is the next best thing.

"Yeah, Smalls. I can do that."

I lay my cell phone on the pillow beside me and lie back, my hand resting on my chest.

"You okay over there?" she asks softly.

"I'm good. You okay?"

"Mmm-hmm. Will you tell me something?"

"Anything."

Whatever can distract me from my dream.

"Tell me about where you grew up."

I take a deep, calming breath and close my eyes, picturing my family's farm in all its peaceful beauty.

"The farm was, well, sometimes I imagine it's what Heaven will be like one day. Peaceful, beautiful."

"Mmm..." I can tell she's relaxed listening to me.

My words become murmurs as I share memories of my younger years growing up on the farm. "My favorite time of year though was wintertime."

"Yeah?"

"Mmm-hmm." I imagine the entire scene in my head as I tell her about it. "When the snow is covering the land, it's like a dazzling blanket of white stretching as far as the eye can see. A full moon makes it look like a dream world. Like the most beautiful snow globe. It's so quiet out there. All you hear is the stillness of the wind. Cold, yeah, but..." My eyes grow heavy. "The perfect time to take a walk. To fill your senses. The cold crisp air, the softness of the snow..."

I inhale a long relaxing breath as I hear Carissa say, "Sounds wonderful."

CHAPTER 19

Carissa

Me: I'm so sorry I had to hang up this morning even though you were still sleeping. I had some work I needed to get started on and needed to use my phone. Please let me know when you're awake.

Me: And thank you for staying on the line with me last night. *heart emoji*

Shit.
I shouldn't have used a heart emoji.
Is he going to read into that?
I was just trying to be nice.

Hopefully, he's not too upset when he wakes up and sees I'm no longer on the line. I'm grateful he's getting some good sleep, though. The last two weeks of away games have been rough on the entire team. It takes a toll when they're not in their hometown, able to sleep in their own beds. Hotel life can be nice, but certainly not every night. I felt bad that Colby was having a difficult time sleeping. Even when they're not real, dreams can really mess with your head.

After Colby dropped me off last night, I spent time opening my mail and compiling all of the latest rounds of bills that need to be paid, cursing my parents as I have every month for the last couple of years. Constantly keeping on top of things is becoming exhausting, but if I ever want to move up in the world or have what I need to be able to afford a better place to live —or, God forbid, a car —I need to tackle the mess.

I've got eight different piles of mail on the floor around me, not including rent, though technically, I should only be responsible for two of them. On my lap is a notebook I use to keep track of my bank account so I don't have to zoom in on my phone. It's the easiest system for me to use so I know I'm keeping track of everything, though I know the rest of the world would probably snicker at my lack of use when it comes to banking apps.

Nope.

Pen and paper.

Old reliable.

I'm three piles in when there's a knock at the door. My brows knit together as I spin through the very small mental Rolodex of who it could be. Chelsea would be pounding on the door and saying something like, "Bitch, open this door," so it can't be her. Colby is still sleeping, as I have yet to see a text from him, so the only other person it could be is Mr. Hastings, my landlord.

Finally.

The leak under the bathroom sink nearly filled the bucket while I was gone, and now the shower is dripping.

"Coming!"

I hop up to answer the door, and when I pull it open, I'm met with the most adorably sexy face.

"What are you doing here? I thought you were still asleep."

Colby hands me a small brown paper bag. In his other hand, a drink carrier holding two large coffees.

"Thought you deserved a breakfast of champions as an apology for last night."

"Last ni—are you kidding me? Colby, I told you, you don't ever have to apologize for calling me. I was glad to hear from you."

With his now free hand, he tips my chin and kisses my lips as he breathes me in. "I missed you last night. I didn't have anyone stealing all the blankets. It was a weird feeling."

"I know what you mean. I got more than six inches of the mattress."

He wraps his arm around me. "As long as you weren't getting more than six inches of something else without me there."

"Nah. Only three or four. It was nothin' really." I give him a wink, and he laughs.

"I really did miss you, though. I got used to sleeping with someone while we were away."

That makes two of us.

"That's very sweet of you to say. I missed you, too. What's in this bag?"

"Ever had a Cachito from Klein's Bakery?"

My eyes widen and I gasp. "You brought Klein's?"

He laughs. "I'll take that as a yes."

"Oh my gosh, bless you, Colby! I could totally go for the taste of their sweet bread and smoked ham. I didn't even know I needed this today, but my mouth is already watering!"

"Good. I got one for both of us, plus a couple of chocolate croissants and a dozen macaroons for later."

"Later?"

"Yeah. You have plans today?" He looks around, noticing the piles on my floor. "Oh, I didn't mean to interrupt. What's all this?"

Internally, I cringe. I think I just cringed externally as well. The last thing I want to do is talk about bills with the rich guy I've been sleeping with.

"Uhh, it's nothing." I put the bag of food on the counter and then hop over to my organized piles of chaos, stacking one pile on top of another.

"Doesn't look like nothing. Are you someone's bookkeeper or something?" Colby's face falls. "Shit, they're not medical bills, are they? Is there something I don't know?"

Standing with the large stack of bills in my hands, I release a sigh and squeeze my eyes closed, knowing I'm about to get myself into an uncomfortable conversation.

"No, not medical bills. I'm fine. But also, yes, there's a lot you don't know."

"Oh." He passes me a questioning glance, and I can tell he's having an inner battle.

Ask her about it or don't ask her about it?

Placing the stack on the floor against the wall, I grab our breakfast bag and pat the seat next to me on my couch, which is really more the size of a loveseat, so having a brute of a hockey player sitting next to me probably looks all kinds of humorous.

I open the bag and pull out our Cachitos, which are basically like fancy rolls stuffed with ham and oh, so good, and hand one to Colby. He sets our drinks on the coffee table in front of us.

"So, back when I was in college, and I'm talking like, freshman year of college, so it's been a while..."

"Okay..."

"My parents stole my identity."

Colby nearly chokes on his bite, coughing a few times before grabbing his coffee to wash it down. "Sorry about that. I guess that's not what I expected you to say at all."

"Well, now I'm curious. What did you expect me to say?"

"Honestly, I thought you were going to tell me you were in some sort of accident years ago, or maybe you got into some bad shit like...I don't know, gambling. Or that you were a stripper at one time or something."

That notion makes me laugh. "Seriously? Me. A stripper. Can you even imagine what short little me would look like swinging from some pole?"

He wags his brows. "Yes. I can abso-fucking-lutely imagine it, Smalls."

"Right." I shake my head. "Forgot who I was talking to."

"So, they stole your identity."

"Basically, yeah. They took my social security number and opened all sorts of credit cards in my name that I didn't know about. Took a few fancy vacations, even purchased a new car for themselves among many other things they couldn't afford at the time, and now here I am...stuck paying for it."

"That's complete bullshit." His brows draw together. "They can't do that to you."

Slowly, I nod. "Obviously, they could—because they did."

"And you never knew it was happening?"

I shake my head. "Not until I graduated and tried to be an adult in the real world. What kid worries about their credit at that age? I didn't need a credit card back then because, as far as I knew, my parents were paying for anything I needed. I just didn't know they were using my identity to do it."

"Did they not have jobs?"

"Oh yeah, they had jobs. Still have them. And how's this for irony? My dad is a lawyer in town."

Colby's eyes bulge. "What the fuck? Are you serious?"

"One hundred percent serious. He works as a public defender. I imagine that's where he got the idea. Probably had to defend some asshole who had done it to someone else."

"What about your mom?"

"I'd love to say my mom wasn't complicit, but she was. She knew exactly what was going on. She works for housekeeping at the Hilton, and knowing what I know now, it wouldn't surprise me even a little bit if she's the type of housekeeper who looks through people's private items and takes what she can."

Colby shakes his head, confounded. "Unbelievable."

"Yeah," I answer softly. "So, now my credit is tanked. Until I pay all their bills —and somehow get them to never do it again —I can't move forward with my life. I'm stuck in this hellhole of an apartment because it's all I can afford if I want to keep chipping away at all the debt."

"Wait. You can't honestly be saying you're going to pay off every penny they took from you? You could be shutting off cards, cancelling accounts. Hell, you could prosecute your parents. Surely your dad knows that."

"I've shut down accounts and all that, but they're my parents, Colby."

"I don't care who the fuck they are. Nobody gets to mistreat you like that, Smalls." He rapidly pulls his phone from his pocket and scrolls through his contacts. "I have a great lawyer, and I'm sure my brother Elias can help out in som—"

"No, no, no, no, no." I lay my hand on Colby's wrist until he lowers his phone back to his lap. "I'm not asking for your help, Colby."

"I know you're not asking. I'm offering. It's no big deal. Hell, I can pay them all off for you right now. There's no amount of money in those bills that I can't pay. You realize I make millions, right?"

"Yeah, I know. And you realize the moment you even think of doing that, I'll feel like a whore."

Colby rears back, like I just slapped him in the face. "That's... fuck! Carissa, that's not what I—"

"I know, but—"

He never calls me Carissa.

That's how I know he's serious.

"No, listen to me." He frees his hands and cups both sides of my face. "If you think for one minute that I see you as someone who wants me for my money, you couldn't be more wrong. I've never ever had that thought cross my mind. In fact, if you recall, the first night we met I tried to give you all kinds of cash for a fucking box of Lucky Charms, and you wouldn't take it."

I give him a shy smile. "Well, don't forget, I didn't know who you were that night. Had I known you were a celebrity rich boy, maybe I would've treated you differently. I might have been happy to take your money."

He shakes his head. "No way in hell. You didn't care who I was, remember? You stood your ground. You fought for what was rightfully yours. Why aren't you doing that now?"

"Because I can't afford the legal fees." I shrug.

"Then let me help you with—"

"No."

"Carissa..."

"No, Colby. I need to do this on my own. I'll figure it out. I'm figuring it out. It's baby steps, but I'm working on it as best I can. Please, just let me."

His shoulders drop, and I can tell he's disappointed. I'm ripping the wind from his sails. "What can I do to help?"

I pat his leg. "You can play hockey, and you can kick ass doing it."

He tilts his head with a scowl. "And how is that helping you?"

"Well, for one, you doing your job gives me content to work with for my job. I like this job, and I don't want to lose it. Support me in doing what I do best and, you know, maybe a hug every once in a while."

He grins. "I can do better than a hug, you know."

Visions of our nightly hotel escapades float through my brain.

Colby's head between my legs.

Colby bent over me from behind.

Pulling my hair.

Fucking me up against the wall.

Growling my name.

"Oh, I am well aware."

Chuckling, he stands and offers me his hand. "I have something planned for us today. I know I walked in on you working, but tell me you're not busy."

"I'm not busy. What did you have in mind?"

This is nothing that can't wait another day.

He pulls me into his arms and kisses my forehead. "First of all, you're going to pack a bag, and I'm taking you home with me."

"Home-home?" I ask in a high-pitched tone, my throat starting to close tight with nerves. "Like, to meet your parents?"

It's a little early for that.

"No, Smalls." He shakes his head with a laugh. "Home, to my

place. You haven't been there yet and after last night, I don't think I like sleeping in my bed without you."

"Aww, you want a slumber party, Nelson?"

He squeezes me a little tighter against him. "Something like that. Maybe I can remind you how much more I can give you than just a hug. I'll even give you more than six inches."

Well, what do you know. My lady bits speak Colby's language, and they just woke up to take notice of his existence.

"Who would I be to turn down an offer like that?"

"Plus," he adds. "I booked us a massage at the house. My apology and thanks for last night."

"Ooooh."

"And then we can either make food or order food, and then cozy up for the night. Fireplace, lots of blankets, large bed... television... hot shower... large bed. Did I mention I have a large bed?"

I giggle. "At least once, yeah. You did."

Colby rubs his nose against mine, and then peppers kisses on my forehead, my temple, my cheek, my chin, and finally my lips, pushing through them and swiping his tongue against mine. Warmth spreads through me and pools between my legs, and it takes more self-control than I care to admit not to climb him like a pole and show him my stripper skills.

"Jesus, fuck," he growls, smoothing my hair back, holding my face in his hands. "Your tongue is fucking fire, Smalls." He leans his forehead against mine. "A man could get lost in your kisses."

"Mmm. A girl could say the same about yours."

"Come home with me."

"Yes please."

"Five minutes to pack? And then you're mine for the weekend."

I rise up on my tiptoes and give him a quick peck on his cheek. "Deal."

"Holy shit. You didn't tell me you lived in a freakin' castle, Nelson." We pull up into his private driveway, my jaw on my lap as I take in the sight of the exquisite home in front of me. A magnificent Greystone home nestled within the trees gives this place the feel of a secluded vacation home, or one only a celebrity would own in order to remain hidden from the paparazzi.

"It's a little large, yeah," he concurs, "But it's often filled with hockey players because, for some reason, my house is where they want to hang out."

"Are you the only one who owns an actual house?"

"I'm the only one who owns a home secluded like this one is. The guys like that they can come here, and chill out, and not fear that their pictures will be splattered throughout the media."

"Paparazzi don't come here?" I ask him when he opens my car door.

He shakes his head. "Maybe occasionally, if they know for sure I'm out and doing something worthwhile, but otherwise no. I don't get helicopters or drones and shit like that flying around the house waiting for me. There are usually bigger celebrities in the city than me at any given time. Those pictures would make more money."

He grabs my bag and throws it over his shoulder, and then takes me by the hand to lead me inside his castle. Amused by his generalization, I nudge him with my shoulder.

"You wouldn't classify yourself as a big enough celebrity worthy of a little attention?"

"Nah. I just play hockey. I'm not some A-list actor in town shooting a movie, or a rockstar taking the stage. And I'm definitely not Oprah, so, you know. I'm usually safe. If I make the paper, it's usually a picture of me doing charity work, and it's a posed picture taken by someone like you."

"More pictures of Colby doing great things. Got it."

He chuckles. "I didn't say that. Come on in. Welcome to my home."

As we step into a spacious foyer, my eyes immediately follow the grand staircase up to the second floor and take in the vaulted ceiling. I can only imagine what a huge Christmas tree would look like nestled next to the stairs, with its peak reaching up to the second floor. Someone would have to hang over the banister just to add the star. The neutral color scheme gives this place more of a homey feel than I would have anticipated coming from someone like Colby, but then, he's always surprising me.

"Where's all the sports memorabilia?"

"What do you mean?"

"This house doesn't look like it's owned by a professional hockey player."

Colby chuckles at my question. "I'll take that as a compliment. You think I should have shelves lined with old trophies and stuff like that?"

I shrug. "Well, I just assumed..."

"Nah. Nobody wants to see that shit when they come here, and I don't want to live in it twenty-four-seven. The guys probably spend more time here than anyone, and they don't need to see my childhood or professional successes. They have their own. My parents don't need to see it. They lived it with me. When I have guests, I want them to feel like they're on vacation. They should feel warmth. Comfort. I don't want to live in a museum."

"Commendable," I tell him. "But you mean to tell me you don't even have a special brag area in this place? Like, nothing that says, I-play-hockey-and-I'm-proud-of-it?"

Colby cringes and then gestures to a door at the far end of the room. "That door leads downstairs to the game room. All my hockey shit is down there. Old jerseys in shadow boxes, trophies, pictures. The usual stuff, I guess. Why, did you want to see it?"

"We'll get there, I'm sure." I squeeze his hand. "Why don't you show me the rest of the house?"

We spend the next twenty minutes or so on a tour of Chez

Nelson. Colby points out a few key details in the design flow of the house while I marvel at each and every incredible space he shows me. Especially the expansive gourmet chef's kitchen, complete with gorgeous granite countertops, and an island I could probably live on all by myself. And my favorite part, a fireplace in every room. Some are gas-heated and some use real wood. There's nothing cozier than the smell of a wood-burning fireplace in the wintertime.

Colby's bedroom is the last room we visit, and it is nothing short of incredible. A king-sized bed sits against the wall in the middle of the room, draped in pearl-colored sheets and a moss green duvet. Floor-to-ceiling windows fill the entire far wall, but what's better, one of those windows is a door leading out to a private balcony overlooking the lake. With another fireplace out here, along with an extra-large lounge chair piled with throw pillows and a fluffy blanket, it is truly a cozy place to spend an evening.

"You haven't said anything yet, Smalls."

"Huh?" My head snaps toward his voice behind me.

"You're making me nervous. What do you think?"

"What do I think? I think you live in the most unbelievably relaxing castle I've ever seen." Gesturing to the lake even as the cold air whips at our faces, I tell him, "I mean seriously, this house is goals for..."

Me.

"A lot of people."

His arms wrap around my waist, and he kisses the side of my neck. "Are you a lot of people?"

"Yeah," I huff out a soft laugh. "Yeah, I am. Do you even realize what you have here?"

"Yeah, I do. It's a safe haven. My place to be me. A place to bring the people I care about."

I turn in his arms and peer up at him. "Are you saying you care about me?"

"You wouldn't be here if I didn't."

"Is that what you tell all the women you bring here?"

"I've never brought a woman here."

My brows shoot up in disbelief. "Never?"

"Never."

He holds my stare as butterflies flit wildly through my stomach. A part of me doesn't believe him, there's no way he hasn't had a relationship before. Not that we're giving that name to whatever it is we are when we're together. But then, Colby's never been one to lie to me either. I gulp back my nerves and try not to make what he's saying seem like a big deal —just in case it isn't, and I'm just overthinking it.

"This really is gorgeous. I imagine the bathroom is a freaking spa?"

He chuckles and takes my hand, leading me back inside from the cold balcony.

"In here."

The extraordinary primary suite comes with its own attached marble bathroom that boasts a whirlpool bathtub big enough for two and a walk-in shower encased in glass doors. Another door leads to a walk-in closet literally larger than my entire apartment. I mean, it's big enough that there's a bench inside. You know, for those times when one must contemplate what to wear. Racks upon racks of shoes line the bottom of the walls, while different sections of his closet seem to be organized by style. Suits, dress shirts, dress pants, jeans, T-shirts, hoodies, and of course, Red Tails branded clothing. My hands run over his collection of neckties, he really does have a cool sense of style.

"Do you buy all these clothes, or do you like, you know, have some sort of stylist who does it all for you?"

Colby shrugs, an uncomfortable smile on his face. "A little of both. But only because I didn't trust myself in the beginning."

"What do you mean?"

"When I first started out, I hired this guy. His name was Patrick. He's a well-known stylist for other professional athletes. Anyway, with my age, I knew everyone would be talking about my 'look,'" he says using air quotes. "You know, before games. After games. During press meetings. My agent reminded me that if I wanted to be taken seriously, I couldn't be dressed like some twenty-year-old kid. I had to look the part. So, Patrick helped me come up with a style I felt comfortable with, and taught me what to look for when I'm out shopping. Now, whatever I buy is handpicked by me. Well, I mean sometimes my mom, too, because I can't ever say no when she brings me something. Lucky for me, she's paid attention over the years and has good taste."

It's sweet hearing him talk so positively about his mother.

"Are you close with your parents?"

"Very. Mom, Dad, Elias. We talk in some way or another just about every day. Even if it's just through a text."

"That's good."

"Yeah."

Colby slides his hands into his back pockets and rocks back on his heel. Unsure of whether or not he wants to answer more questions about his family, I look away to think about something else to talk about when a glint of red catches my eye. Stepping toward the hanging material, I push back a black garment bag, revealing a glimmering red floor-length gown. Three pairs of Louboutins sit on their respective boxes underneath.

My brows fold.

I thought he said he's never brought another woman here.

"Is this..." I start, gripping the hanger and pulling the garment off its hook. "Is this your mom's, or...?"

Colby shakes his head, a nervous smile spreading across his face. "No, silly. Look at the tag."

I lift the black tag hanging from the hanger and read my name printed in small white letters. My head snaps his direction. "I don't understand. You bought me a dress?"

He steps toward me and takes the dress from my hands, turning me toward his floor-length mirror and holding the garment in front of me. "You can say no, Smalls. You can always say no. But...I was kind of hoping you might be willing to accompany me to a charity event. I knew you would need a dress and didn't want you to feel stressed about shopping for one, so, I called Patrick and had him come up with something for you."

"Colby, this dress had to have cost you a small fortune. And the shoes! Those are Louboutins! Do you even know how expensive those are?"

"Doesn't matter. You're worth every penny, Smalls."

"Colby—"

"Just say yes, Carissa."

"Of course I'll go with you. You don't even have to ask. When is it? What is it?"

"It's for an organization called Amateur Empowered."

"Oh my gosh, I've heard of that! That's the organization that helps underprivileged kids learn to play all kinds of sports, right?"

He nods. "Yeah. A lot of different sports programs run through the organization. Football, basketball, baseball, hockey, golf, tennis, you name it."

"Yeah, I'm only vaguely familiar. Several of DePaul's athletes would often spend time volunteering there. Some of the people on the staff had done pieces and social media posts about it over the years."

Colby smirks. "But not you?"

"No, not me." I cringe. "Someone else took care of the sports media stuff. I was always doing other campus events. Sports weren't my area."

But no way do I want to stand here and talk about Gretchen right now.

"Anyway, so when is this event?"

"Umm..." Colby frowns and backs up a step as if I might slap him. "Tomorrow night?"

"Tomorrow night?" My eyes bug out as a million different things run through my mind about what I would need to have ready before then.

"I'm sorry, Smalls. I know it's last minute I just didn't want you to say no, so I—"

"No, no. It's fine. I can do it." I wave my hand shaking him off, my mind already reeling with thoughts. "I'll just need to take a few notes about what things you want posted, and if there are certain people you want me to make sure I get pictures of you with, and then—"

"No, Smalls." He hooks his arm around my waist when I step past him. "You're not working tomorrow."

"What?"

"I want you to come with me... as my date."

He watches me cautiously as I ponder his idea.

"Your...date."

Pulling me against his chest, he smooths my hair back and lifts my chin with just a finger until I'm gazing into his soft, comforting eyes. "As my date, Smalls. You and me."

"And the other guys?"

He shakes his head. "Won't be there. This isn't their charity. It's mine. Something special I've been doing for years now. Elias will be there, but that's only because he's loaded, so I always make sure he and his office partners get an invite, so they'll give all their riches to the kids."

"Smart plan."

"Damn right it is."

His date.

In public.

Pictures will be taken.

People will talk.

What will Valerie say?

"I know what you're doing in that pretty little head of yours, Smalls."

"Yeah?"

"Yeah. Stop overthinking everything. I'll take care of talking to Valerie if that will make you feel better. Just say yes, wear the pretty dress and the come-fuck-me heels, and be by my side for the evening. Then wear those heels tomorrow night while I'm balls deep inside you."

And there go my lady bits again.

"That's very presumptuous, don't you think, Mr. Nelson?"

"Mr. Nelson is my dad. He's the proper one. I'm just the asshole hockey player who likes to play with his food before he eats it."

Why does it turn me on when he says things like that?

"What if the dress doesn't fit?"

"It'll fit. I promise."

"How can you be so sure?"

"Trust me, Smalls. It'll fit like a fucking glove, and I won't be able to keep my eyes off you all night."

"Is that a threat or a promise?"

"Yes."

That's all he says before he lowers his mouth to mine, capturing me in a penetrating kiss. His hand twists through my hair, tugging my head back for a better angle. He pushes his tongue deep into my mouth, licking me, twisting with mine, before softly sucking my bottom lip. When I wrap one hand around his bicep and palm his chest with my other, a growl grows from deep inside him. The sound of his hunger, his desire, ignites my soul. I don't know how we don't combust right here in this closet, setting the entire room on fire with the sparks shooting through us both. I can tell he wants me. If I asked him to take me right here, right now, I have no doubt he would satisfy me in ways I can't begin to dream of.

He finally pulls back, smoothing his thumb over my bottom lip, and I am literally putty in his hands.

It's official.

I would do anything for Colby.

Because I'm falling for him.

And fuck, I'm falling hard.

CHAPTER 20

Colby

So far so good.

She didn't freak out when we pulled up to the house, and she hasn't judged my decorative skills yet. I won't tell her that a lot of the house was put together with the help of my mom. Since she seems to be happily impressed, I'll take all the points I can get.

I'm lighting a vanilla candle when I hear the door creak open behind me.

"Why is there only one table?" She gestures to the massage table set up in one of my guest rooms and pulls the tie to her fluffy white robe tighter around her waist. "And why are you still dressed?"

Looking down at my gray sweatpants, I frown. "I'm only partially dressed. I can take my pants off if you prefer me that way, but you should know—I'm totally commando under here." I wag my brows at her, but she only blushes in response. "And I told you, Smalls. This is my thank-you for putting up with me last night. Besides, you work hard, and I want to do this for you."

She rolls her eyes. "Says the guy who literally keeps himself steady on ice for hours a day and is constantly being knocked around by other players."

"Semantics." I shrug and give her my best grin. "Besides, I have people who are paid to massage my aching muscles. You don't have that luxury, but you deserve it, so..." I motion for her to come closer to me with the curling of my finger.

She saunters to me, taking note of the low lights and scented candles. "This feels so..."

"Relaxing? Soothing? Sensual?" I suggest the few words that come to mind. "Erotic?"

"Well, I was going to say unfair."

"Are you kidding? This is a win-win for both of us."

"How so?"

"Because you get to lie here and have your body rubbed from head to toe by a handsome-as-fuck hockey player, and I get to have my hands on you for as long as you can stand it." Slowly, I loosen the tie to her robe, inviting it to open, so her sensuous features are on display. "I get to touch every damn inch of you."

"For as long as I can stand it, huh?" She gives me a teasing half smile. "You know I can probably lie on this table all day, right? Somehow, I have a feeling it won't be me that gives in first." She lowers her gaze to the already protruding bulge in my sweatpants and then raises a brow in challenge.

Her confidence and sass are what draw me to her.

God, she's so fucking sexy.

I slide my hands into her robe, pushing it off her shoulders, and holding her stare as it falls to the floor. She gasps as the cool air penetrates her skin. Her nipples harden and goosebumps pepper her arms.

"You might be right about that, Smalls. Your sexy little body does things to me. So, be a good girl and climb under this blanket so I can get started before I have no choice but to spread your legs and work those muscles in other ways."

She bites her bottom lip as her cheeks grow a deeper shade of pink. Her desire is evident, but it's her damn confidence that has me so turned on.

"You'd like that, wouldn't you?" I growl. "For me to fill you up and make you mine?"

"I'm already yours, Colby." Her satisfied smile takes my breath away, but I reel it in and stay in control for now, because she deserves to be pampered.

"Fucking right you are. Now get under that blanket. I won't

say it again."

Carissa climbs onto the massage table, and I help cover the bottom half of her with a heated blanket. I gently pull her hair up and secure it with an elastic band, and then squirt a dollop of vanilla oil into my palm. The moment my warmed hands touch her shoulders, just below her neck, she softens into the table and releases a satisfied moan.

"Oh my God, that is amazing."

She can't see the smile she brings me with her words, but I show her how much I appreciate her with my touch, working my way down her neck and across her shoulder blades. The soft, silky feel of her skin coupled with the vanilla scent filling the room plays with my senses. I'm a kid in a candy store who can't wait to lick everything he touches.

My hands warm and slick, I rub down her lower back in a wide circular pattern, watching her skin redden beneath my touch.

"How does that feel?"

She sighs. "Like heaven."

I lean down and kiss her neck, mostly because I can't help myself when I'm this aroused around her. "Good. I'm glad."

"Where did you learn to do this?"

"I didn't." My confession makes me chuckle. "I watched a little YouTube this morning and then got a few pointers from Derrick, my masseuse."

"Well, Mr. Nelson, is there anything you can't do? Because God knows you're fucking good at this."

"I'm not perfect, Smalls. Far from it. Just trying to show my girl a little appreciation."

If she only knew the things I'm not good at.

The things that scare me.

She would probably run for the hills.

I spend the next fifteen minutes massaging her arms and hands, and then move to her legs and feet, rubbing her soles until her body is practically jelly on my table. And then I move back up to her ass.

Her glorious, round, perky little ass.

My fingers knead into her muscles, pushing her cheeks together and driving the stress from her body.

"Ohmygod, Colby. Please never stop." She's so relaxed her words start to slide together.

"That good, huh?"

"Mmm." Her moans make my already raging hard-on more of an unyielding rock. "I mean, I wouldn't advise you to quit your day-job, but holy hell, your hands."

I laugh under my breath. "I'm glad you're enjoying it. And I'm equally glad you're allowing me to enjoy it as well. The view is... incredible."

Breathtakingly so.

"Who would I be to deny you what you want?"

"Do you really mean that?" I ask with an incredulous laugh.

"Of course."

"Then flip over."

She follows my command, her beautiful naked body now on full display.

"Fuck, Smalls. I've never seen anything more gorgeous."

Her eyes lazily open, and her breath hitches when I take her leg in my hand and lick my way up her thigh.

"Colby..."

"Shhh. So sweet, Smalls."

She gives in as her eyes fall closed and her lips part. She starts to squirm on the table, but for her safety I can't allow her to move too much. I grab her waist and tug her toward me at the edge of the table and hitch her legs over my—

"What are you doing?" she asks, her eyes big and round and heated.

Licking my lips, I finish what I started, hitching her legs over my shoulders, her sweetened glistening pussy in line with my face.

"Rewarding my good girl."

"Fucking yes," she hisses.

She's right here. Her body mere inches from my tongue. I am

desperate to taste her, devour her, take every drop of her she has to give. But as I said before, I'm a man who likes to play with his food.

Teasing her just a little, I feather my finger at the junction of her thighs, coating it in her arousal, and circle her sensitive nub. "Is that what you want, Smalls?"

She sucks in a deep breath as her back arches off the table. "Colby."

"So wet for me already and I've barely touched you."

"That's a lie. You've done nothing but touch me for the past hour at least. Turning me on with every rub." Her body squirms. Her hips move side to side but I still her with my palm.

"And you want more, you greedy little minx." I bring my hand down to her slit and gently spread her with two fingers. Sliding one briefly inside her, I curl it against her wall until she emits the moan I was waiting for.

"Oh my *God*... yess."

"So goddamn wet." I pull my finger out of her and wrap my tongue around it, getting my first taste of her. "The sweetest pussy. Fuck, you're making me hungry, Smalls."

Her legs wrapped around my neck, she pulls me toward her body. "Then fucking bon appétit, Nelson."

"That's my girl," I tell her, beaming at the feast in front of me. With a flattened tongue, I plunge forward with one long languid stroke from one end to the other, circling her clit for good measure.

"Fucking Christ, Colby!" she cries, gasping for breath. Her knees start to shake on my shoulders. "It's too good. You can't—"

"Oh, yes, I can. And I will. A man always cleans his plate." I stroke my tongue through her once, twice, three times. One slow lick after another, and then flick her clit in quick succession as she writhes underneath me.

"Colby..."

"I know, Smalls. You're almost there. Fuck, if you only knew how hard you're making me right now. I can't get enough of you."

I dip my tongue inside her, licking her, eating her, ravaging her as she screams for mercy. Slipping a hand into my sweatpants,

I grab my cock and squeeze like hell as I eat her out like it's the last meal of my goddamn life.

"Fuck! Fuuuck, Colby!" Her knees tighten around my head and her body shakes beneath me as she finally lets go. I want to continue to lap her up, with soft gentle licks this time as she comes down from her high, but fuck if I have the will power or wherewithal for any of that right now.

I scoop her exhausted body from the massage table and carry her the few steps to the guest bed and toss her onto the mattress. I grab a condom from the pocket of my sweatpants and then kick them off in front of her, her eyes taking in the size of me.

Yeah babe.

All yours.

"I'm sorry, Smalls. I really didn't plan to do this," I tell her, sheathing myself and climbing onto the mattress, holding myself above her. "But if I don't get inside you in the next ten seconds, I swear to God this might be the first time you see me cry."

"Well, we can't have that, can we?" She spreads her beautiful legs for me, and I line myself up and then plunge inside her. My hands squeezing her thighs. My head falling back at the tight warmth enveloping my cock.

"Motherfucker, Smalls." A white-hot heat shoots through my chest and up into my brain, as if it's the signal my body has been waiting for to take what I so desperately desire. I crash my lips to hers, her tongue meeting my every swipe as if she is eating me this time. Our bodies thrust together in a ravenous panic. A race I must win. A cliff I have to jump off of. The guttural groan that comes from inside me only fuels me forward, plowing into her harder, faster, as if I'll never get far enough inside her. And then she touches me.

Fucking Christ, she touches me.

Her hands slide down my pecs to the arrow like V leading to our junction, and then they're on my ass. Palming me. Squeezing me. Pulling me into her, her hips meeting me thrust for thrust.

"Fuck, Smalls. It's so good." Watching her breasts heave as

our bodies move together, I lean down and take one of her nipples into my mouth, sucking, nibbling, licking.

Her mouth flies open and her back shoots off the bed, her gasps and pants becoming louder and stronger. With my free hand, I grab her other breast and squeeze her nipple between my fingers, and she surprises me with a second climax, her body clamping down around my cock, milking me in response.

"Ah fuck, yes!" My balls tighten and my dick throbs, and a sheen of sweat breaks across my back, chest, and forehead. The literal growl that comes out of my mouth is a surprise, even for me, as I explode inside her, my body shaking as I struggle to hold myself up.

"Smalls..." My forehead drops to hers as we both try to catch our breath. She kisses my lips and then my chin and then my cheek, her hands cupping my face in a tender embrace.

"That was incredible."

I force myself to open my eyes so I can see the gorgeous beauty staring up at me.

"You're incredible."

She's like a goddamn angel, smiling at me as if I've just given her the most precious gift. And for just a moment, I wonder if this is all real.

Is she really here with me?

Did she really let me do all that?

Devour her?

Ravage her?

Was it really my name she was screaming?

Is this really happening the way I feel like it is?

Or is this all just a dream?

CHAPTER 21

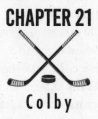

Colby

"Bumfuzzle?" Carissa's cackle fills the room. "Is that even a real word? There's no way that's an actual word."

"It is so a word."

"I don't believe you."

"Bet me."

She shakes her head, still giggling. "You're on. What are we betting?"

"A nipple twist."

She guffaws. "A *what*?"

"You heard me, Smalls. If I'm right, I get to twist your perky, pink nipple."

She crosses her arms over her chest, and I almost bust a gut wondering if she did that self-consciously. "And so, what do I get if it's not a word?"

"Then you can twist my nipple. As hard as you want."

Her brown eyes narrow as she hedges the bet, and then she smirks at me. She's goddamn adorable. "You're on. Nipple twist it is."

We shake hands, and then I reach for my phone. "Hey, Siri..." My eyes never leave Carissa as I talk to the ghost in my phone. "What does bumfuzzle mean?"

"I found the word you are looking for," Siri reports. "Bumfuzzle: to confuse, perplex, or fluster."

"Fucking serious! It's a word!" Carissa slams her hand down on the coffee table, nearly upsetting the Scrabble tiles, and all I can do is laugh. Oh, and add up my points of course.

"That's a double letter score for the F, so that's twelve, and then a ten-point Z. No points for the blank Z, plus the other letters, so, we've got thirty-two times three, since I also hit the triple word score, which gives me..." A shit-eating grin spreads across my face. "A whopping ninety-six points!"

Carissa pouts playfully. "I cannot believe you're going to win this game over a fucking bumfuzzle."

"Hey," I scold her with a wink. "Don't knock the bumfuzzle. What did bumfuzzle ever do to you?"

She rolls her eyes. "It's about to get my nipple tweaked. So, there's that."

"Damn right about that, Smalls."

Letting out my best maniacal laugh, I pounce on her, pushing her backward onto the couch as I hover above her, my hand snaking under the only article of clothing she has on.

One of my Red Tails T-shirts.

I palm her warm breast in my hand, and she hisses at my touch. Pinching one of her nipples between my thumb and forefinger, I give it a little twist until she squeals.

And then I lift her shirt and suck the sting away.

Because I'm a nice guy like that.

"Can't go that way, Smalls. The knight can only move in an L-shaped pattern in Chess— two plus one, or one plus two."

"Who made up that stupid rule?" she huffs. "Horses can go in all sorts of directions. They're horses, for Pete's sake."

"Yeah, but they're mathematically challenged horses who only know how to count to three, so..." I shrug at my bullshit answer and laugh when Carissa tosses a couple pieces of popcorn my way. Finally, she decides to move a pawn instead, and it's just the move I was hoping she would make. I slide my bishop diagonally until it puts her king in check. "Checkmate."

She studies the board and realizes there is truly not a move she can make that will save her king, so she lays him down, conceding her loss, and lifts one side of her T-shirt, ready for nipple tweak number two.

"Just do it."

Smiling like a motherfucker, I kiss her neck this time while palming her breast. "Game day with you is so much fun, Smalls."

"Uh-huh."

"What's your favorite holiday?"

She takes a bite of her egg roll and then gives me a beaming smile. "Mardi Gras."

Of all the holidays.

I chuckle at her answer. "Mardi Gras? Why Mardi Gras?"

"I mean, what other holiday revolves around eating fatty foods while parading down the street?"

I cock my head and give her a half grin. "Uhh, Thanksgiving?"

She almost spits out her food laughing. "Ooh, touché. I guess you got me there." She sits back, thinking about the question a little more. "I don't know. I guess I've always viewed Mardi Gras as a big party, you know? At least that's how it always looked on TV when I was a kid. A little risqué in the whole... you know, flashing for beads thing, but fun. Carefree. Plus, there's just something about New Orleans. The music. The people. The mystery and intrigue around the city."

"Have you ever been to Mardi Gras?"

She cringes. "Would you believe me if I said no?"

I smile back at her. "I guess I would."

"I've never been there." She digs into her sweet and sour chicken. "My parents never allowed me to go to Mardi Gras. They always said it was too adult-ish for kids. I guess they were right, to an extent. So now, it's on my bucket list of places to see before I die."

"Wow. How many places are on that list?"

"A fuck ton. I don't plan to die anytime soon."

I laugh. "That's good news. Maybe we need to plan a trip there sometime. Start working on that bucket list together."

She chews her bite, her long lashes batting back at me as she holds my stare. Once she finally swallows, she nods and says, "I think that would be amazing."

"Yahtzee!"

My jaw practically falls off its hinge. "How the fuck is that your fourth Yahtzee of this game?"

She sweeps the dice off the coffee table, into her hand, and then kisses her fist. "Luck be a lady, I guess."

She's all grins and giggles, and I can't remember a time that I was ever this happy hanging out with a woman. "You're adorable, you know that?"

"That's what all the guys tell me." She shrugs and nods like I'm not saying anything new and fuck, she makes me feel so goddamn light.

"All the guys, huh?"

"Yep." She smacks the P between her lips.

"How many guys are we talkin', Smalls?"

I don't really want to know this answer, but then again, I'm genuinely curious.

Her eyes grow into saucers. "Loads of 'em."

"Really? That many, eh?"

"Oh yeah. I was getting a lot of dick before I met you, Nelson."

I let out a loud cackle. "A lot of dick. Is that so?"

"I mean, I don't lie, so..."

Crawling to her on all fours, she braces herself underneath me, her hands on my pecs, still all grins and giggles. I spread her legs and then maneuver myself between them.

"Maybe I need to remind you what a lot of dick feels like."

"What's that? I think I'm getting amnesia. You may have to remind me more than once."

A low growl builds in the back of my throat as I lean down and suck on her neck.

"It would be my pleasure."

How lucky am I to have someone like her in my life?

Her body is warm and protected as she lies asleep in my arms.

In my bed.

Like an angel.

Even after our long, hot shower, remnants of vanilla from this morning's massage scent her skin.

Her body is soft, like silk, and I can't keep my hands off her.

I don't want to be without her.

I can't be without her.

And I think it's time for me to tell her.

"Stay with me, Smalls."

And then it happens again just as it always does, yet this time... it's different.

The sound of the ice cracking bellows through my ears. She screams, and I wake to an empty bed.

She's not here?

"Carissa!"

Where is she?

She was just in my arms.

Her body next to mine.

"Carissa!"

"Colby! Help her!"

"I know, Eli! I fucking know! Stay there!"

Why is Eli even here?

"Carissa!"

"Colby! There!" Eli points to the balcony door, and my heart bottoms out in fear of what I know I'm about to find. My gut twists

as I watch in horror from afar. She thrashes through the icy water, trying to pull herself up, but to no avail. The frigid waters of the lake are overpowering her, and I don't even know how she got out there.

"You were supposed to protect her!" Dad shouts to me.

"Dad, I... I"

"Co...Colb..." She catches water in her mouth, and it takes her breath away. She coughs and reaches for me.

And then I'm there.

At the lakeshore.

I don't know how I got here.

Did I jump?

My body shakes as the cold wind whips across my face.

She's too far out. I'll never get to her in time.

"Help me, Colb!"

"Stay with me, Smalls! Just hang on!"

She slips through and dips back under the water.

"Fuck! No! Carissa!"

"Eli! Go get dad!"

"Why aren't you protecting her?"

"Please don't leave me, Smalls! Please...!"

I spring up in my bed, gasping for breath. Goosebumps canvas my sweat-soaked skin. I'm trembling in fear. Horror. Confusion.

What just happened?

Carissa.

Terrified, I pull the covers back just enough to see her sound asleep next to me. I squeeze my eyes closed and release a deep breath, my shoulders relaxing as my body goes limp.

Thank God.

Just a dream.

A horrible dream.

I'm so fucking tired.

I swipe my hand down my face, trying all I can to rid my mind of the epically scary last few minutes and the absolute despair I felt at the thought of losing her. If I could cocoon her with my body and sleep peacefully for the rest of the night, I would scoop her into my arms right fucking now. But I fear my dreams will continue to haunt me every time I close my eyes.

Climbing out of bed, I grab my sweatpants and pull them on before padding to the restroom. A decanter of scotch rests on one of the built-in shelves for nights just like these. Nights that have been plaguing me more often. I only wish I could figure out why. I pour a small glass of the amber liquid into one of the three glasses with the set, and then quietly step out onto the balcony. The cold air strikes my chest, but I welcome the chilly assault.

Punishment for not doing enough in my dreams, I suppose.

Reaching for the switch on the wall behind me, I turn on the overhead heater, and then flip on the gas fireplace in front of my chair. The instant warmth is like a robe, shielding my body from the stinging chill of the winter air. I glance quickly in the direction of the lake, and though I hear the wind moving, some waves crashing, and the ice moving, all I see is black. Plopping down in my chair, I hold my head in my hands, the weight of my demons feeling extraordinarily heavy in my mind.

It's been twenty years since my big brother died on that ice.

I grieved his passing.

Thought I dealt with it.

But now, instead of Alex, it's Carissa taking his place in my dreams.

What the hell is it all supposed to mean?

You know what it means, Nelson.

I like her.

I'm fooling myself if I try to say otherwise.

I think I even more than like her.

She's become someone I look forward to being around any moment of the day or night. I've grown accustomed to feeling her next to me in bed. I've memorized her body, inside and out. And now, I find myself not only caring what happens to her, but also freaking out subconsciously over the mere idea of losing her.

I've somehow allowed her the ability to break me to pieces.

She has the power to rip me apart.

And I don't think she even knows it.

"Colby?"

My head jerks up, and she's standing in front of me, naked but wrapped in the throw blanket from the bed. Her brows draw together when her eyes land on my pained face. "What is it? What's wrong?"

A flutter in my chest, I sit back in my chair and reach for her to join me. She straddles my lap and wraps her blanket around us both, the hardened peaks of her nipples warming against my chest. Her skin feels amazing against mine. This feels...right.

"Nothing is wrong, Smalls. I just had a bad dream."

"Do you want to talk about it?"

Yes.

No.

I don't know.

"I just need to hold you for a minute."

She doesn't say a word when I wrap my arms around her back and smooth my hands up and down her spine. The desire to be honest and transparent with her about my feelings grows stronger the more I'm with her, and definitely now as I'm holding her here in the safe space of my balcony.

But I'm afraid to say the words.

What if I say the wrong words?

What if she doesn't understand?

What if she doesn't believe me?

What if she doesn't feel the same?

There's only one way I know how to truly convey my feelings to her. To get her to feel what I feel. To recognize the difference between carnal desire and an intimate moment between us. I pull her tightly against my chest and bury my head in her neck, breathing her in. Memorizing her scent and placing gentle kisses behind her ear, on her cheek, her chin, her lips, and all around her face. A tiny whimper sounds from her throat, and she shimmies over my covered cock.

"I don't want to lose you, Smalls."

She leans back a tad so she can look into my sorrowful eyes. "Why would you lose me?"

"I..."

It's now or never.

"I want to tell you about my brother."

"All right."

"Don't let go of me, all right?"

"Never, Colby. I'm right here, okay? I promise I'm not going anywhere."

She curls up against my chest, and I continue to stroke her back. "Our family farm in Wisconsin had this magnificent pond on the far side of the field. It was on the edge of the forest that led into the neighbor's property. We'd spend hours on that pond every year once it froze over. Especially Alex, but then, he was the oldest, so of course, he had been doing it the longest. Anyway, he wanted to be the first big hockey star to come out of Appleton, Wisconsin."

"Sounds like a good dream to pursue."

"Yeah. And when Alex had an idea, he went one hundred percent balls to the wall until he accomplished it."

She squeezes herself against me a little tighter as the wind blows, and I immediately feel like a prick for being out here. "Shit, I'm sorry, Smalls. We can go back insi—"

"No. I like it here. With you. Chilly, yes, but...it's peaceful. And you're doing a great job keeping me warm."

I place a kiss on the top of her head. "I'll always keep you warm, Smalls."

"Tell me more."

"Umm, well, Dad always set up the net once it was safe to be on the ice. He tested it all the time. To be honest, though, I don't know if he checked it that particular day or not, but there we were, shooting pucks as far across the pond as we could. When we shot the last puck, Alex told Elias and me to go collect them all." I huff a silent laugh. "Fuck, Elias was so pissed. He was almost a teenager, which meant he was above picking up the pucks. Tried to make me do it all, but Alex made him help me."

"Typical brothers."

"Yeah. So, there we were, collecting pucks. Holding them in our jerseys as we skated around to pick them up."

A knot forms in my throat when I relive the next moments in my mind, a feeling of absolute dread overcoming me. "I, uh... I took a quick break, plopping myself in the snowbank at the edge of the pond as Elias got the last couple of pucks. I remember thinking there was snow getting into my glove and was about to take it off to check when I heard Alex swear, which was odd, because I had never heard him swear before."

"How old was he?"

"Sixteen. I was so startled by his using the big bad F-word, I looked up and he was in this stance... this, frozen stance. He looked at me and then looked at Elias, and screamed at him to get off the ice."

"Get off the ice, Eli! Stay back!"

"He was scared. I had never seen my brother scared before, but he was scared that day. God, he had to have been so fucking scared." Tears begin to slip from my eyes down my cheeks, but I don't want to let go of Carissa to stop them, so I let them exist. "But he was so brave. He hunched down, just like Dad had taught us. Lowered himself so he could crawl across the ice to the edge where we were, but as soon as his knees hit the ice, it broke, and he went through."

"Alex!"

"Eli, help him!"

"I know, Colby! I fucking know! Stay there!"

"There was nothing I could fucking do. I was completely helpless standing on the bank that day. Scared out of my fucking mind that Elias was going to ask me to crawl onto the ice to help save him because I knew I wasn't strong enough. I was so young."

"Colby." Carissa tightens her blanket around me, trying her best to warm me as I tremble against her.

"He came up to the surface, gasping for air and trying like hell to grab ahold of something...anything, but the ice kept breaking, and his wet gear made him so heavy."

"Colby, go get Dad!"

"Elias screamed at me to go get Dad, who was working with some of the guys in the barn, so I ran. I ran as fast as I fucking could, but the snow drifts were..." Heavier tears slide down my cheeks, and Carissa finally notices. I feel her inhale against me, and then she slides her hand to my cheek, tenderly trying to wipe them away. "They were so deep, and I was just a little kid. It took way longer for me to get to the barn than it should have. I remember my legs felt like they were cement blocks."

"Dad! Gary! Bill! Help! Alex needs help!"

"Dad didn't even have to ask what was wrong. He saw me huffing and puffing, a sobbing mess, and they all just...knew. They went running, and I couldn't even fucking keep up. By the time I made it back to the pond, Dad was coming out of the water with Gary, and Bill was helping Eli. There was nothing anyone could do. He was..." I shake my head, the unbelievable grief smacking me in the face all over again. "Alex was gone."

"Oh, Colby, I'm so sorry."

"If I had just... I don't know. Run fucking faster. Maybe..."

"No, Colb." Carissa sits up and takes my face in her hands, wiping my tears and kissing my cheeks. "Don't go down that road. It will do you no good. You were a kid, do you hear me? You did everything you could've possibly done. This wasn't anybody's fault."

"I didn't even get to say goodbye. Eli sent me away and I didn't—"

"He loved you, Colby. Alex loved you. You have to know that."

Somewhere in the very back of my mind, I know what she says is true, and I nod. "I miss him so fucking much."

"I would be surprised if you didn't, but listen to me, Colb," she says, still holding my face in her hands. "Some people bring so much light into your world that even when they're gone, their light stays with you." She passes me a sympathetic smile. "He's not gone for good, Colby. He lives inside you. If I had to guess, he's the reason you've become the athlete you are. One of the strongest, most popular, and most accomplished hockey players in the league. Don't think for a second he didn't have something to do with that."

"Elias never played hockey again after that day. We used to talk about all three of us being professional hockey players together when we got older, but he just couldn't do it."

"But you did," she whispers. "He's with you, Colby. He's in you. You don't have to grieve him anymore. You can celebrate him instead. Celebrate the memories you shared, and appreciate the passion, and the drive he taught you to have. I have no doubt, if he were here right now, he would tell you how proud of you he is. But since he's not, hear me instead."

She brings my forehead to hers, her hands pushing through my hair. "I am so, so proud of you, Colby Nelson. Proud of the man you are. Proud of what you do for others. Proud of the leader you are for your teammates, and proud of the young child inside you who was so brave to carry himself through all that snow that day to try to save his big brother. I'm proud of you, Colby."

She wipes away my falling tears, presses her lips to my mouth, and then whispers against them, "So fucking proud of you."

"Carissa." Her name is a warm sigh, a blanket of emotion covering the two of us in an intimate bubble. I slide one of my hands up her back to the base of her neck and the other down to the swell of her ass and focus on the feel of her against me.

Her skin on my skin.

Her breath on my lips.

Her breasts brushing against my chest.

Her beautifully naked body wrapped around me.

Holding me.

Comforting me.

Loving me.

"Carissa," I breathe against her mouth. "I need you."

"I'm right here, Colb. You have me."

"I want you. Need you. Please, Carissa."

In the silence of the winter night, under the flickering glow of the fireplace, she lifts off my lap enough for me to free my thickened cock from my sweats and rub the tip along her entrance. Then she sinks down over me, sheathing my shaft in her tight warmth, inch by inch, and it's fucking incredible.

Jesus fuck.

We sigh in tandem, and she wraps her arms around my neck, holding me to her chest.

I can't even think of the right words to say in this moment, because she's taking them all away.

She kisses me, her lips soft but yearning, and with every gentle swipe of her tongue, she takes away my pain, my guilt, my confusion, my pent-up anger. All of it.

Sifting her fingers through my hair, she melts me.

I groan into her mouth.

She moans inside mine.

"I should grab a condom. I'm sorry, I—"

"Shhh." She pivots her hips, and my eyes roll back at the unbelievable feeling of her sliding against me, taking me inside her. All of me. As far as she can. "I've been on the pill for years, Colby. We're always careful. It's okay. Just this once, I want to feel you, too."

"Carissa..."

There's no dirty talk this time. No spanking, no biting, no fucking.

We are two people in the dead of winter, sharing the most intimate of moments on my balcony.

"Feel with me, Colby. Free yourself of what pains you. I'll hold it all for you. Just... be with me. Here. Now."

She releases her hold from around my neck and brings her hands to my shoulders. I push away the blanket around us, allowing the bite of the wind to swirl around our naked bodies, but I don't succumb to the chill because this woman is enough to keep me warm. To keep me grounded. To make me whole.

She's everything.

I palm each of her breasts, and her head falls back when I swipe my thumbs across her nipples.

"You are so goddamn beautiful like this. Bared for me. God, look at you. You're everything I didn't know I would ever need in my life."

"Colby," she sighs my name, and I swear to God, my dick grows another two inches.

She circles her hips, riding my cock, bringing me to a state of pure bliss. I want to hold on as long as I can. I want her to feel how much I feel for her.

I pull one of her nipples into my mouth, flicking it with my tongue, and then I suck and lick, and suck and lick, with all the reverence I have in me.

She moans again. The urge to thrust is almost overpowering.

"God, Colby, yes. More, baby. I want more. Need more. I want to feel you."

Thank fuck.

With my hands on her hips, I hold her as she pistons against me a little faster, and I pump into her, every thrust enhancing the pleasure.

It's so goddamn good.

Intimacy with a woman has never felt like this before.

I've never had a woman at my house, let alone my private balcony.

I've never trusted a woman with my feelings.

Never laid myself bare for her.

But I need it all with Carissa.

I want it.

Crave it.

She closes her eyes and throws her head back, her teeth slipping over her bottom lip.

Such a turn-on.

I could watch her like this forever.

Her tits bobbing up and down as she moves, her messy bed-hair cascading over her shoulders.

She's gorgeous.

She's everything.

"Colby..." she cries. "I'm almost there."

"I know you are, babe. I feel it. I'm right there with you."

I watch as her hands travel up her body, skimming over her breasts and then slipping into her hair. She gathers it on top of her head and holds it there, her body completely bare for me, and then pistons even faster.

"I'm so full, Colb. It's never felt like this before." She gasps when I palm her breast, a languid, satisfied cry falling from her lips. Then her pussy clenches around me, taking my breath away. My jaw falls open, and I unleash a huge moan.

"Fuck, Carissa. It's too good. I'm going to come, babe. Shit, I'm there. I'm there. I'm..."

I wrap my arms tightly around her body, holding her in place as I empty everything I have inside her.

All my fear.

All my regret.

All my pain.

All my love.

I give her everything.

And she takes it.

She takes all of me.

With no judgment.

Only respect.

And kindness.

And love.

CHAPTER 22

Carissa

Me: Well? What do you think?

I send a picture of myself in my new red dress, standing in front of the mirror, to Chelsea. The long-sleeved dress, with a plunging neckline and a split thigh, hangs perfectly on my body. It shows just enough skin to be sexy and alluring without being trashy and inappropriate. I'm high-class tonight, and I feel like more than a million bucks. I don't know how he did it, but Colby —or rather, Patrick —really knows how to pick a dress.

Chelsea: Holy shit! You look HOT! Where are you going in that slick little number?

Me: Charity event with Colby.

Chelsea: So, things are going well I take it?

Me: Last night was a night I'll never forget. So yeah, it's going very well!

Chelsea: Well, you look amazing!
Hair up or hair down?

Me: I'm thinking mostly up? Maybe
a few loose strands down?

Chelsea: Yes Queen! And those
shoes are to DIE for!

Me: RIGHT?! OMG I still can't
believe he did all this for me.

Chelsea: He's a good guy, Rissa.
He cares for you.

Me: I think you're right. *wink
emoji*

Chelsea: Have all the fun tonight!
Don't do anything I wouldn't do.

Me: LOL I'll try! Love you babe!

Chelsea: Ditto that!

"Wow. You look..." Colby slides his hand down his face and then covers his mouth as he watches me come down the stairs. He shakes his head, then hops up the last few stairs to offer me his arm. "Stunning, Smalls. You look stunning."

"Thank you, Colby. You don't look so bad yourself. A far cry from the white towel of the locker room or the pads of a hockey uniform."

He kisses my neck with a smile. "Don't think I don't know how many pictures you have of me wrapped in that white towel, though."

I give him an innocent shrug. "Hey, a girl's got to have something to look at when she's all alone in bed with nothing but her battery-operated friends."

"I am your battery-operated friend, Smalls. Remember that."

"Oh, I haven't forgotten."

But what he doesn't know won't hurt him.

Though, it'll certainly be my pleasure.

"You ready to go?"

"Ready. Let's get this show on the road."

Colby takes my hand and leads me down to his heated garage where our chariot awaits. A fancy, black SUV. He opens my door and helps me inside, ever the gentleman, and then walks around to hop in the driver's seat. He lays his hand on my thigh and doesn't move it for the entire drive, and I'm a heart-thumping, giddy mess inside.

I wasn't lying when I told Chelsea last night was a night I'll never forget. Hell, the whole day was a whirlwind. A dream come true. Rescued by a prince, taken to his castle, given one hell of a massage followed by a few raging orgasms, and then an afternoon of fun. I'm convinced there's nothing he can't do well.

And when he was at his most vulnerable last night on his balcony, spilling his heart to me through tear-filled, trembling words, I fell in love with him. I fell for the man who so easily trusted me with his heart. With his soul. With his fears. His guilt. His anxieties. His pain. I'm so in love with Colby Nelson, I can't see straight. I've been nothing but smiles all day, and now, dressed up for a special night, I'm grateful he chose me to do this with him. To stand by his side.

As his girl.

I swallow the small knot in my throat, anxious about what Valerie will say on Monday when I finally spill the beans about us. Maybe she already knows. Maybe she doesn't. I've been as careful as possible until tonight.

Tonight, we go public.

Tonight, everyone will know.

I just have to hope Valerie will understand and accept what Colby and I want to be.

"Hey." Colby squeezes my leg. "What are you thinking about over there? You're quiet."

I clear my throat. "Do you have to give a speech tonight?"

"Nothing formal. They may ask me to say a few words. All depends on who will be in attendance. They try not to make it all about one sport or the other. They'll have a few celebrities from several different sports there to show their faces as sponsors for the organization."

"And we're sharing a table with Elias?"

He nods. "Yeah. Elias and his business partner, Beckham, and probably a partner or two of his firm, and then whoever else they put at our table. It's usually a great night."

"Sounds good."

"You sure you're okay, Smalls? You seem... I don't know. You're usually giving me grief with that sharp wit of yours, but you're quiet tonight."

A soft chuckle escapes me, and I place my hand on top of his resting on my thigh. "I'm sorry. I guess I am a tad bit nervous. This is a big step for me."

"For us," he corrects. "Don't forget, I've never done this either. I always go to these things alone. Or sometimes I invite my mom."

"Are you nervous, too?"

"Hell, no. Are you kidding? I'm happy as fuck to finally have you by my side. Officially."

His excitement warms me.

"Don't worry about a thing, Smalls. I'll take care of you tonight. I promise. And if you want me with you when you talk to Valerie on Monday, I'll be there. Anything you need, okay? We're doing this together."

His optimism and confidence are heartening. I squeeze his hand again and pass him a sincere smile. "I really am excited to have some fun tonight."

"Good. Me too."

"Mr. Nelson! Over here! A picture, please!" We walk the red carpet hand in hand, finally reaching a small group of photographers stationed in front of the backdrop for Amateur Empowered. Nerves heighten as my eyes dart to everyone, wondering who might be around noticing that I'm here with Colby.

Do I know any of them?

Do they know me?

My grip on Colby's hand tightens, and he takes notice instantly. Without missing a beat, he lets go of my hand, wraps his arm around me, and places a chaste kiss on my temple. He squeezes my hip against him protectively and whispers, "Smile and relax, Smalls. I'll be right next to you all night. I promise."

Shouts come from the photographers, asking who he has on his arm tonight. For a fleeting moment, I feel like a modern day *Pretty Woman*. Like I'm Julia Roberts, the arm candy for the rich man's event, but then I remind myself he's not paying me to be here.

He wants me to be here.

"Gentlemen, this is Carissa Smallson." He gazes at me lovingly for a second and then continues. "My girlfriend."

If the photographers and staffers weren't excited a minute ago, they certainly are now. Flashes go off around us like we're the hottest new Hollywood celebrity couple, and they're calling my name to get me to look at their cameras specifically. This might be the most surreal thing I've ever done.

"Does this mean you'll have helicopters and drones flying around tonight?" I murmur to him.

Colby shrugs. "Maybe. Want to give them another balcony show just in case?"

His comment frees the butterflies in my stomach, and I laugh out loud. "Go big or go home, right?"

"Sweetheart, you've got big." He winks. "And my home is your home."

Even though that's so far from the truth, as we practically come from opposite ends of the financial spectrum, I can't help but think he actually means it.

With his hand on the small of my back, Colby leads me into a grand ballroom elegantly decorated for a party. Flags and banners from many area sports teams —major leagues, minor leagues, and even collegiate sports—hang from the ceiling around the room. It's an array of color that symbolizes a celebration of self-growth, determination, personal effort, and teamwork.

A full bar stands along the west wall of the room, the rest of the space filled with round tables and a small stage. Along the wall where we just entered is a group of long tables with all sorts of different sports memorabilia, signed merchandise, and many other gift-like items.

"Silent auction?" I ask Colby, holding onto his arm.

"Hell no," he chuckles. "They want the rich boys to compete to win. It's a regular auction, so everyone can hear how much they're spending."

"Ah." I smile. "Of course. How silly of me."

"See something you like, just say the word, Smalls. I'll bid on it."

I quickly peruse the table as we walk by. "Hmm, I don't see any big stuffed teddy bears up there."

"Is that what you want? A big stuffed teddy bear?"

"Nah." With an arm already hooked through his, I squeeze it with my other hand. "I already have one right here."

"Fuckin' right you do." He kisses my temple, and his eyes drop to my chest briefly before rising back up to meet mine. "You look absolutely amazing tonight. In case I haven't told you enough already."

"It's a compliment I never mind hearing twice. Thank you, Colb."

"Carissa? Is that you?"

I turn my head in the direction of the voice calling to me, and there, standing in a floor-length black velvet dress, is Gretchen Prong.

Colby squeezes my hand, I'm guessing to remind me I'm not alone, and I force a smile. "Gretchen! Oh my gosh, it's great to see you!"

She gives me a haphazard embrace, which I return in kind. "It's great to see you as well. I didn't think about the fact that you could be here tonight. How nice of the Red Tails to send you toni—" She catches a quick glimpse of Colby holding my hand. "Oh. Maybe you're not here in any official capacity."

"Officially my girlfriend, if that's what you're asking." Colby grins and offers her his hand. "Colby Nelson."

Her jaw only hangs open for a few seconds before she's stumbling on her words. "Oh, of-of course. Your girlfriend. That's... that's wonderful." She turns to me, nudging me with her elbow. "You must be so excited, right? You got your dream job and the dream guy all at the same time, huh? Colby Nelson... captain of the team and everything. Not bad, Smallson." She winks.

That's right, Gretch.

I deserve to be happy after the shit I've gone through.

So, I'm not mad about where I am or who I'm with.

"I'm one hell of a lucky girl." I smile at Colby and then shake my head. "I'm sorry, Colby. Where are my manners?" I gesture to Gretchen. "This is Gretchen Prong. She's on the PR staff for DePaul. I worked with her for several years before coming to the Red Tails."

"I'm sure she's mentioned me." Gretchen huffs out an uncomfortable laugh. "We go way back. Worked together for years. Of course, I always did the sports events. Carissa was never much for sports."

I see what you're doing, Gretchen.

And it won't work.

"Hmm, I'm sorry," he answers her. "I don't recall her

mentioning you at all, actually. But then again, we spend a lot of time not talking if you catch my drift."

"Oh." Gretchen's brows pull together, and I feel my cheeks pinken. I, for one, certainly caught his drift.

"With a pussy as sweet as hers, I'm a kid in a candy store twenty-four-seven." He winks and squeezes my hand, bringing my bumfuzzled brain back to reality. "You ready, babe?"

"Yep. Ready. See you around, Gretchen."

Colby nods to Gretchen as I give her a small wave and then follow Colby to our table.

"You really had to talk about my pussy?"

Should I be embarrassed about this?

"Smalls, I normally don't kiss and tell, because nobody out there deserves to know what goes on behind closed doors, but I could read that girl immediately. She's just like all the other puck bunnies of the world, and she's totally jealous of you, by the way." He shrugs with a smirk. "So I decided to rub a little salt in her wound. Now she's jealous of your pussy, too."

I cackle a little too loudly for a woman at a fancy dinner, but I don't even care. When we reach our table, Colby's brother and his friend are already smiling at us.

"Sup, bro?" Colby gives Elias a fist bump, followed by a hug, and then shakes the other guy's hand as well. "Beckham. Good to see you guys. Thanks for coming."

"Wouldn't miss it," Elias tells him before turning to me. "Carissa, you look amazing tonight. It's good to see you again." He gives me a hug and whispers in my ear, "Thank you for what you do for my brother."

I don't respond to his thanks but let him know with my eyes that I heard him. "Pleasure to see you both again. I hear this is a fun night."

"Always a riot. We like to watch the rich guys get drunk and piss on each other over how much they're going to spend on those fancy auction items."

"Yeah," Beckham chimes in. "Saw your signed Crocs up

there, Colby. Nice touch."

"Thanks, man."

"That's a creative contribution," I mention as Colby helps me to my seat.

"It's something I try to give in hopes it'll go to a kid. Most adults could care less about the Croc thing. It's the kids that get excited about gifting or trading charms."

"That's very nice of you, Colb."

He shrugs, and Elias smirks at him across the table.

"What?" I ask, watching them hold a conversation without ever saying a word.

"Ah, nothin'," Elias says, bringing his elbows to the table. "It's his other entry that will bring in the big money... just as it does every year."

My eyes widen. "Ooh. Did you donate something else? Now I'm curious. What is it?"

Colby bows his head, smiling, and softly says, "I switch places with someone for a day."

"What? What do you mean?"

"He means he legit trades places with the lucky winner for one day. So, whoever bids the highest will get to show up and practice with the team that day, doing all the things the team usually does. Watching plays, merch promos, charity work, team meetings, you name it. They spend the day with the entire Red Tails team... well, minus Colby."

"That sounds fun!"

"Yeah." Elias nods. "And then, in return, Colby does whatever job the winner has for an entire workday. And let me tell you, over the years, he's gotten to experience many interesting jobs, to put it mildly."

I narrow my eyes. "Okay, maybe I'm not understanding something, but if it's mostly rich guys who bid on and win the experience, doesn't that mean Colby would spend a workday in some high-rise office somewhere?"

"That used to be the case, yeah," Beckham says, smiling. "But then Elias bid on it a few years ago and won, and decided to gift it to someone more deserving. So, Colby spent the day working alongside the guys at Roto-Rooter. Slingin' shit and cleaning drainpipes."

Beckham and Elias laugh, clink their glasses together, and sip their bourbon.

"Well, that is... wow. Equal parts disgusting and humbling. What a great idea to gift the experience to a deserving person."

"Yeah. It's become a thing now," Elias adds. "And now the rich guys try to outbid each other so they can choose the worthy person to gift the package to, which also means they're looking for the oddest or grossest or funniest job to have Colby do."

My smile morphs into an all-out beam. "Like what? What kinds of things have you had to do?"

Colby takes a deep breath and taps his fingers lightly on the table. "I taught kindergarten for a day."

"Oh my! Kindergarten? You?"

"Otherwise known as the booger brigade, by the way, and yes. Can't you picture it? Me singing 'Itsy-Bitsy-Spider'?"

I snicker. "I can totally picture it. What else?"

"Let's see... I spent the day working at Victoria's Secret, which they loved, by the way. Every guy in town lined up to buy something for their significant other because they wanted me to pick it out. Now old Vicky calls me every year to ask me to come back."

"Oh my God!"

"Yep. I've ridden the trash truck through downtown Chicago. I delivered outhouses to Lincoln Park, and I've worked as the entertainment coordinator for a local nursing home."

"A nursing home? Holy shit, Colby!" I can't stop the giggles. "What kind of entertainment did you provide?"

"Bingo, baby! And they loved it, by the way."

"That is amazing."

Elias nods, laughing right along with me as Colby recalls his experiences. "Tell her what you did last year, bro."

"I don't think so. She doesn't want t—"

"Oh yes, I do. There's no turning back now, Nelson. Tell me what you did, or I'll just look it up on the internet. There's no way it's not out there."

He concedes. "You're right. It's out there. And, to be honest, I'm surprised you haven't seen it yet."

"Okay, seen what?"

He shakes his head, slightly embarrassed. "I performed in the Magic Mike show that was in town for a few weeks."

"What?" I squeal. "Okay, wait. First of all, you can dance? And secondly, how the hell did that even happen? That is hilarious, and I'm kinda jealous I wasn't there to witness it."

He slides his hand up my leg under the table. "Happy to give you a show later if you want. And, yes, I can dance."

Elias laughs. "So, it turned out one of the dancers in the show is a Chicago native, and he's a huge Red Tails fan. So, he hung with the team for the day, and Colby had to learn an entire dance routine and then perform that night. It was a fuckin' riot to watch!"

"Oh man, you were there?"

"Fuckin' right I was there. No way was I going to miss it. The show sold out that night, of course."

Without hesitating, I turn and take Colby's face in my hands. "This is truly amazing, Colby. The things you do. You're incredible, you know that? Absolutely incredible. It's no wonder the community adores you."

I lean forward and connect my mouth with his. "I adore you."

He moans against my mouth and returns my soft kiss. "Right back at you, Smalls. And, thank you. I'm really glad you're here."

"What about me, bro?" Elias holds his hand to his chest. "Aren't you glad I'm here, too?"

Colby laughs. "Fuck off, brother."

CHAPTER 23

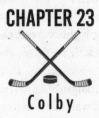

Colby

"Homebuilding, huh?" Carissa follows my lead as we dance with the many other party attendees. Now that the dancing portion of the evening has started, every rich couple, corporate party, and professional athlete in attendance tonight is here on the dance floor. Overcrowded, but fun nonetheless. "I feel like you got kind of lucky with that one."

"Hell yeah, I did." I huff out a laugh. "I'll get to spend the day rockin' out with my caulk out. What's not to like about that?"

Her sweet laugh fills the air around me, and my heart couldn't be fuller. The evening has been a wonderful success. Amateur Empowered raised nearly three million dollars tonight, a new record. Watching the grumpy rich guys fight it out during the auction was almost better than the Stanley Cup Finals, and here I am ending the night with a stunningly sexy woman in my arms.

Life is good.

"A day holding your caulk in your hands? Sounds lonely, but you do you, Colb."

I throw my head back in laughter, and then squeeze her tighter against me so I can whisper in her ear. "I would rather have my caulk in your hands, Smalls."

"Mmm. Is that so?"

The music changes to a sultry number, performed by some girl I'm sure I've heard of before, but can't recall her name. Carissa pulls part of her bottom lip into her mouth, a mischievous grin spreading across her face, and I'm immediately intrigued.

What could she be up to?

She turns around, her back to my chest, and dances against me, her petite little ass rubbing against my hardening cock.

Fucking hell. She's a temptress tonight in her sexy red dress. I haven't been able to stop eye-fucking her since we left the house. And all I've been able to think about is sliding my hands through her plunging neckline or thigh-high slit. Intriguing accommodations for my pleasure.

And hers.

Patrick did a bang-up job choosing her attire. I'll have to remember to thank him again later.

"I can only imagine what's going on in that dirty mind of yours, Smalls." I wrap a hand around her, palming her abdomen and holding her against me as we move together. My mouth at her ear so only she, and she alone, can hear me.

"Wouldn't you like to know?"

"You know I do. You know what else I want to know?" Moving my hand down toward the slit of her dress, I sneak my hand inside and feel her gasp against me.

"What?"

"I want to know how wet you are for me right fucking now."

"Colby," she sighs as my fingers flutter between her legs, my hand hidden beneath the fabric of her dress.

I lean my head forward over her shoulder and kiss the side of her head before whispering, "Relax, Smalls. The floor is way too crowded. Nobody is watching, and the risk of being seen turns me the fuck on. Are you turned on, Smalls?"

"You know I am," she breathes.

I bring my free hand up to the bottom of her deep neckline, my palm resting just below her breasts. Underneath her dress, I swipe my finger between her legs, expecting to find her thong, but instead, there is no barrier.

"Fuck. Someone's not wearing panties."

She shakes her head with a smirk. "Didn't want panty lines showing through the dress."

"Well, isn't that genius? I think my good girl deserves to be rewarded."

"I think she does, too. And she knows exactly what she wants."

"She can have anything."

She turns her body around so she can speak directly into my ear. "Your cock in my mouth as soon as possible."

"Fuck, Smalls." My eyes nearly roll back in my head at the suggestion, and then I'm grabbing her hand and pulling her from the dance floor. "As you wish. Let's get out of here."

I lead her off the dance floor toward the door, not giving two shits about saying goodbye to anyone, but she tugs my hand, giggling. "Wait, Colby. My phone and purse are at the table. I just need to grab them."

Slightly annoyed because my dick is uncomfortable in my pants, I follow behind her so she can collect her things... and so I don't look like a sixteen-year-old boy with a mega stiffy.

"Leaving already?"

"Already?" I scoff. "We've been here for hours, and we have..." I look to Carissa and then back to my brother, his brow cocked. "Things... to do."

Elias chuckles. "Things."

"Yeah, things."

"All right, well, it was good seeing you guys. Oh, and Carissa, there was a girl here looking for you. Long black dress? Said she ran into you earlier?"

"Gretchen, yeah." She nods.

He gestures to Carissa's phone. "She took a few selfies with your phone... said it was a long-standing joke from college? And then I think she sent you a text. Just a heads up."

I lean over Carissa's shoulder as she scrolls through the new selfies of Gretchen.

"Was that really a thing with you guys?"

"Yeah," she answers, continuing to scroll through pictures and messages. "We used to do it to each other if we left our phones out while we were working. We would see who could take the most ridiculous selfie. Dumb, but it was entertaining at the time."

She reads Gretchen's text that simply says, "Great to see you tonight. Let's catch up soon!" Tossing her phone in her purse, she takes my hand and waves to Elias and Beckham with her other hand. "See you at the next game?"

Elias nods. "We wouldn't miss it. G'night guys."

I get us home as fast as I possibly can, my mind reeling from one of the best days, nights, and weekends I've ever had. All because of the woman in my passenger seat. I'm already wondering what kind of fun we could get into tomorrow when we pull into the garage. I help Carissa out of the car, and we walk hand-in-hand into the house where I lead her to the main living room. It's one of my favorite rooms in the house with its oversized furniture, plush carpets, throw blankets, and a gas fireplace that I turn on with the flip of a switch.

I saunter over to Carissa and slowly run my finger down the bare neckline of her dress all the way to the top of her sternum.

"You were ravishing tonight. Absolutely breathtaking."

Her cheeks pinken, and a smile spreads across her face. "Well, that's quite the compliment."

"You deserve it." I step back, looking her over from head to toe once more. Her brown waves gently pulled up behind her head show off the slope of her neck and the sparkling diamonds hanging from her ears. The plunging top of her dress revealing the swell of her breasts. The cut of the fabric flaunting her figure perfectly.

"But as beautiful as you are in this dress, I've done nothing all night but imagine peeling you out of it."

With soft hands, I reach behind her and tug the zipper until it stops just below her waist. Then, I gently slide her shoulder straps down her arms until the dress falls to her feet, leaving her completely naked in front of me, with the exception of her Louboutin shoes.

Deep red come-fuck-me heels.

"Goddamn, Carissa. You're every fantasy I've ever had." I

lean down and tip her chin, crashing my lips to hers. Breathing her in, exhaling into her mouth, our tongues tangling together.

She moans.

I groan.

I want to touch her everywhere... and nowhere.

Keep her sensitivity heightened.

Keep her wanting.

Waiting.

I release her lips and step back, staring at her doe-like eyes as I unbuckle my belt, unzip my pants, and palm my hardened cock.

"On your knees, Smalls."

CHAPTER 24

Carissa

Drip. Drip. Drip.
   Drip. Drip. Drip.
   Drip. Drip. Drip.

"Mr. Hastings, I really need someone to come look at the leak under my sink. It's dripping faster now and filling my bucket almost every day. I seriously think—"

"Yes, yes, yes," my landlord cuts me off. "I'll come take a look at it this afternoon, Ms. Smallson. Don't you worry. We'll have it fixed in no time."

Somehow, I don't believe him. This conversation feels like one of the good ol' boys patting me on the back just to get me out of his office. I roll my eyes and huff out a deep sigh.

"Okay, well, while you're here, please take a look at the leak in the shower as well. It's a small, steady stream from the shower head."

"Will do. Will do."

"If you can tell me when—"

CLICK.

I hold my phone away from my ear to see the call has ended.

"Fucking son of a bitch hung up on me." I blow my hair out of my face and sit on the edge of the bathtub, frustration oozing out of me. "I hate this place."

Compared to the Nelson Palace I visited this past weekend, this place is a fucking dump, and I know that. I want more for myself, but getting there with the shit hand I've been dealt by my parents is making my goals feel incredibly unreachable. Up until today, I've tried to take my life in stride. Fix the problems. Have the drive to build a better life for myself despite my setbacks. But this morning feels like the Monday-ist Monday in the history of the world, and all I want to do is scream and cry about it. Throw a tantrum for just a damn minute.

As happy as I was with Colby this weekend, cozied up with him in his castle, being here just reminds me that, in reality, we come from two different worlds. He's the celebrity athlete, the prince of the ice, and I'm just the poor little girl dealing with real-life issues, causing her to forever be the wannabe princess.

There was a day when I was excited to have my own place. To be on my own and finally away from my parents, but today? Today I hate them even more if that's possible. I hate them for putting me in this predicament. I hate them for stealing my identity and ruining my credit, so a place like this hellhole is all I can afford.

And I super hate that there isn't much I can do about it right now.

I slept through my alarm this morning and woke to find the bucket under my sink overflowing. That meant having to call work and tell them I'd be late, then I spent an hour sopping up the mess on the bathroom floor. Once that was done, I had to clean everything as much as possible to make sure nothing rots or grows moldy, because the last thing I need is an apartment filled with mold.

I can tell Colby is worrying about me because my phone has been going off like crazy with texts I haven't looked at or answered yet, as I'm finally getting ready for work. In my haste, I pull my clean hair up into a ponytail, dab on minimal makeup since it's not a day filled with executive meetings, and grab my stuff to head out. Finally grabbing my phone off my coffee table to let Colby know I'm fine and on my way, I see the latest string of texts aren't from him at all.

Chelsea: Uhhh, you okay?

Chelsea: What happened? Want to talk about it?

Chelsea: I can be free at a moment's notice. Just say the word.

Chelsea: Okay now I'm worried about you. Why aren't you answering?

Chelsea: OMG are they firing you? Is that why you're not answering?

Chelsea: You didn't really do it, right? It couldn't have been you.

Chelsea: Is it a setup?

Chelsea: I mean the pictures are... phew. Fucking hot, Rissa, but still. Is it photoshopped? Would somebody do that?

Chelsea: Okay, I need to know you're okay. Can you please write me back?

Chelsea: You're really starting to worry me.

"Pictures? What the hell is she..." I quickly write her back.

> **Me: WTF are you even talking about? I'm fine. Leak in my bathroom. Running late to work.**

Chelsea: Oh Rissa...you haven't seen?

My stomach drops, and my heart rate picks up.

> **Me: Seen what?**

Chelsea: It's all over social media this morning babe. Hold on. I'll screenshot.

Within seconds, Chelsea is sending me a text of several different photos. Front pages of the morning's tabloid paper, the front page of *The Chicago Tribune*, and several other online news sources.

"Chicago Red Tails Staff Sexual Scandal Exposed."

"Red Tails Marketing Rep's Relationship with Team Captain."

"Red Tails Marketing Staffer Exploits Team Players."

"Carissa Smallson: Chicago Red Tails'

Newest Puck Bunny."

"Red Tails Hockey Team Behind-the-Scenes Pics Sold for Staffer's Financial Gain."

"What?" My heart sinks, and a wave of nausea hits me as I lower myself to my coffee table and flip through every picture Chelsea sent. Pictures of Colby and me from Saturday night.

Dancing.

His hand inside the slit of my dress.

His hand near my plunging neckline.

My mouth open and my eyes closed, like I'm... fuck. Like I'm being pleasured.

The two of us kissing at our table.

Us kissing on the dance floor.

Our picture on the red carpet.

Colby's hand on my abdomen like he owns me.

My hand on his chest like I own him.

My embrace with Elias.

Him whispering something in my ear.

A close-up of my hand around Colby's arm that looks like I'm clinging to him.

"But this isn't..." I shake my head, bewildered. "They're making this look like more than..."

And then I flip through more pictures.

One of the players holding a towel around his waist in the locker room. Nobody can tell who it is, but I know it to be Quinton Shay. There's another picture of me dancing with Dex at Pringle's. A video of our beer chug competition. Of Dex and Hawken twerking. Selfies with me and just about every guy on the team. More drinking pictures from our away games. Selfies of Colby and me in bed. Other photos clearly edited to look like we're all in precarious positions. Even one made to suggest I'm intimately involved with several of the guys.

"How did they get these?"

"I don't understand."

Tears fall from my eyes without my having to think about it.

I know what this looks like.

Valerie will have my ass.

"Fuck! Valerie." I hadn't even given her a thought until now, and then another thought stabs me in the chest. "Colby!"

What if he thinks...

What if...

Does he know?

He must know by now.

But why hasn't he written me?

Surely he wouldn't think...

Would he?

Shit! I have to get to him.

I make it to work as fast as the L will get me there and literally run from the station to the arena in my heels. I fly past Mr. Cagnis, the doorman, noticing he's not smiling this morning, but giving me a sympathetic glance, and I nearly throw up with that realization. He's the sweetest older man, and he's always smiling. We've always been friendly with each other. If Mr. Cagnis isn't smiling, there's a reason.

Does he know?

He has to know.

They all must know. Rumors spread like wildfire, and I wasn't here to extinguish them right away this morning.

If that doesn't look like pure guilt...

Fuck!

My chest on fire and my body wanting to give out, I force myself to run to the team meeting room, but when I fling the door open, nobody is inside, so I double back to the dressing room. Slams of lockers and voices propel me to pull the door open and step inside, where I'm met with several familiar faces.

But not the one I'm looking for.

Not one of the guys says a word to me, but they all stare me down like I'm dying prey, captured and about to be eaten alive by its predator. All the air is sucked out of my body.

Do they believe it, too?

How can this be happening?

If they believe it...

I find Zeke among the group and steel myself to finally ask, "Where is he, Zeke?"

His shoulders fall, and he gives me a sad glance confirming what they must all be thinking. He gestures out the door. "Weight room."

Holding his stare, I say the only thing I can spit out, and even as I think the words in my head, my throat tightens, and tears roll down my face. "You know this wasn't me, right? I would never..."

None of their expressions change. Each of them watches me as I back up to the door, shaking my head. "I'm so sorry."

I exit the locker room and walk cautiously to the weight room, where I can hear the clanking of weights and the grunts of one man. When I step into the room, Colby notices me in the mirror as he holds his deadlift. Sweat dripping from his body. His skin glistening. His hair wet.

This isn't his first workout this morning, I can tell.

He's overworking himself again.

It's what he does when he's stressed.

I did this to him.

"What are you doing here?"

"I... overslept, and then the leak in my bathroom was..." I shake my head, covering my face with my hands. "It's been a shit morning, and then this... shit. I didn't know about this, Colby. I didn't know about any of it. You have to know that."

"Do I?"

I step closer to him. "What? What do you mean?"

He lowers his weight to the floor and then wipes his face with a towel, never once cutting eye contact with me. His deadened stare pierces my heart.

Sucking out my soul.

"Just tell me one thing. Were those pictures from your phone? Yes or no?"

I swallow, unsure of how to answer. "Yes, but—"

"Then we're done here."

"But Colby, I—"

He throws his towel on the floor and shakes his head, his jaw tight with anger. "Was this what you meant when you said you were 'dealing' with your financial problems?"

Shaking my head at the absurdity, I open my mouth to respond. "Wha—"

"You sold your private pictures." He gestures between us. "Our private pictures. To the media. To solve your debt?"

I rear back. "No. I would never—"

"You know, it's bad enough you used me. It's bad enough you fooled me into thinking you truly cared, so I would bare my soul to you. And for what? A few grand in your pocket? But you sold out the team, Carissa." He gestures to the locker room. "Those guys in there? They're my family! My best friends. My br—br—brothers." A lone tear slides down his cheek, and my heart shatters.

He can't honestly believe I would do this.

Why is he reacting this way?

My chest tightens, and I struggle to breathe through my sobs. The only thing I want to do is throw myself at his feet and beg him to believe me.

"Colby, I—"

He stands up a little taller and raises his chin. "Well, nobody fucks with my family. Not you. Not the media. Not anybody."

"Please, Col—"

"Get out."

"Colby."

"Get the fuck out," he sneers, his nostrils flaring. "I don't want to ever see you again."

I shake my head fiercely. "You don't mean th—"

"The fuck I don't! Get out!" he shouts at me. "Right fucking now, Smallson."

Smallson.

My last name is a punch to the gut.

To the heart.

He never calls me Smallson.

He watches me as I slowly back up to the door. Swallowing the knotted lump in my throat, I take a deep breath through my ugly sobs before I leave and say to him, "I love you, Colby Nelson."

CHAPTER 25

Colby

"Fuck!" I put all my weight into striking the punching bag more times than I can count, as hard as I can without breaking my damn hand. Once my arms give out, I stumble to one of the benches in the gym and hold my head in my hands. I try to rein in my breaths, but my chest constricts, and it hurts to breathe.

I should get a drink of water.

But I can't get my body to get the fuck up and do what it needs to do.

Everything hurts.

And I'm so pissed off, I can't think straight.

How did I fucking get here?

How could I let her do this to me?

Is there any truth to what she said?

How can there be?

Those photos were on her phone.

They were her private pictures.

How could it not be her?

No. She did this.

Sold me out and sold out the team.

And this is why I don't fucking date.

"Motherfucking shit!"

A water bottle dangles in front of my face when I finally raise my head. I lift my eyes to the mirror to see Milo and Zeke standing behind me. "Drink, asshole. Small sips."

I grab the water bottle and swig large gulps, because I'm a

grown-ass man and do what I want. Milo merely shakes his head, releasing a quiet huff.

"Or not. It's your stomach."

Zeke watches me from behind for a moment, and when I don't say anything, he straddles the bench beside me. "She was here?"

I nod.

"What did she say?"

"I don't even know. Didn't want to hear it."

"Colb."

"What, Zeke? She sold us out."

"Do you know that for sure?"

"I'll tell you what I do know, man. I know she's in debt up to her eyeballs because her parents stole her identity and used it to buy all this shit in her name." I scoff. "I mean, if that story is even true. I don't know what to think anymore. Maybe she made up the whole thing. Maybe the entire several months is one big scheme."

Milo counters, "You don't really believe that."

"Don't I?" I snap.

"No. You love her."

I nearly spit my water. "I don't love her. I hate her."

"You don't hate her." Zeke cocks his head. "You're hurt and disappointed. There's a difference."

I don't answer him because I'm so fucking emotional right now. I don't know what to think, or what to say, or what to do.

He's right though.

I was falling in love with her.

I thought about telling her more than once this past weekend.

I loved every single moment with her.

I pictured a future with her.

A forever with her.

And now...

"For what it's worth, she looked pretty beat up when she stopped in the locker room."

"Good."

Milo folds his arms over his chest. "Can I ask you something?"

"You're going to anyway, Milo, so just get on with it."

He chuckles softly and then takes a deep breath. "What did you tell her?"

"What do you mean, what did I tell her? I told her to get the fuck out. I told her we were done. I told her nobody hurts my family. My brothers."

Milo bows his head for a moment. "And what if you find out later it wasn't her?"

"There's no way it can't be her, Milo. You saw those pictures! They were her private pictures from her own fucking phone. Nobody could've sent them to the media except her."

"Okay. We're hearing you," Zeke says, his hands up in defense. "I'm just saying, she doesn't seem like the type of girl who would hurt someone she clearly loves even if she's never said it."

"She did say it." I swallow.

"What?"

"Right before she left." My shoulders fall. "She told me she loved me."

And it was a fucking punch to the gut.

Too little too late.

But a small part inside me, maybe the little boy who so desperately wanted to save my brother, wanted to scream back at her that I loved her, too.

"I called Strongfield."

My head turns to Milo. "What for?"

He shrugs. "First of all, he's our agent and he'd already seen everything and was coming up with a plan for damage control. Secondly, he has connections. I thought if anybody could do a little research and find some answers, he can. Then we'll know for sure."

"Answers?" I spit out. "What kind of answers? It's pretty cut and dry, man."

Zeke shakes his head. "We're not convinced."

"Who's we?"

"All of us."

I give them a hard stare, and Milo shrugs. "I'm sorry, Colb, she just doesn't seem the type of human to do something like this. Now, we could be completely wrong, but wouldn't you rather know for sure?"

I take one last swig of water and then stand. "Whatever. I can't imagine he'll find anything, though."

"Maybe not. But... maybe."

Leave it to Milo and Zeke to have hope.

They're always glass-half-full.

I would rather break the fucking glass.

CHAPTER 26

Carissa

I stand outside Valerie Wellman's office, envelope in hand, face red and splotchy from crying. I should've known Colby would react the way he did. I deserve his anger. His disappointment. Though I wasn't the one who sold our pictures to the media, I still kept them on an unlocked phone, and for that, I am paying the ultimate price. Never in a million years did I see myself in this position, but I know I have to do this. Not for myself.

For Colby.

For the team.

For the organization.

I knock on the door lightly, pushing it open slowly. "Valerie?"

When she looks up, it's hard to read her face when she realizes who is standing in her doorway. Anger? Indifference? I don't know. But I step inside and hand her the envelope.

"My letter of resignation. Effective immediately."

She stares at the envelope and then back at me. "Would you like to have a seat?"

"With all due respect, Valerie, I would rather not. I think it's just best if I leave. I've caused a big enough mess around here. I'm not sure how I could ever begin to fix it."

"Can I ask you something?" she asks.

"Of course."

"Why did you do it?"

My shoulders fall. "I didn't. I didn't sell those pictures. Not one."

"That's not what I mean."

I glance up at her with my puffy, tear-filled eyes. "Oh. I'm sorry, I—"

"I meant, why did you get involved with Colby Nelson? After I specifically warned you about the ramifications."

I shake my head. "I didn't do it on purpose. I swear to God, I didn't wake up one morning and decide to sleep with him because you told me not to. It just... we started talking, and then spending time together, and... I even told him I worried what you might think and that I needed to talk to you, but then one thing led to another and—"

"Do you love him? Or was it just casual fucking? How bad of a mess do we have to clean up here?"

I swallow back the lump in my throat. "I love him. I'm in love with him. I'm crazy about him." I bow my head. "But none of that matters now."

"Why not?"

"Because perception is reality. What the media perceives through those pictures and videos is that we're having some illicit affair, and that I sleep around to climb the proverbial ladder. So, to our fans, and those on the outside, that's reality. You know that. I know that."

"Did you explain this to Colby?"

"I tried. He doesn't want me around."

"He didn't believe you?"

"No."

"Why not?"

"Because he thinks I had motive."

"Which was?"

Ugh. Why can't she just take my letter and let me go?

Squeezing my eyes closed and wiping the tears from my face, I plop down in the chair across from her desk.

"Because while I was in college, my parents stole my identity and opened a number of credit cards in my name. Took a few lavish trips, you name it. Now my credit is in the shitter, and I'm trying to climb out of it."

Valerie's eyes grow huge. "You didn't know this was happening?"

"No." I shake my head, embarrassment heating my cheeks. "Not at all. Not until I got a job after graduation and tried to finance a car. That was the first time I ever needed my credit checked." A resigned sigh falls from my mouth as well as a few tears from my eyes and sniffles from my nose. "I get it. He thinks I betrayed him. He thinks I betrayed the whole team. Thinks I sold them all out for money to pay my debts...er...my parents' debts or whatever. Like I said. Perception is reality." I stand up from my chair and wipe my face again. "So please...please just accept my resignation and let me go."

She holds my sad stare for a long moment and then finally accepts the envelope from my hand. "I'm sorry about this, Carissa. For what it's worth though, you've done great work around here. But I can appreciate where you're coming from and the decisions you're making now."

"It's not for me. It's what's best for the team." I shrug. "For the entire organization."

"I understand."

"Thank you." I start to leave Valerie's office and then turn back. "And thank you for the wonderful opportunity to work for you. It was a dream come true."

"Oh, Rissa." Chelsea wraps her arms around me in a tight hug. "I'm so sorry this is happening."

"I don't know what else I can do to fix it, Chels," I cry. Now that I'm with my best friend, who knows better than to think I would ever do something so terrible to another human or humans, I'm free to ugly cry as much as I want without judgment. "He's not hearing me. He didn't want to believe me when I told him I didn't do this."

"He's hurting right now, babe. He's confused. I'm sure he'll come around."

"You didn't see his face this morning in that gym. You didn't hear his voice yelling at me to get the fuck out."

She cringes. "Yikes. He said that?"

I nod. "And told me he never wants to see me again."

"Oh, babe." She smooths her hand down my back, comforting me. "Do you want me to talk to him for you? Set him straight?"

As much as I would love for that to happen, I just don't see it working. "Thank you, Chels, but no. He's either going to believe me or he's not. Besides, as crazy as I am about him, I can't force him to love me. I know that."

"I don't like to see you hurting like this, Rissa. What can I do? Do you want to eat all the chocolate Chicago has to offer? Do you want to drink ourselves into oblivion? You say the word, and I'll make it happen."

I give her a sad smile and then bring my knees up to my chest. "You're the best friend a girl can have, you know that?"

"Always, babe. You would do the same for me."

CHAPTER 27

Colby

"Colby, are you and Ms. Smallson romantically involved?"

"Colby, over here! Is there a wedding date?"

"Did you break up with Ms. Smallson, Colby? Your fans want to know!"

"Did you know she was sleeping with other members of the team, sir?"

"How is this impacting your game?"

"Is she here tonight? Have you seen Ms. Smallson?"

My stomach churns.

Though I've purposely avoided any and all press while this mess blows over, it doesn't stop the reporters from hanging out at the entrance to the arena. Thank God, security has been amped up to help get the team through the barrage of questions that none of us want to have to answer.

This shit has been hanging over my head for several days now, and it doesn't seem to be getting better. Or maybe it's my mind that isn't allowing me to move past it.

Do I miss Carissa? Yeah. I do.

I haven't been able to sleep in days.

My words to her play on repeat in my brain.

"I never want to see you again."

"We're done here."

Part of me has wanted to reach out, but the other part wants to scream at her until she breaks apart and feels even remotely how I'm feeling at the moment.

Hurt.

Betrayed.

Angry.

No, not angry. Goddamn pissed off.

Confused.

Lonely.

There's nothing lonelier than knowing the one you think could be the one... isn't the person you think she is.

It's been a fucking lonely couple of days.

The room spins when I slide my jersey over my head, so I lower myself to the bench, willing the dizziness to go the fuck away. I check my phone again and finally see a message from my agent.

Aaron: Hang tight, Nelson. Still in clean up mode over here. Will hopefully have more news soon.

Sighing, I place my phone back in my locker. We have a game to play tonight. I'll be damned if I'm going to let Carissa Smallson distract me from playing my best and leading my team to the win we need.

Coach hasn't been around for a good portion of the day, a fact that has been in the back of my head all afternoon.

Where has he been?

Who is he talking to?

And why isn't he screaming at me?

She may have sold pictures of us to the media, but it doesn't change the fact I was in those pictures. Touching her in inappropriate ways for two professionals in public. I should've known better, and I'll have to take ownership of damaging not only my own reputation but also that of the team.

Guilt consumes me as I look around the locker room, my teammates busily dressing themselves. Nobody joking around like we usually do before a game. No Taylor Swift playing for Dex to dance to. No grunting or chest bumping or hype of any kind.

They're all so serious.

They're all thinking about it.

About Carissa.

About what she's done.

"One hour till game-time, gentlemen!" Coach roars through the locker room as we finish putting on our uniforms and lacing our skates. "Foster and Shay, you two are doing the pregame press conference. They're ready for you in ten. Nelson..." My head snaps up. "In my office, now."

Fuck.

Here it comes.

I check my phone one more time. I've checked it more times than I care to admit today, hoping my agent will have something to tell me that will help me wake up from this nightmare of a day. But when I don't see a message from Aaron, I slide it into my locker, roll my shoulders, swallow the knot in my throat, and step into Coach's office.

"Sit," he says. Once I'm seated across from him, he pierces me with his bright blue stare. "You got something you want to tell me, Nelson?"

"I'm sure I don't have anything to tell you that you don't already know, sir."

"I'm positive that's not true."

I shift in my seat. "What do you mean?"

"Do you love her?"

I scoff and roll my eyes. "Not today."

He leans forward, his elbows on his desk, his clasped hands against his mouth. His stare never wavering. "Did you love her or were you just fucking her?"

A wave of nausea hits me, and I glance down at my restless leg, bouncing lightly. "We weren't just fucking, Coach." I shake my head. "We... I thought we..."

Coach sits back in his chair and sighs. He smooths a hand down his face. "Did you know she resigned?"

Silently, I bob my head. "I had heard mumblings about it. Haven't seen her around, so I assumed."

"Did you tell her to quit?"

"No, sir."

"What did you tell her?"

I swallow back my emotions and look him square in the eye. "I told her to get the fuck out and that nobody hurts my brothers. My family."

A hint of a grin hits the corner of his mouth. "How noble. So, you think she did this? She really did it?"

I shrug. "I want to believe she didn't, but..."

"Yeah. I know."

We both sit in Coach's dark office staring at each other. Neither of us really knowing what to say.

"For what it's worth, I liked her, Nelson. There's not a person associated with this organization that hasn't seen how you've changed over these last few months. I had a feeling you two were fooling around. I just wasn't aware there were feelings at play."

"Yeah."

"Valerie was pissed." He chuckles. "Said she told Smallson not to get involved."

"It's not her fault, Coach." I sigh. "I pursued her. She knew it was risky. She worried about what Valerie would think. I promised her I would take care of it and then..."

"Then the shit hit the fan."

I shift in my seat again, unable to get comfortable. "Yeah."

"You going to be able to play tonight?"

My head springs up with his question. "What?"

"You think you can really pl—"

"Not a fucking question in my mind, Coach. I'm ready. We've got this. I've got this."

He holds my stare and then slowly nods. "All right. Let's get through this game, then we'll talk about how we're going to clean up this mess."

I nod silently and then stand, waiting to be dismissed from Coach's office.

He gestures to the door. "Get outta here. Lace up. We've got a game to play."

"Thanks, Coach."

Our warmup is swift and focused. The guys look good. Our formations are tight. Zeke is blocking practice shots left and right. The energy in the arena is high as we take on Pittsburgh. We've been told my childhood idol, Mario Lemieux, is in the house tonight. Although his heart is always with the Penguins, I can't help but feel energized to play in front of him. Alex would've loved to be here tonight.

He is here.

I feel him with me.

When our warmup time is over and the buzzer goes off, we head off the ice and back to our dressing room to await official game time. I don't know what makes me do it, but I quickly open my locker to check my phone again for any word from my agent. But there are no new notifications.

Get yourself in the zone, Nelson.

Do not let her knock you off your game tonight.

I toss my phone back into my locker, slamming the door, and then sit on the bench, chugging another few gulps of Gatorade. My body is already sweaty from the warmup. Coach strides in for one more pep talk and then it's time. Time to line up in the tunnel to take the ice.

"Colby!" I hear my name being shouted from down the hall, but I'm already in the tunnel waiting for our team to be announced.

"Colb!" I hear footsteps running down the hallway as we all turn to see what's going on.

"Who the fuck?" Dex starts to ask, but just then Elias rounds the corner huffing and puffing.

My eyes bulge and my heart drops. "Eli! What's wrong? What's going on?"

Though he has access to the area down here, he rarely hangs out, especially not before a game.

"Carissa!" He huffs. "It's Carissa!"

For a moment, I worry that something may have happened to her, but then I refocus my mind and remind myself she's not important anymore.

"Eli, I'm sorry. I didn't call you today. But Carissa and I aren't—"

"She didn't do it, Colby!"

My teammates turn toward my brother and me in the middle of the tunnel. "What?"

"She didn't do it, Colb. Carissa didn't sell her pictures to anybody. It wasn't her!"

I shake my head, bewildered. "How... Eli, how would you even know that? The pictures were on her phone, bro."

"Yeah, I know. I saw them. But I knew something had to be up, so I pulled a few strings at the Tribune and, well, it's going to cost you a private dinner for the reporter and ten of his closest friends, as well as a suite for the next four games, but I got him to give me the name of the source that sold them. Her name was Gretchen."

He smiles and continues. "Isn't that the girl from—"

"Saturday night," I finish for him.

"Yes!" He nods. "Remember? I told you she took a selfie on Carissa's phone that night. But what if she... I don't know, somehow stole pics from her phone? It's possible, right? I mean she had to have done it then. "

"Impossible," Zeke says, shaking his head, "If Carissa has her phone password protected then—"

"She didn't have it protected that first night at Pringle's," Dex says. "Remember? I gave her a hard time about it."

"I did too, not that long ago," I murmur and then shake my head as the Pittsburgh Penguins take the ice. "But Eli, why are you telling me this? Why now?"

"Dumbass." He shakes his head and gives me a brotherly punch to the shoulder. "I know you, bro. I assumed you would be a hot mess about it. You've been a tool for days according to Milo."

I turn my gaze to the snitch who decides now is the appropriate time to wink at me.

Asshole.

"Anyway, I wanted you to be able to play a good game knowing she didn't do it, Colb. I think that girl's crazy in love with you, if you ask me. And based on the way you were eye-fucking her all night long, you feel the same way about her. So go... go play your heart out. And then you can get your girl."

"Put your hands together for our very own RRRRRRRRRRRED TAILS!"

I don't have even a second to thank Eli before the guys scream and grunt our gameday chant, "Hustle, hit, and never quit!" and then fly onto the ice in perfect formation as the crowd roars around us.

Our first period is mediocre, but Milo manages to score twice for us against Pittsburgh's one. We're not up by a great margin, but still in the lead heading into the second period. I need to get my head into this fucking game. I've done a lousy job at even pretending to be interested in my job. All I can think about right now is Carissa's face. The tears sliding down her pink cheeks because I didn't believe her.

I didn't protect her.

I wasn't there for her when she needed me.

I promised I would take care of us. Promised I would clear the air with Valerie, and when shit hit the fan, I recoiled and pushed her away.

We take to the ice for the start of the second period, and my body already feels overheated. Sweat pours from my face and down my back, and my hand shakes inside my glove as I grip my stick and prepare for faceoff. Milo wins the faceoff and passes to Hawken who moves the puck down the ice to Quinton's territory. He shoots for the net, but it's blocked by their goalie who sends it back up the ice. Milo tries to send it my way, but I miss it, and it hits the wall, quickly rebounded by Pittsburgh.

We fight for control of the puck for a solid two minutes,

and the crowd is cheering us on. I finally break the puck free and prepare to shoot it to Dex when I'm slammed into the wall by another player.

"Motherfucker!"

The crowd along the ice pounds on the glass as I try to get my bearings, but for the life of me, I can't seem to catch a full breath. My head hurts. My leg muscles tense, and the ice a blur.

More pounding on the glass as jerseys of both team colors head my direction. I slide out of the way just in time and swing around to find the puck, but I can't even see the faces of the players around me.

What the fuck is happening to me?

Why didn't you protect her?

"Colby! Help her!"

"I know, Eli! I know! Stay there!"

"Get Dad!"

"Carissa!"

My heart rate spikes, and the room spins as I turn myself around on the ice. I hear voices on both sides of me. My name being shouted. From where? I can't tell.

I think I might throw up.

I can't...

Can't breathe.

"Carissa"

"Colby! Help her!"

"Why didn't you help her?"

"Nelson! You all right?"

It's Milo. I hear his voice. I know he's here with me as players whiz past us. "Colby, come on! We've got to move!"

"Yeah."

"Nelson!" I move my stick to catch a puck, but nothing hits it. I spin into the wall, grasping it for dear life. Pain ricochets through my body and I clutch my chest, and that's the last thing I remember.

Before the world disappears.

Before my mind goes blank.
Before everything is black.

CHAPTER 28

Carissa

"What the hell, Miller!" Chelsea yells at Zeke through her television. "How did you let that one through? Ugh! Get it together, Red Tails!"

She's busy following the whole team, but my red eyes have only been trailing one particular player. The one who told me to get the fuck out and never come back.

The one who doesn't want me anymore.

The one who thinks I betrayed him.

My heart can't possibly shatter into any more pieces than it already has today but just watching him glide around on the ice makes me cry over and over and over again. Like he's gone on with life without me. Not another thought. Not another worry.

And as much as I deserve that, it doesn't make me hate it any less.

The buzzer goes off, signifying the end of the first period, and the teams leave the ice. For a moment, I consider texting Colby, knowing he could potentially check his phone. But the last thing I want him to do is block my number, if he hasn't already, so I fight the urge and grab another beer from Chelsea's fridge.

"You doing all right?" she asks me when I curl up on her couch under one of her many heavy throw blankets.

I shake my head and wipe a few stray tears. "No. But... yeah. I'm sure I'll be fine. It just..."

"Fucking sucks?"

"Yeah." I nod. "That."

She turns toward me, resting her knees under her feet. "Okay, let's talk this out again. There must be an explanation here. Some way for you to absolve yourself."

"What difference does it make, Chels?" I shrug. "Perception is reality, and people are going to believe what they want to believe. The fact of the matter is, the pictures exist, and someone took them from my phone and..."

Her brows crease. "And what? Why did you stop talking?"

"It can't be that easy."

"What? What can't be that easy?"

"She wouldn't..."

"Who wouldn't? Oh my God, Rissa, use your words."

My eyes snap to hers. "Gretchen Prong."

She shakes her head. "I don't get it. What about her?"

I sit up a little higher on the couch. My brain working a mile a minute, and my mind becoming clearer. "She was there, Chelsea."

"Where?"

"At the event! The charity event! She was there! We spoke! She flirted with Colby right in front of me."

"Bitch! Why would she even do that?"

"Because she's—"

"Jealous," Chelsea finishes, nodding her understanding. "I mean, if she was there, I suppose it's possible, right?"

"It's more than possible. I left my phone and purse at our table while Colby and I were dancing."

"Those were hot as fuck pictures, by the way."

I tilt my head and give my best friend one of those not-right-now expressions.

"Okay, sorry. Go on."

"Anyway, when we got back to the table, Elias, Colby's brother, told me she had been by looking for me. That she had taken a selfie on my phone... You know, like we used to do when we worked together."

"So, you think she could've stolen your pictures then?"

"Yeah..." I trail off, because the movement on the television captures my attention just in time to see Colby slammed against the wall. I cringe, knowing that had to have hurt like hell, and silently tell him to shake it off and go for the puck, but he doesn't.

He's slow in his response as the game flies around him, and then it looks as if he's floating on his skates to the middle of the rink for no good reason.

"What the hell is he doing?" Chelsea asks. "Is this some new play?"

I shake my head. "I don't...think... oh my god!" We watch in horror as Colby tries to latch onto the wall and then falls to the ice, motionless. "What... what's going on?" I jump up from the couch. "What's happening? Colby, stand up!"

"Whoa. It's okay. He probably just got winded from being checked against the wall. Give him a minute."

But a minute passes... and then two... then three. The entire team surrounds Colby, still lying motionless on the ice as the team's medical staff check him out. The sportscasters on the television don't know what's happening, and the entire arena looks on, waiting... watching... wondering what comes next for Colby Nelson. Within minutes, there's a paramedic team coming onto the ice with a stretcher, and my stomach turns inside out.

"Colby." I curl into a ball on the couch, hugging my knees and watching through my blurry tears as they take him off the ice.

"Where do you think they're taking him?" Chelsea asks softly.

"I don't know. That didn't look good, and they don't mess around. Hospital would be my guess."

Chelsea stands. "Do you want to go? I'll take you."

Fucking yes, I want to go. I want to be there. I want to be holding his hand. I want to be telling him it's okay. That he's going to be okay. I want to remind him to breathe. I want to be his support person. I want to be his rock, because when all is said and done, I've seen Colby at his most vulnerable. I know the person he is inside. I know what scares him. What fuels him.

But he doesn't want me.

"I can't go."

"You're a fucking adult, Riss. You can go if you want to go. They're not going to kick you out."

"They very well could. The media will inevitably be there. It'll be a hot mess. I'll be thrown to the sharks, and they'll all want answers about shit they don't need to be wondering about when Colby is lying in a hospital bed. Besides, I don't want to make it worse for him. My being there won't help him one bit."

"Do you want to text someone? Milo? Dex?"

"No." I sigh. "As far as I know, they're all unhappy with me right now. They think I sold them out, remember? I'll just have to wait for updates from the media... just like everyone else."

"I'm really sorry you're going through all this. I wish there was something I could do to help."

"There is. You can drive me home, so I don't have to take the L and risk people recognizing me."

"You don't want to stay the night?"

"It's not that. Mr. Hastings hasn't come to fix my bathroom leak yet, so I need to go empty the bucket under my sink and check my shower. Otherwise, I'll be dealing with much worse tomorrow, and I don't want him to charge me extra for that."

"Fucking landlord," Chelsea sneers. "You need to find a lawyer... I mean other than your father, of course, and take the guy to court. He's a slumlord if you ask me."

"Yeah, well, that all costs money, and as of today, I'm fresh out, so."

Chelsea's shoulders drop, and she gives me a comforting hug. "I'm sorry, friend. You know I'm here for you, whatever you need, right?"

"Yeah. Thanks, Chels."

CHAPTER 29

Colby

I come to as a flurry of activity unfolds around me, and I gasp for breath.

"He's breathing!"

"Get his pads off!"

"Colby!"

"Get him some oxygen."

"Ambulance is here."

"Are we thinking heart attack?"

"Colby, I'm right here."

"Don't know yet."

"Colby?"

"Are you family?"

"I'm his brother."

My eyes finally focus on a paramedic straddling me. I'm being transported down the hallway on a gurney with a crowd of people around me. Somehow, I manage to lift my arm and grasp Elias's hand.

Fuck, he looks scared.

I'm alive, Eli.

I'm here.

"I've got you, Colby. Just stay with me, okay?" His brows draw together, and his eyes look red.

Is he crying?

"Eli."

"Don't try to talk Mr. Nelson. We want you to breathe as best you can," the paramedic above me explains. "I'm going to cover your mouth with this oxygen mask to help you breathe. You're going to be okay, but we're going to get you to the hospital for a few tests."

Large doors open, and a cold breeze hits us all as I'm lifted into the back of an ambulance, my brother at my side, and whisked away.

"Just breathe, bro." Eli squeezes my hand. "Breathe." My eyes meet his before the doors close, and I hear him whisper, "And don't you fucking leave me."

My throat is scratchy, and my body feels like it's been through a marathon. I turn my head and notice my brother in the chair next to me. His hand is on my arm, and his head is bowed.

"Hey."

His head snaps up and his shoulders fall as he releases a heavy sigh.

"You son of a shit bitch fucking bastard cunt."

Even in my sleepy state, my eyes bulge in shock, and I huff out a quiet chuckle. I don't think I've ever heard him swear like that. "What's that for?"

"Because I thought..." He shakes his head, pinching the bridge of his nose.

Yeah. I know what he thought.

"Hey. I'm here, Eli. Okay? I'm right here."

"Yeah." He nods. "I know, but for a minute I thought—"

"Yeah. Me too."

His eyes dart to the machine behind me and he checks the numbers.

"What happened? Did I have a heart attack?"

"I'm guessing not, or you wouldn't be here. They would probably have you in some cathlab or something. They gave you some meds that made you sleepy though. You've been out over an hour."

"Mom and Dad?" I ask, leaving the rest unspoken.

"They saw. They called. They're on their way."

My eyes squeeze closed as guilt overcomes me again.

"Carissa?"

Elias shakes his head. "Haven't seen her."

I deserve that.

But deep down I wish she were here with me.

I wish I hadn't snapped at her.

I wish I had heard her out.

I wish I had believed her.

"Mr. Nelson?" the doctor asks, stepping into my private room.

Elias and I answer in tandem. "Yes."

The doctor eyes us both, and Elias explains, "Sorry, I'm Elias Nelson. Colby's brother."

"Ah. Yes. Good to meet you, Elias. I'm Doctor Rendmire."

He turns to me. "Good news, Colby. Your EKG shows no signs of a heart attack, and your blood work says you're healthy as a horse." He takes a quick peek at the machine beeping behind me. "Pulse is back to normal. How is your breathing?"

I inhale a deep breath and then clear my throat. "Uh, it's good, I guess. Feels a little tight."

The doctor nods and lays his charts at the foot of the bed. He pats my leg and gives me a reassuring glance. One I could see my father giving me after a rough day. "That's to be expected with a panic attack. Your body went through its own trauma while you were also exerting yourself on the ice. You probably feel a bit like you got hit by a truck."

"Understatement of the year, Doc."

"A panic attack?" Elias repeats. "That's really what this was? No heart attack?"

Doc shakes his head. "Anxiety attack. Panic attack. That's my best guess given your test results and that your body isn't still in some sort of flaming shock." He turns to me. "Were you feeling anxious or stressed before the game started?"

I sigh and glance knowingly at my brother. "You could say that."

"Ah." Doc nods. "I'm guessing then, what happened during the game was your body's way of dealing with whatever stress was going on in your head. Do you experience anxious feelings often? Feelings of dread? Of worry?"

I use the next few minutes to explain my recent nightmares to the doctor as Elias keeps his hand on my arm for brotherly support. I also share my embarrassing mistake with Carissa. Doc listens intently, nodding his head in all the appropriate places, and then he shares his thoughts.

"Son, I'm going to give you a little advice. My daughters aren't professional athletes, but they're about your age, so I hope you'll humor me for just a moment."

"Sure."

"First of all, I should say, as your doctor, I think we need to get you on an anxiety medication short-term." He holds up his hand. "Not forever, but long enough for you to feel like you're in control of yourself and of your mind while you work on step number two."

"Okay." I nod. "What's step number two?"

"Therapy. You have a lot on your plate that you have to deal with on a daily basis, given your career and therefore your celebrity status. But more than that, it sounds like you still harbor feelings of grief, as well as something we call survivor's guilt, over your brother's passing that perhaps talking to someone could help you work through."

I don't love the idea of therapy, and the doctor reads it on my face right away.

"I promise you, Colby, there's nothing to be embarrassed or ashamed about when it comes to talking with a therapist. I'm well aware of the stigmas that exist on mental health, but your overall wellbeing, and therefore your game as well, will improve once you're able to talk through your anxieties and your stresses and then learn how to process and overcome them."

I suppose what he's saying doesn't sound so bad. If talking

with someone will help me get rid of the nightmares plaguing my sleep, I guess I'm willing to give it a shot.

"All right, Doc. Anything else?"

"Yes. One more thing, and this one comes from me as a father of three adult women."

"Okay." I chuckle at his teasing eye roll and accompanying smirk.

"This girl you mentioned."

"Carissa."

He nods. "Yes. Carissa. Look, arguments happen all the time in relationships. Miscommunications. Things said that you don't mean and vice versa. But, in the end, after whatever fight or argument blows over, if you can look at her and know in your heart she's still the one, chances are, you're going to be okay. And if she loves you, she'll forgive any of your shortcomings or, as my wife calls them, dickish moments."

He gives me a wink and pats my foot.

"Thanks, Doc."

"You're welcome." He turns his head and takes notice of the group of people waiting outside my room. "Now, I'm going to get out of your hair and let the gentlemen waiting in the hall check up on you. It looks like they're eager to see you."

I thank him again, shaking his hand, and watch as he welcomes my closest friends into my room. One by one, their burly bodies file in and surround my bed. Milo, Dex, Hawken, Zeke, and Quinton.

"Did they bring you your JELL-O yet?" Dex asks. "I hear their JELL-O is a goddamn delight."

He never fails to make me laugh. "Hey guys. Thanks for coming. Did we win?"

"Fuckin' right we did," Quinton says. "Once they took you off the ice and we took a short break, Milo went on a damn rampage."

I lift a brow and give Milo some side-eye. "This guy?"

The guys nod and Zeke speaks up. "You should've seen it, man. I had nothing to do the whole third period. I could've painted my damn nails with all the free time I had. These guys were a bunch of hot-headed penguin fuckers who showed no mercy. We won six to one."

"Outstanding. I'm sorry I failed you guys."

"Hey." Milo lays a hand on my shoulder. "Enough of that. You haven't failed anyone."

"I told Coach I was okay to take the ice when I knew my head wasn't on straight."

"We've all done that, Colb," Hawken says. "But you gave us quite a scare. The media is saying it wasn't a heart attack though. That true?"

"Yeah." I roll my eyes. "Apparently, I had a panic attack."

I expect the guys to laugh but none of them do. I take a deep breath and sheepishly tell the guys, "On top of everything that happened yesterday, I fucked things up with Carissa."

"Confession time, brother," Zeke says. "We all kind of fucked things up with Carissa."

"What do you mean?"

"She came into the locker room looking for you that day."

"Yeah?"

He nods. "None of us said a word to her. I think we were all a little shell-shocked by what the media was saying, and we didn't know what to think. If it was true, and she really used you...and us..."

"Yeah," I murmur. "I get it."

"But we should've known better," Dex adds. "Carissa has never been anything but great to all of us. I feel like we kind of owe her."

"I told her to get the fuck out." I bow my head, ashamed. "That I never wanted to see her again."

"Is that true?"

"Fuck no, it's not true. It pained me to say it then, and it's killing me now to know she's God knows where thinking I hate her."

"Do you think we can get her job back for her?" Milo asks.

"She would have to want to come back first, and after the way I treated her..."

"She loves you, Colb," Elias reminds me. "There's no doubt in my mind she's crazy about you."

I nod silently, too embarrassed to speak. "She told me she loved me."

"Whoa!" Dex steps back, his hand on his chest. "She did?"

"Is that so hard to believe, asshole?"

He bobs his head with a shit-eating smirk. "Well, I mean... you are a dick sometimes."

"Yeah, yeah. Keep talking."

"So, she loves you. She told you that," Hawken recalls. "And how do you feel about that?"

"I've been crazy about her since the day she denied me my fuckin' Lucky Charms. I just have to get her to believe me."

"You need a grand gesture?" Milo asks. "I read about them in my books all the time. I could come up with a few good ideas."

I shake my head. "Nah. She's not necessarily the grand gesture type. I just need to do something... genuine."

And I have just the idea.

"Elias, I might need your help."

He smiles. "I'm here for you, bro. Whatever you need."

"Can you do a little research for me? Find a way for me to talk to Attorney Bill Smallson? He's Carissa's father. He's a public defender at the courthouse."

"Sure. I can do that."

"What else do you need?" Milo asks.

"I need to get the fuck out of here, so I can get my girl back."

CHAPTER 30

Carissa

Though it's only been a few days, it feels like it's been weeks since I left the Red Tails arena for the last time. I haven't heard a word from Colby. Not that I expected to.

But one can hope, right?

The media reported that he's in good health and taking the next week off to recover. I don't think I've ever felt more relieved hearing the news. But with the reports of his health status came more rumors about me, our hidden affair, and my possible affairs with other players on the team.

It makes me want to throw up every time I hear about it. For someone, anyone, to think I'm that kind of person, it's a crushing blow. And if this isn't the perfect time for my parents to kick me when I'm down, I don't know what is. I'll be keeping a close eye on my credit report for the next few months just in case.

In the meantime, I have to do my own damage control if I want to continue to find work in my field. Before I left DePaul, my boss, Dr. Sweeny, gave me a piece of advice I've never forgotten.

"Ain't no one looking out for you in this adult world, but you. You'll do good to remember that always."

He was right. At any moment, that person you at least trusted as a colleague can turn on you. That friend you tell your secrets to can turn around and shout them to the world. One misstep, one mistake, one false statement can change your life. I know how bad rumors can spread through the media. I know I could let this drag me down.

But I also know I'm strong enough to face it head on and do something about it. Now that I have an inkling of who, what, and why Colby and I were dragged through the mud, I know exactly what I need to do to try and fix it.

For my career.

For Colby.

For the team.

"Thank you for the ride," I say goodbye to my Uber driver and head inside my old university PR office. I may not be able to get Colby to believe that I didn't purposely expose our pictures to the world, but I can certainly try to find Gretchen's motives for doing what she did.

I enter the PR office to find the entire media team for the university sitting at the conference table. Even my best friend, Chelsea, is among them. Her proud smirk fueling me forward. Dr. Sweeny, my old boss, notices my entrance right away.

"Carissa Smallson! What a pleasant surprise!"

"Good morning, Dr. Sweeny. I was in the area and thought I would pop in for a quick moment. I hope that's all right?"

His smile is answer enough for me. "Of course, it is." He springs up and walks toward me, wrapping me up in a comforting hug from an old professor. Then he holds my shoulders at arm's length, giving me a pensive gaze. "Is everything okay with you, Carissa? I'm sorry to say you've been the talk of the social media news lately. Well, you and…"

"Colby. Yeah." I nod. "I know. That's why I'm here." I give a side eye to Gretchen, who is shifting in her seat, probably wishing she wasn't here right now.

"Oh? Something we can help you with?"

"Something Gretchen can help me with, yes."

"No problem. We can leave you two alone if you want to chat."

"No, no. That won't be necessary. I just have a few questions, and I think you should all stay and hear them for yourselves."

Dr. Sweeny pivots from Gretchen to me and then back to the table, an inquisitive brow raised. "All right. The floor is yours, Ms.

Smallson."

I roll my shoulders and stand tall at the end of the table and then glance solely at Gretchen. "I just want to know why she not only stole pictures off my phone, but then turned around and sold them to the media."

Dr. Sweeny's jaw drops. "Carissa, that's quite an accusation."

I tilt my head, my gaze never leaving Gretchen. "And yet, she hasn't denied it. Because she can't."

"I don't have to deny it, Smallson," she gloats. "The media never reveals its source, so you have no proof it was me. Besides, why would you even think up such a preposterous idea like that?"

"Because you had my phone that night. At the Amateur Empowered Event. You even left a fucking selfie for me." I turn my phone around for everyone. "See?"

Her face goes white.

"And then I thought to myself, 'But how did she get my pictures?' So the other night, I checked the settings on my phone, and wouldn't you know it, your contact icon came up as my most recent AirDrop."

"Carissa, I—"

"Save it, Gretchen. I don't want your excuses or your bullshit lies. I just want to know why."

She chews the inside of her cheek, her eyes darting around the room as everyone stares at her. Finally, she concedes. "Because I deserved that job. You don't even know anything about hockey. You never followed sports while you were here. Yet there you are, being put up on a pedestal by Dr. Sweeny, as always. I could've done your job a thousand times better than you ever did." She looks to Dr. Sweeny. "But you never gave me the chance, professor. You always overlooked me for Smallson."

Chelsea rolls her eyes, which almost makes me laugh.

Except I'm too pissed to laugh.

She tried to ruin my life.

Dr. Sweeny sits up in his chair, a look of disbelief on his face. "So, your professional jealousy gave you the right to steal someone's private property and sell it to the goddamn media?" He raises his voice. "Do you have any idea what you've done, Gretchen? To Carissa? To Mr. Nelson? To the entire Red Tails organization? To this university?"

She shakes her head. "I... I—"

"They could turn around and slap us with a lawsuit. They could slap you with a lawsuit. Hell, Carissa has every right to press charges against you."

"But I didn't *do* anything illegal."

"You're fired, Gretchen. Effective immediately. Get your belongings and leave."

"But—"

"And a report will be made to the university. What they decide to do with you is up to them."

As Gretchen gathers her things, her hands shaking, tears flowing down her face. I steal a glance at my best friend, who simply throws me a wink.

Atta girl, Smalls.

This has been the longest week of my life, and even at the end of it, I have nothing to show except a tarnished reputation, a tiny bit of vindication in Gretchen's firing, and—

Pssshhhhhhhhh

"What the hell is that?" I spring out of my bed immediately to see where the sound is coming from.

It's like a water park in my bathroom. The pipe under my sink finally burst open and water is spraying everywhere—bucket be damned. And with one burst pipe comes another, as my shower pipe explodes as well.

"Fuck! Fuck! Fuck! Fuck!" I scream and cry and scream some more because, "I am so fucking over this! Why me, you fucking piece of shit shower bastard!"

Soaking wet and still in my pjs, I grab my phone and call my landlord, Mr. Hastings. Of course, he doesn't answer, so I'm forced to leave another message.

"Mr. Hastings!" I shout into my phone. "It's me again! Carissa Smallson? Remember that leak I've asked you to look at more times than I can count? Well, I now have a couple burst pipes and there's water everywhere, and I'm sure if there's water up here, then there's water in the store below me. Would you *please* get here and fix this! I don't know what to do!"

Once I end my call, I lay my cellphone on the counter and then unlock my door so Mr. Hastings can get in. Then I do the only thing I can think to do. I head back to the bathroom, under the spray of two burst pipes, and try like hell to keep some semblance of control.

It's fucking pandemonium in here. Everything is wet. My makeup bag is wet, my curling iron is wet, my towels are wet, my robe is wet, the floor is a mess. At least some water is in the tub, but at some point, if Mr. Hastings doesn't get here, the tub will overflow and then what the fuck am I supposed to do?

My emotions get the best of me as I stand in the bathroom sobbing, with my foot against a bucket by the sink, and my hand covering the spray coming from the wall of the shower. I'm a sad, wet mess.

Worse than a drowned rat.

"I can't fucking stand here forever!"

There's a loud knock on my door, and my head falls back. "Finally," I shout loud enough for him to hopefully hear me. "It's about fucking time, Mr. Hastings! I need a little help in here!"

I hear the door shut and await his hurried arrival, but the person now staring at me from the bathroom door isn't my landlord.

My breath hiccups, and a third pipe bursts somewhere inside me when our eyes meet, causing all the water to flow through me as I sob his name. "Colby."

His initial look of shock morphs when he sees me start to cry. He drops the flowers he was holding onto the floor and walks right into the wet mess, lifting me from the tub and wrapping his arms tightly around me.

"What the hell is going on?"

Letting go of all my pride and inhibitions, I sob into his chest. "I hate this place so fucking much! And what are you even doing here and oh, shit —are you okay? I saw you. I saw what happened, and I was so scared for you, but I knew you didn't want me there, and I'm so sorry, Colby. I'm sorry. It's just been a shit week and I—"

"Hey, hey, hey," he murmurs into my ear, trying to calm me down. "Shhh. I'm okay, Smalls. I'm right here. I'm okay. And I fucking missed you."

I lift my head, wiping tears from my face, not that it does any good as I'm still a drowned rat. "You did?"

"I should've believed you. I should've heard you out. I should've been there to protect you when you needed me, and I'm so sorry, Carissa. I'm sorry I was such a dick to you."

"It's okay, Colb. I get it. I deserved it."

"You didn't deserve shit, Smalls. I should've believed you. I should've known better than to think you would ever hurt me."

"I would never."

He smooths my wet hair off my face. "I know. You would never hurt me, because you love me."

I eye him, speechless.

He heard me?

"You told me you loved me that day... in the gym. I heard it. Is that still true?" he asks. "Do you still love me?"

I swallow my sobs and choke back my tears. "I never stopped loving you, Colb."

"Thank Christ," he whispers, lowering his forehead to mine, his eyes closed. "Because I'm goddamn crazy about you, Smalls."

I raise my head, shocked at this new revelation. "What?"

He smiles. "I'm saying I love you, Carissa Smallson. I love you so much it fucking hurts. Literally...chest pains and blackouts."

My brows fold in. "Wait. Are you saying the other night on

the ice was..."

"A panic attack, yeah." He laughs.

I can't believe he's laughing.

How is he laughing?

"I found out right before the game that none of this was your fault, and I couldn't stop thinking about you, Smalls. What I had said. What I had done. That I hadn't protected you when you needed it most." He shakes his head. "I should've fucking been there with you. For you. The guilt got to me. You were my brother all over again. I didn't save you."

"Colby." My heart breaks for him.

"Instead, I was a complete asshole. And I'm sorry. I'm so sorry. Please forgive me, Carissa."

My legs wrapped around his waist, sopping wet and dripping in his arms, I cup Colby's beautiful, vulnerable face in my hands and kiss him like my life depends on it. Because he's everything I need.

Everything I want.

"Forgiven. I love you, Colby."

"I love you too, Smalls."

"What in the..." Mr. Hastings stands at the bathroom door with an old blue toolbox in his hand. His jaw askew, and his eyes the size of saucers. "What is going on here?"

"There's a leak in the bathroom, Mr. Hastings," I report from Colby's arms. "I've been trying to tell you for months!"

"This is a whole lot more than a leak!"

"No, sir," Colby interjects. "This is what happens when you ignore a leak. And now Ms. Smallson's apartment is uninhabitable, so she'll be moving out immediately, and you will absolutely be repaying her security deposit."

"Colby," I murmur against him, shaking my head. "I can't afford to—"

"She's not staying here one more minute." Colby doesn't even look at Mr. Hastings. He only has eyes for me. "She'll be moving in with me."

"What?"

"I have more than enough room, Smalls. You know it, and I know it. I live in a castle, remember?" He gives me a sideways smile. "No fucking way are you living in this dump with a slumlord who doesn't listen to his tenant." He kisses my forehead. "Besides, I like you in my bed. I haven't slept well at all since you've been gone."

Neither have I.

"You really want this?"

The last thing I want to do is impose on someone else.

"More than anything. Please, Smalls."

CHAPTER 31

Colby

"You have to let me pay rent, Colb. I can't just stay here rent free."

"You're already living rent free in my head, Smalls. Morning, noon, and night."

"You know what I mean."

I roll over onto my side, so we're facing each other after the best make-up sex I could ever imagine having. Like, I wonder if it's worth it to break up again just so we can have that kind of incredible make-up sex every time.

Nah.

We're never breaking up again.

Not as long as I can help it.

"I do know what you mean," I tell her. "And you're not paying rent. You sleeping next to me at night is payment enough. You belong in my bed, Smalls. You belong with me."

"But if Valerie is giving me my job back, then I should totally pay for—"

"She is giving you your job back. You should have an email in your inbox now. Oh, and before I forget, I have one more thing to tell you." I lift her petite body so she's straddling me. Her warm, sweet pussy covering my cock. "I met with your father."

Her eyes bulge. "You did what?"

"Yep. We met. Had lunch earlier in the week, and let's just say you'll never have to worry about making another payment towards those debts again."

Her shoulders fall "Colby. I told you I didn't want your help. I don't want your money."

"It's not my money, Smalls. Your father will be paying his own bills."

She gasps. "What?"

"I let him know if those bills aren't completely paid in sixty days, I will be paying for the best goddamn lawyer money can buy, and you will be pressing charges against them both for identity theft and whatever else we can throw at them."

Her jaw hangs open. She's speechless.

Good speechless?

Or bad speechless?

"Uh," I chuckle nervously. "I'm going to need you to say something here, Smalls. You're making me nervous."

Her chin wobbles and tears spring from her eyes. "You're my hero, Colby Nelson. Literally my knight in shining armor."

"No, Smalls. You're my hero." I tuck her hair behind her ears and smooth my hand down the sides of her body. "My perfect person. The partner I need in this life. And I swear to God, one day soon, I'll make you my wife and the mother of my children."

"That sounds like a dream come true."

"For me too."

She stares up at me with her beautiful brown eyes, and I can feel her love. "For tonight, though, can I just be your lover?"

"All night, Smalls. All night. Every night. As long as we both shall live."

THE END

**Want a fun epilogue of the team's first annual
ASS-travaganza?
Join my newsletter at authorsusanrenee.com**

CHICAGO RED TAILS BOOK TWO

UNFAIR GAME

SUSAN RENEE

Want more of the Chicago Red Tails?
Keep reading for an excerpt of Milo Landric's story in
Unfair Game.

Chapter 1

Milo

"Did you just spank my monkey?"

Dex cackles. "Damn right I did. Felt pretty good, too!"

"Just wait, Milo," Colby mumbles next to me. "I'm gonna bone him so hard he won't know what hit him."

"HA!" Dex hurls his whole body to the right instead of simply turning his controller. "You're jealous, Colby, because you don't have a monkey for me to spank."

"That's because his monkey belongs to me!" Carissa bellows from the kitchen. A minute later, she places a few bowls of chips, veggies, and some assorted dips on the coffee table in front of us and then gives Colby a peck on the cheek. "Don't worry, baby, if you need to bone someone later, I'm all yours."

Colby tosses his controller on the couch. "Fuck it, I'll take that bone right now. Take over, Quinton."

"What the fuck?" Quinton scrambles to pick up Colby's controller as he and Carissa canoodle their way down the hall, her giggles still heard from a couple rooms away. "Am I on the top or bottom?"

"Depends, man," Hawken says with a smirk. "You want to watch her drive or not?"

My phone dings on the coffee table with an incoming text message, but my eyes are too glued to the screen to look away. It's most likely my sister, anyway.

"Last lap, suckers!" Dex laughs. "I'm about to smoke all of you!"

I watch my Donkey Kong character roll through the

hieroglyphic square and end up with my favorite power-up. Hitting the button on my controller, I smile to myself as I fly through the air.

"Make way for Bullet Bill!" I shout.

"Dang!" Colby laughs, having rejoined us in the living room with his wife. "He brought you to the end fast and hard."

Carissa playfully swats her husband's ass. "Never underestimate those bullets, babe."

Watching Dex hit the finish line only a half second in front of me, I sit back against the couch, my controller in my lap. "Well, at least I wasn't last."

My phone dings again.

"Who could possibly be texting you?" Hawken asks me. "All the dudes you hang with are in this room."

"Not Elias," Colby states. "Or Zeke."

I nod, reaching for my phone. "True. They're probably up to their elbow in baby blow-outs."

Turning my phone over, I glance at the text on the screen.

> **Daveed: Hey man. You busy? I need a favor. Pretty big one.**

"Oh. It's not Elias." I tap my thumbs across my phone, returning his text.

> **Me: Veeeeeed!! Long time no talk! Not busy. What's up?**

Daveed Bryce is an old friend and teammate. He played for the Red Tails for about four years before he was traded to Seattle a couple seasons ago. It's been several months since any of us have heard from him, though understandably, staying in touch with anyone during a busy hockey season can prove difficult.

"It's Bryce!" I tell everyone, my brow furrowed. "Says he needs a big favor."

"Son of a bitch," Dex chuckles. "Tell him no, Wongs will not deliver to Seattle, nor will it stay fresh in the mail." That dude has to be going through withdrawal as much as he loved their food. It's no question that Wongs has unequivocally the best Chinese take-out in the city, and when Daveed was on the team, we were eating that deliciousness multiple times a week.

Quinton shrugs and grabs a tortilla chip, dipping it in the bowl of salsa in front of him. "I'm sure there's equally good Chinese food in Seattle... somewhere."

"He didn't say what the favor is?" Colby asks.

I'm about to answer him, but my phone rings in my hand. Holding it up and standing from the couch, I respond, "He will now, I guess." I tap the button on my screen to accept the call. "Veed! How are you, you big son of a bitch? Nice of you to keep in touch."

"I know, I know. My apologies. The move was a lot, mid-season, and Jada and I were house hunting and dealing with all that bullshit. It's been a busy year."

"Nice game last night. Heard you obliterated Miami."

"We sure as hell did." He laughs. "Ten to one. And that one was just a pity goal, because I slid the wrong way and swear, I somehow crushed a nut in the process. Hurt like a bitch."

"Ouch." I wince out of sympathy. "All right, you're forgiven. Hey, the guys are all here. You should say hi!"

"Oh, man, I'm sorry I'm interrupting—"

"No, no, no. It's all good. We're literally just hanging out at Colby's and dicking around with Mario Kart and snacks. We have a few days off and none of us wanted to really deal with the weather tonight, so we're staying in."

"Sounds like my kind of hangout."

"How's Jada?"

"She's great. Really great. Found herself a sweet job at the hospital and seems to be loving it."

"Good! I'm really glad to hear that. Anyway, what's this favor you need help with? Whatever it is, I'm in."

"Well, you might want to hear me out before you say yes."

Dex calls out, "Ask him if he needs my nut juice!"

"What the fuck is he on about?" Daveed chuckles.

I flip Dex my middle finger. "He called for me, Asshat. If he needed your nut juice your phone would be ringing right now and oh, look at that... it's not."

Daveed laughs on the other end of the line. "Tell that fucker I'll take his nut juice any time he wants to send it to me."

"I wouldn't throw that gauntlet down, Veed. He may very well pick it up."

"You're right." He's silent on the line for a second and then says, "All right, well, I'm just going to rip off the BAND-AID here."

Uh oh. That sounds ominous.

"All right."

"Jada and I have a friend who needs a place to stay. You still living in that monster penthouse?"

"Absolutely, man. I've got tons of space. You know that."

"Yeah, but I'm not talking just a few days. We could be talking weeks, or maybe even a month or more, Milo."

"Hey, if you know someone who needs help and you trust it won't be a problem, then it's all good. It's not like I don't have the room. Is everything okay? Is he suspended? Injured? Being traded? What's going on?"

The guys are now watching me as I have this conversation with Daveed.

"Uh, yeah, everything will be okay, I think. And no, she's perfectly healthy. She just needs to get out of a messy situation until she can figure things out on her own."

She...

"She? Veed, we're talking about a girl?"

"Oh shit. Yeah, it's a girl. Fuck, I should've asked first. I'm sorry. Are you single? I don't want to put you in a precarious position if you have someo—."

"Yeah, no. I'm single, Veed. It's fine." *Is it fine though? Am I really okay with this? Living with some girl I don't know, sharing my space with a stranger?* "So, what are we talking about when you say messy situation? She in trouble with the law? Because you know that would be a hard pass given our reputations."

"She's squeaky clean, I swear. It's nothing like that. She wants out of an unhealthy relationship. She's a good friend to Jada, but the guy she's with is an asshole. She needs a clean break. I don't know if her financial situation is strong enough to support an apartment in the city or not. This is going to be a quick getaway, so she hasn't had time to apply for places to live just yet. She has a job connection in Chicago though, so Jada and I immediately thought of you when she was talking about places she could go."

"You did? Why me?"

"Of course, we did. You're a good guy, Milo. You're honest and helpful and compassionate. Fuckin' boy scout as far as I'm concerned. I told Jada if she was going to help her friend, we had to talk to someone we both would trust with our own lives."

"Wow." Warmth spreads through my chest. "I guess I'm speechless. That's nice of you to say."

"I wouldn't say it if I didn't mean it. So, can you help? For Jada? For me?"

As Daveed and I are talking, I'm writing out a note on paper for the guys about the possibility of gaining a female roommate. The guys have been whispering question after question at me ever since.

"Is she hot?"

"What's her name?"

"What does she look like?"

"How hot do you think she is?"

"I take it she's single?"

"What if you think she's hot?"

"If she's hot, can I date her?"

"Where is she going to sleep?"

"You gonna give her your bed?"

"Wonder if she gives good head."

"Are you going to do it?"

"Are you saying yes?"

"Of course, I'll help out. You know me, Veed. Always willing to help a friend. Or, in this case, a friend of a friend."

"You're a good man, Milo. I owe you one. A big one."

"Don't sweat it, man. When should I expect err...what's her name?"

"Charlee. Her name is Charlee. And she and Jada will be in town tomorrow. They're already on the road."

I chuckle softly. "Motherfucker, was I that much of a forgone conclusion?"

"Nah. I just had a strong feeling you wouldn't say no. I'll give Jada your number so she can keep you updated in case of a delay."

"Sounds good."

"Hey, thanks again, Milo. I really appreciate this. And I know Jada does, too."

"Sure thing, Veed. Happy to help." Well, I don't know if I'm that happy to help knowing I've now opened my home to a complete stranger, but when have I ever turned a friend in need away?

Never.

Daveed used to be one of our goalies when Zeke Miller and I joined the team. He took us both under his wing and helped us get our feet wet in the NHL. I've always admired his leadership, but more than that, I've always looked up to his way of life. He truly cares about people. He's constantly giving back to his community, and his love for hockey is unmatched. He's an all-around great guy. Someone I aspire to be like.

"So, you're shacking up with some chick?" Hawken asks, grabbing a handful of pretzels and tossing them into his mouth.

I smooth my hand down my five o'clock shadow and nod.

"Yeah, I guess I am."

"So, what's the story?"

I shrug. "Some friend of Jada's, I guess. Needs to get away from a douchebag and wants to start over in Chicago. She just needs a place to stay while she does some apartment hunting."

Dex chimes in. "Did he say if she's hot?"

"I hardly think that's important."

In fact, it would be better for me if she's the ugliest human I've ever set eyes on. The last thing I need right now is a distraction from my job on the ice. Gaining a roommate when I've never had one is one thing. Gaining a hot roommate I struggle to keep my eyes off of is a whole other set of issues.

"Maybe not." Dex bobs his head. "But having something nice to look at once in a while ain't a bad thing."

Colby wraps an arm around Carissa's shoulder. "When is she arriving?"

"Tomorrow."

Everyone's brows shoot up.

"I know." I run a hand through my hair. "So much for preparing."

"Don't worry about a thing." Carissa waves off my concerns. "Your guest room is just fine. As long as she has a place to sleep and a bathroom to clean up in, she'll be fine. And I'm happy to help in any way I can."

"Thanks, Carissa."

She gives me a reassuring smile as she takes Colby's hand in hers. "Absolutely."

"I guess it's not like my sister hasn't spent time at my place before. If I can handle her being all up in my business..."

Colby chuckles. "If you can handle your sister, you can handle any other woman who walks through your door."

God, I hope he's not wrong.

Continued in *UNFAIR GAME*...

OTHER BOOKS BY SUSAN RENEE

The Anaheim Stars Hockey Series
What If We Do (novella): Jilted Bride
What If I Told You: Best friends to Lovers
What If I Knew You: Coach's Daughter

The Red Tails Hockey Series
Off Your Game: Angry Meet Cute
Unfair Game: Strangers/Roommates to lovers
Beyond the Game: One Night Stand/Surprise Pregnancy
Forbidden Game: Teammate/Best Friend's Sister
Saving the Game: Fake Relationship
Bonus Game: Single Dad/Nanny

The Bardstown Series
(Prequel) *I LOVED YOU THEN*: Second Chance at love
I LIKE ME BETTER: Enemies to Lovers/workplace
YOU ARE THE REASON: Second Chance
BEAUTIFUL CRAZY: Friends to Lovers
TAKE YOU HOME: Boss's Daughter

The Camel Club Series
Smooch: One Night Stand/Strangers to Lovers
Smooches: Single Mom/Ex's Best Friend
Smooched: Fake Relationship/Surprise Pregnancy

The Schmidt Load Novella Series
You Don't Know Jack Schmidt
Schmidt Happens
My Schmidt Smells Like Roses

Stand Alone Novels
Hole Punched: Strangers to Lovers/Hidden identity
Total Ship Show
(part of Love at Sea multi-author series)
Kamana Wanalaya for the Holidays
(She-grinch/sunshine trope)
No Egrets: Grumpy Sunshine
(Part of the Tuft Swallow Multi Author Series)

The Village series
I'm Fine
Save Me
*The Village Duet comes with a content warning.

Solving Us
Surprising Us (a Solving Us novella)

ACKNOWLEDGEMENTS

You guys!!! I just wrote my very first SPORTS ROMANCE!!!! I really loved every minute of bringing Colby and the team to life, and I'm even more excited to provide all of their stories for you in the near future. I know not everyone reads acknowledgements anymore, but I would be remiss if I didn't thank a few people who truly helped me work on this project.

First of all, my new group of alpha readers, Jenn, Jennifer, Stephani, and Kristan. I don't know why in hell I waited this long to reach out to some of my readers for help, but you ladies have been a fucking godsend! Sincerely, THANK YOU so much for reading when I needed you to, and for always giving me your honest opinions as I move through the words. You are truly my biggest asset, and now you may very well be stuck with me forever. MWAAAAHAHAHAHA.

Secondly, to Brandi, Kandy, and Sarah, my team of ladies who are always there to not only be my friend but to talk me through issues whether they be story related, cover related, or just...life related. THANK YOU so so so much for always being a never-ending group of encouragers.

To my dear friends, Carrie and Joel, THANK YOU for inviting me to a few Columbus Blue Jackets hockey games and for allowing me to sit there and develop my hockey team in my head while you enjoyed the game! Haha—You two will forever be my hockey experts!

Brandi, I know I thanked you above, but you really are the BEST editor a girl could have, and I will recommend you and your services to anyone who asks! I love reading your comments good or bad and appreciate your skills! I learn something new from you with each book!

To my ARC readers, man do I LOVE and hate sending you things to read!! You are the BEST cheerleaders, and although it always scares me that you might not like what you're reading, you never fail to send me your hugs, smiles, and virtual high fives. You also know how to make a girl feel loved when she's the most vulnerable.

Kimberly, you're literally sitting on the hotel bed next to this desk as I write this because oops, I forgot to do this last thing before uploading the book and we're on a bestie weekend. THANK YOU doesn't even begin to say all my feelings, but thank you for being my person. The Christina to my Meredith. The Beavis to my Butthead. I don't know why I just typed that, but it just came into my head and made me chuckle, so there you go. I hope we continue to grow old together in our pjs, lying in hotel beds and watching ghost stories together on the TV.

To my TIKTOK following, SERIOUSLY FUCKING THANK YOU FOR every single message, like, comment, and share. It has been an absolute pleasure getting to know so many of you, and I can't wait to experience more BookTok craziness because there is so much fun to be had! Some of you come up with the best one-liners to start my books, and I am here for it!!

To my readers and friends, THANK YOU for continuing to read my books. Thank you for continuing to share my words, and THANK YOU for continuing to talk about my books. It only takes a spark to light a fire, and I appreciate every one of you for being that spark for me!

KEEP IN TOUCH

Website: authorsusanrenee.com
Instagram: @authorsusanrenee
Twitter: @indiesusanrenee
Tiktok: @authorsusanrenee or @susanreneebooks

ABOUT THE AUTHOR

International bestselling author, Susan Renee wants to live in a world where paint doesn't smell, book boyfriends are real, and everything is covered in glitter. An indie romance author, Susan has written about everything from tacos to tow-trucks, loves writing romantic comedies but also enjoys creating an emotional angsty story from time to time. She lives in Ohio with her husband, kids, two dogs, and a cat. Susan holds a Bachelor and Master's degree in Sass and Sarcasm and enjoys laughing at memes, speaking in GIFs and spending an entire day jumping down the TikTok rabbit hole. When she's not writing or playing the role of Mom, her favorite activity is doing the Care Bear stare with her closest friends.

STORIES WITH IMPACT

WWW.PAGEANDVINE.COM